DEATHRUN!

Tarron entered the pass. He feared it would be lined with men. But not a gun spoke and the trees lay silent and dead before him. Suddenly, he heard a triumphant yelling. He had run into a trap! He turned the next winding of the path and saw that they had heaped up fallen trees and brush into a mighty mound.

Twice Monte, seeing the obstacle before him, buckjumped and shuddered with fear. But then the mustang flung himself high into the air. He struck the upper part of the heap. Head over heels pitched Monte, flinging Tarron from the saddle at the first impact. Screams and shouts surrounded them! Tarron leaped to his saddle as the gelding regained its feet. Bullets roared behind and before them . . . all misses!

A rifle flashed before Tarron! Another miss! No! Monte staggered. It seemed to Tarron that the hindquarters of the gallant mustang had fallen away beneath him. But the horse gathered himself and lurched ahead. Never had Monte's heels flown so fast . . .

Only Tarron knew, running beneath him Monte's every stride was marked with heart's blood—the great horse was dying!

Warner Books

By Max Brand

MAX BRAND

Flaming Irons

WARNER BOOKS

A Warner Communications Company

WARNER BOOKS EDITION

First published in magazine serial form in 1927

ISBN 0-446-98019-6

This Warner Books Edition is published by
arrangement with Dodd, Mead & Company

Cover art by Roy Anderson

Warner Books, Inc., 75 Rockefeller Plaza, New York, N.Y. 10019

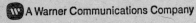 A Warner Communications Company

Printed in the United States of America

Not associated with Warner Press, Inc. of Anderson, Indiana

First Printing: September, 1976

Reissued: January, 1979

10   9   8   7   6   5   4   3   2

Contents

Chapter I

A Fine Pair

IF THE COLT had stood still and taken things calmly all would have been well, and they could have worked it out in time. But the colt was not much over three years—just old enough to have its strength and not old enough to have full sense. Except to one person, it was as wild as any unsaddled mustang from the farthest range of the mountains. And when it found itself caught in the treacherous mud at the edge of the water hole, it began to flounder and fight with a terrible energy.

Tarron and his older boy got a lariat of stout rawhide over its head and tried to pull it out in that way, but it was sunk much too deep.

Then they ventured into the slush and tried to quiet the fine gray, but their presence only made the handsome fellow more wild with fear.

It was down to the shoulders; then down to the very withers, and such were the furious efforts which it made that its strength was rapidly ebbing, and before long its exhausted head would sink.

A horse is too intelligent in some crises. A mule, when in a tight corner, will stand quiet and trust to Providence whose special care has always been mules. But when a horse cannot solve a riddle, like many a high-spirited and high-strung man, it gives up, surrenders completely, and so is lost.

A very little more and the gray would surrender in just that manner, and Tarron knew it.

He was desperately put to it. From his little place, where he managed to provide for his family only by dint of the most constant exertions, he could not afford to lose a sheep or a calf, to say nothing of the finest horse that mare had ever foaled in those mountains.

Suddenly he cried: "Where's Les? Where's Les? Get Les down here, Joe!"

Joe, with a nod, leaped on the back of his cow pony and spurred over the hill.

When he reached the house he shouted, as he sprang from the saddle, "Where's Les?"

Mrs. Tarron, dishcloth in hand, came toward him in a flurry.

"Poor Les has a dreadful headache. He's still in bed, I guess."

"Oh, dash his headaches! The gray's drowning in the tank!"

And Joe Tarron hurried up the ladder to the attic room.

It was still semidark in that room. The atmosphere was close, and in a corner an outline could be dimly discerned under a huddle of bedclothes.

"Les!" Joe yelled.

There was no answer.

Hurrying to the huddle of clothes, he tore them off the prostrate form of the sleeper.

"Les!"

There was a faint groan, and then a feeble voice muttered: "Sick, Joe. Can't get up—"

"Damn you and your sickness! Get up! Get up! I know the kind of sickness that keeps you in bed on frosty mornings!"

Les Tarron groaned softly again, and, turning on his side, his heavy breathing announced that he was already falling into soundest slumber.

His brother, in an impatient fury, stretched out a hand to strike, but something withheld him.

"You fool!" he shouted. "It's the gray, your own colt, bogged down at the edge of the tank—"

You would have said that he had struck some vital nerve, not of a man, but of a cat, so quickly did Les Tarron spring to his feet. He was past his brother in a bound. Half dressed, his long hair flying behind him, he dropped from the trap door, disdaining the ladder—fled through the kitchen, and, springing into the saddle on the mustang, rode furiously away while Joe afoot labored heavily behind.

When he got to the edge of the tank, he could see his father keeping the lariat taut, but it was patently a useless effort to maintain the head of the colt above the edge of the slime. The eyes of the gray, usually so fiery bright, were now glassing over.

"Jim!" called the rescuer.

The mud-covered ears of the colt pricked, and he uttered a feeble whinny, as Les Tarron jumped from the saddle and stood on the edge of the tank.

"In bed—by heaven, I might of knowed it!" sneered his father. "Now save the gray, or it's the last day that I keep and feed your useless carcass!"

Les Tarron hardly seemed to hear. He reached one hand over his shoulder and plucked away his shirt. The garment, not coming free at once, was ripped in twain by the force of that grasp. A strange thing to see, for the shirt was of stoutest wool, and one would have guessed that the united strength of two men could hardly have accomplished so easily what a single gesture had done now. However, now that the shirt was off and the sun glinted on the naked torso of Les Tarron, the explanation was not far to seek. He was no giant in bulk, but Nature, which makes so many forms in slipshod haste, had here worked with the delicate hand of an artist and composed all in a perfect harmony and a perfect balance. The muscles stirred and moved like living snakes beneath his skin.

He had come barefooted. Now he stepped straight into the slush.

"Keep a pull on Jim's head," he directed. "Not too hard, y'understand, but hard enough to take advantage of what I'm gunna do."

"What *are* you gunna do?" asked the father, seeing his son already sunk hip-deep in the mud.

Les did not answer. Bending low, he seemed to find a grip on the horse and made an effort to move him.

It caused the muscles along his neck to stand out like knotted fists, but it only drove Les Tarron shoulder-deep into the mud.

"Steady!" shouted the father in alarm. "It's no good! Anyway, you ain't fool enough to think that you can lift the weight of a horse, are you? Get out of that mud before you're drowned, you blockhead."

Still Les Tarron made no reply. He squelched through the mud. He straddled a little farther apart and felt a firmer bottom beneath his gripping toes. Then he took a great breath, and, leaning over, he sank shoulders, neck, and head beneath the surface of the slime.

In the filthy darkness beneath, his hands fumbled, and presently he found his grip—both hands and wrists thrust under the barrel of the gray behind the elbows.

Then he began to lift, with flexed legs that stiffened and straightened, and with bent back that struggled to straighten also.

A groan from the colt told of a body half crushed by the gigantic pressure. The gray tried to rear to avoid the pain, and so some of its weight was transferred to the hind quarters. Suddenly he was thrust up, head and neck, clear of the mud.

There was a shout of triumph from the shore. Then beside the colt rose the mud-covered head of Les Tarron. He had to tip his head up to clear his face; then, wiping away the filth from mouth and eyes and nose, he breathed a great gasp of relief, and waved a blackened arm toward his father and brother.

"Great work, Les! Now, get out of that and come ashore. I thought that you'd never come up again. You were down a whole minute!"

"Leave me be," said Les Tarron. "He ain't cleared yet!"

The colt had begun its desperate struggles once more, but now a single word from its master quieted it. Back to the sunken hind quarters went Les Tarron, moving with desperate flounderings. Once more he sank beneath the surface of the mud. Once more he bent and strained —and now the colt was fairly dragged out from the deeper mud which had imprisoned it.

The strain on the lariat could tell, from this point. The struggles of the gray itself were helpful, and last of all was the gigantic strength of Les Tarron moving the horse and lifting it forward.

In five minutes the rescued colt was on firm ground, and stood with sinking head and trembling legs while all three washed off the thick layers of mud with water.

Once clean, a horse was revealed eminently worth even such efforts as these had been, a compactly built, powerful animal, with legs which mean speed.

"My, but ain't you a mess?" sneered Joe at his mighty brother.

"That's nothing," answered Les.

He ran down to a point where firm ground came to the edge of the little artificial lake. There he plunged in, and presently he came up white, freed from the black mud. He stood, dripping, beside the dripping colt, and his father, with a sort of happy sadness, admired the magnificent group.

"Ah, Les," said he, "if you could ever come into yourself and be worthy of sitting in the saddle on that horse, what a man you'd be! But there ain't much chance of it, I'm afraid. And one of these days you'll just be bogged down and lost—like Jim here nearly was. Lost doing something useless and foolish, and men are gunna be glad that you're done for!"

These bitter words seemed to slip unregarded over the youth's head. Now that the limbs of the colt had ceased to tremble Les Tarron leaped up and sat sidewise on its back. There was no need of bridle to guide Jim; a word or two and he broke into a gliding pace that carried them softly over the hill, horse and rider, still dripping wet, flashing like a precious stone in the morning sun.

"Watch 'em go," said the rancher to his older son, "watch 'em go! And where would you find a finer pair than them, Joe? Where would you ever see a finer horse— that won't cut a cow, or work with a rope? Where would you ever see a finer man—that won't ride herd or handle a lariat or a branding iron or a pitchfork? Aye, strong

13

enough to lift a horse, as you and me have seen this day, but what good'll his strength be put to, I'm asking you? And yet they say that God made all things with a purpose—even the flies in the air!"

"Aye," said Joe bitterly, "and He made Les so that we could have our foretaste of hell on earth!"

Chapter II

A Successor to Samson

LES TARRON LEFT the colt in the small paddock near the house. It followed him along the fence, whinnying piteously, for it knew as clearly as a man would have known that it owed its life to the intervention of its young master.

At the kitchen door, Mrs. Tarron raised her work-reddened hands.

"Les Tarron! What d'ye mean running around the country more'n half naked to make folks think you're a monkey or something? And what—"

The boy walked lightly past her. It required a good deal to rouse him from his habitual apathy, but the enormous effort he had made to free the colt had set his blood in circulation, and he was stirred even to the point of mirth. He smiled at his mother, and going into the front room measured the distance from the floor to the trap door of his attic, took a running step, and leaped. He missed his hold with one hand, but the left gripped the edge.

"Les Tarron!" cried his mother, following him to the door. "Did you hear me speak to you? Did you—oh, land love us!"

She paused in the doorway and looked up to him, where he hung swinging by one hand.

"Les! Wait till I move the ladder. You'll fall and hurt yourself!"

"No, leave the ladder alone. I'm all right."

"Wait one minute! Can you hold yourself with one hand?"

He merely laughed.

"Oh, I can hold myself I think—if you move quick!"

Panting with haste and dread, she dragged the heavy ladder close to him.

"Can you manage now, son?"

"I'll try," said he.

And then, with one arm—

You young man who have chinned yourself with both hands often, have you ever chinned yourself with one? And have you ever hung at the full strength of your single arm and then drawn yourself up head high? And, worst of all, have you let yourself dangle for a couple of minutes and then tried to make your numbed muscles work?

Les Tarron lifted himself slowly, still laughing down at his mother, and hoisted himself through the trap door into the attic above.

His mother, staring up at him a-gape, grew furious as she saw that he had been making a mock both of her and of his danger.

She stood beneath the trap and hurled angry words up at him until she heard a blithe and unconcerned whistle rising from the room over her head.

Then, quite at a loss, she shook her fist at the gap in the ceiling and went silently back to her kitchen work. She was the only member of the family who had the slightest sympathy for Les. He was her son; therefore, while the others called him fool and sluggard, and though she could not deny that he was both, at least she would reserve the right to love him still.

She did not understand him. Most people thought that there was nothing worth understanding in the youth, but his mother felt that he was a mysterious problem that might be solved by a wise head at some future time.

There had never been a half-wit on either side of the family. She could trace her own blood back for several generations, and all her kin had been mentally alert. The same was true about the line of Tarron.

Whence, then, this anomaly had come?

She could not tell, she could not even guess; but she was fond of watching and waiting, and when she saw her lazy boy developing into a lazier man, and a worthless idleness consuming all his days, she still would hope that one day he would change, and rouse himself to better things.

Today, however, she despaired. She knew enough of men and of their physical prowess to feel sure that few persons would have been able to do the thing which she had seen her son accomplish with such ease.

It did not rouse her admiration. Rather, it filled her with awe and unrest.

She remembered that when Les was a mite of seven he could master his tough, work-strengthened brother of ten. And thus far throughout his life, when he cared to call upon his reserve powers, he could accomplish things which were beyond the capacity of other men.

So thought the mother, working in her kitchen while, meantime, she listened to the whistling of her son.

It was a pleasant sound, but quite unlike the whistling that one hears from the average boy in the morning. One could not call it a tune, but there was rhythm and music in it. The whistling stopped, and through the window, far away over the fields, she could hear the song of birds, unseen among the shrubbery.

Mrs. Tarron dropped her dish mop with a soft exclamation and glanced over her shoulder in terror, for it seemed to her that the song of the distant birds was like the echo of her boy's whistling.

Just at that moment, there was the soft padding shock of a heavy weight falling upon the floor of the next room, and she winced again. When Les dropped from the trap door of the attic, the shock sent a crash through the entire house. And it had never before occurred to her that when her lumpish younger son did the same thing, it was like the muffled fall of a cat.

Now, Les came yawning into the doorway, and as he stretched, and the old clothes which he had donned cracked at the seams, she lost her momentary awe of him.

17

"Go comb your hair!" she commanded. "You look a sight."

"Hungry!" he responded. "Lemme have something to eat."

"If you eat in this house, young man," she replied, "how often have I told you that you'll have to be on time for meals?"

Raising her voice, she added harshly: "And what about the cows? What about the cows? Ain't you going to take them down to the pasture, you lazy good for nothing?"

"Eh, yah!" yawned Les Tarron.

He opened the bread can and took out half a loaf of stale bread. Munching that, he walked away contentedly. His mother stared after him, shaking her head over him for the ten thousandth time. For, certainly, he was not like the others of his kin. There was no resemblance. She had had to cater to her husband and her first son with meticulous care. Good cooking and plenteous fare were essential to them, but this wastrel could get on as well with dry bread as they could with beefsteak! Aye, and he throve better than they on any diet. He could eat like a wolf, and then curl up and sleep for twenty-four hours; and could go for three days thereafter without tasting anything but water. And if—

But she closed her mind upon such memories. They were too upsetting. About everything else in her family she was fond of gossiping to the neighbors, but about Les she never would say a word; because she feared lest the uncanny thoughts which she herself often had about the boy should spread abroad and be reflected in the minds of others.

In the meantime, Les Tarron had gone down to the corral and called out the cows.

He did not drive them before him, as a cowherd should; but waited until the great red bull, the master of the little herd, had lumbered through the gate. Then with a bound he seated himself astride the fleshy hump across the shoulders of the monster.

The bull lashed his tail fiercely and lurched his head from side to side, with deep-mouthed bellowing; but he had attempted to shake off this clinging pest many a time before, and now he quickly gave up the battle and rolled on down the road with his accustomed majestic gait.

The cows followed. Sometimes the calves would race ahead for a short distance, keen to get the good grass of the pasture, but Les Tarron paid no heed.

He sat on the bull's back with his eyes closed. Stretching forth his arms blindly, once more he tensed his arms and smiled with joy as he felt the slight ache in his muscles.

The bull stopped before the pasture bars. The boy swung down, pitched off the bars, and let the herd through.

It was a difficult task, this of herding in the pasture. For one half of the ground had been summer-fallowed, and the other half was covered with tender green growing wheat. On the summer fallow the herd was welcome to reach for the bits of grass beneath the plow furrows. But there was the constant temptation of the tender wheat field beyond.

Young Les Tarron selected a pleasant shady tree at a corner of the pasture, and there stretched himself, his eyes half closed. The bull made straight for the wheat field, with the whole herd behind him, but as he came within half a dozen paces of the forbidden land a sharp, biting whistling from the herdsman stopped his majesty.

The bull paused, changing uneasily from foot to foot. But after pawing up the dust a few times, he turned sullenly and rambled back into the plowed area. The herd followed his example; and Les Tarron, secure in the knowledge that no one of the dumb brutes would dare to disobey his whistled warning, completely closed his eyes.

Not to sleep, but to see more clearly.

For it was the very greatest day in his life. He had known that he was stronger than other men, but the greatness of his strength he had not realized. Now, for the first time he had put forth his utmost might, and the sure consciousness of his muscular prowess sent a tingle along his blood and through his heart.

It had been a great joy. And perhaps—who could tell? —there would be other occasions before very long in which he could use all of his powers; use them to their utmost!

So he lay there on his back, enjoying himself in these reflections, until a voice called from beyond the edges of his daydream:

"Hello! Boy! Oh, Boy!"

He opened his eyes, but he did not sit up.

"Hey, boy! Hey, kid! Come here!"

Les Tarron closed his eyes again.

"You sassy brat! Will this fetch you?"

And a bullet sung above his head and spattered solidly into the tree trunk!

Chapter III

By Process of Deduction

HE LOOKED UP with mild interest at the smoking gun in the hand of the rider.

Then he turned and regarded the neat round hole which had been drilled through the tree.

"Come here, you young fool, or I'll send the next one through your thick head," came the ringing invitation from the roadway.

Les Tarron stood up and regarded the strangers with a closer attention. There were five of them altogether, mounted on dripping horses; and th ugh he was used to seeing the roughest mountaineers, he thought that he had never before seen such a set of fellows ready for anything.

He smiled at them. For all strong, swift, sure things appealed to Les Tarron. The eagle above the peaks or the mountain lion beneath the forest shadows brought a thrill to his heart.

Like five lions, or like five eagles, were these men; all brave, bold, powerful, and cruel. His own life, he felt, came tinglingly close to the tips of his fi gers—a thing to be given away with hardly a thought.

He thought, also, of the revolver at his hip. But he did

not touch it. Instead he walked slowly forward to the fence and leaned against it, still smiling his appreciation of the riders.

"We got all day, maybe?" queried the leader of the five furiously. "Why the deuce can't you come when you're called?"

"I was thinking about coming," said Les Tarron, unconcerned; "but I took a while to get here."

"He's a half-wit, Ingram," said one of the men. "Take it easy with him, or you'll scare him to death."

"No, you won't, Bert," said another. "He's too foolish to be scared."

The wild rider, Bert Ingram, who had during these seconds eyed the boy up and down in a sort of contemptuous disgust, now growled: "Did somebody come down this road?"

"When?" asked Tarron.

And he looked absently past the questioner into the distant heart of the sun-whitened sky, where a buzzard had been sailing the last time he noticed. It was circling there no longer. But from all corners of the sky came other black specks, tiny with distance, swinging through the heavens in loosening circles.

"When do you think I mean?" barked Bert Ingram. "Yesterday or last month? No, I mean inside of the last hour or so!"

"You're kind of rough, ain't you?" remarked Les, looking Ingram in the eye.

He did not stare in fear or in anger, but with the same curious intentness which he had first displayed. For anger and fearful danger did not seem to horrify or appall or disgust him; it merely fascinated him to the bottom of his soul.

The leader, however, had not time to take further note of the peculiarities of this youth. He now declared, with a savage vehemence:

"Talk out, kid, or I'll have a rope throwed and daubed onto you! And then we'll teach you a lesson that you had really ought to of learned at home!"

Les Tarron said: "Wait a minute!" Dropping his chin in his hand, he seemed lost in thought.

This curious vagueness seemed to irritate the leader

more than ever, and he roared: "Half-wit, did you call him! I tell you, the kid ain't got a brain in his whole head!"

Les Tarron looked up and nodded.

"You agree with me, eh?" asked the leader, and there was a roar of laughter from his companions.

"A man went by here a while ago," said Tarron.

"How long?"

"About forty-five minutes."

"You remember seeing him, do you? What sort of a man, then?"

"Big man. Pretty big, I'd call him."

"Aye, aye!" cried Ingram, his eyes flashing. "I begin to think that there's *some* sense in you. Yes, if it's the fellow that we're after, he's big enough for two. Go on!"

"What else?" asked Les Tarron.

"What sort of horse was he riding?"

Tarron's eyes wandered a little, and then lighted as though in memory.

"A big brown horse," said he.

"Good! One big brown horse! I think that I know the one!"

Tarron added: "With white in the tail, too."

"That's it! You've named it! What shape was the horse in?"

"Near tired out," said Tarron.

There was a yell of delight from the entire group at this news.

"We'll have blood before night," said Bert Ingram, rolling his eyes at the neighboring mountains as though his fierce thoughts were already busy roaming there in search of prey. "You say that horse was tired out?"

"Tired so bad that when he got to this little grade here, the big man jumped down and walked and he had to drag the horse after him, the poor nag was so dead beat."

Bert Ingram growled in utter satisfaction.

"I never heard anything better than that!" he said. "Kid, seems like you got some sense, after all. And now tell me one more thing: What shape was the big man in?"

"He seemed to be hurt bad," replied Tarron.

"Hello! What makes you think that?"

"Because he was bending over and walking with short steps. He seemed to be in a lot of pain."

"Darn him!" shouted one of Ingram's followers. "I told you that I nicked him back in the old draw."

"Kid," said Ingram, "I think that you sure enough did, and I'll just make that the luckiest shot that you ever fired."

He turned back to young Tarron.

"How was he armed?"

"He carried a double-barreled shotgun."

"Hey?"

"A double-barreled shotgun."

"You lie!"

"No, I don't lie."

"Boss, I believe it. He must have stole it at the last farm that he touched up. So he's carrying a double-barreled shotgun? It means that Dorn is meaning to fight like sin if he's cornered. You savvy that, boys?"

"Sure, that's pretty likely."

"Now, kid," said the leader, "you say that the horse and the man was both pretty near done for?"

"Down-headed and dragging their feet, both of 'em," said Tarron.

"Better and better. What else?"

"Half blind with tiredness and hurt," said Tarron, "so that they hardly knew where their feet were falling, y'understand?"

"Aye, and ain't I been that way myself, so bad that I could hardly wish the same for any other man in the world!"

"Except that hound!" exclaimed one of the followers with an oath.

"Aye, except for Dorn. That swine—he needs all that he gets. And now tell us one last thing. Which way did he head?"

"I don't know," said young Tarron.

"Hey?"

"I don't know."

"Well, kid, did he bribe you to tell everything but that? But you can't keep secrets from me, young man. You don't know me, maybe? I'll let *you* in on a secret, then.

I'm Albert Ingram. Will that be news enough to start your tongue working to tell us all you know?"

Les Tarron shook his head.

"Look there," he said, and pointed to the side. "The trail splits down yonder. I only know that he went that way."

"Through those rocks!" exclaimed Ingram. "How can a trail be followed here?"

He turned to his men.

"We got to get to that trail and split. I'll go down one side with Chet. The rest of you take the other, and you can make your own choice of which side you'll travel on."

"No good, chief. We'd come to another split in the trail, and then we'd have to divide up again, and what would happen then? We can't comb all the trails in the mountains."

Ingram, his face dark with discontent, scowled and tugged viciously at his mustache.

"This kid could tell us more, if he would," said he.

"Not me," said Tarron.

The leader yanked a revolver from his holster and thrust it suddenly under Tarron's nose.

"You lie, you sneaking brat!" he shouted.

Les merely glanced at the revolver; then he laughed in Ingram's face.

"It don't seem to bother you much—a gun?" asked Ingram, sneeringly, as the coolness of the youngster brought a murmur of astonishment and admiration from the members of the band.

"Why, it sort of tickles me," confessed Tarron.

"You've told all that you know about this gent?"

"Yes, about all."

"About all? What's the rest? Out with it!"

"Only that his second horse died in that valley, yonder."

"Hello! He stopped to talk to you, then?"

"No."

"You mean to say you know that he had a second horse that dropped dead in the other valley, yonder?"

"I guess that was it."

"And he didn't tell you that?"

No."

"What are you getting at, kid?" said Ingram. "If he didn't tell you, how could you possibly know?"

"How could he tell me," asked Les Tarron, "when I didn't so much as see him?"

This statement reduced the group to a dead silence.

"Hold on, chief," said one of the men, "he's just simple, as I was telling you before. I wouldn't hold it too much against him!"

"The sneaking little rat—" began Ingram, who was a burly fellow. "If you didn't see him, he added, "how do you know so much about him?"

"I seen his trail, not him," said Les Tarron. "And I made him out of his sign."

Chapter IV

A Minor Prophet

THE LEADER SNORTED contemptuously.

"You seen him in his sign, did you?" he sneered. "That told you the color of his horse, maybe? Why, you—"

He raised the quirt in his hand; Les Tarron stood alert and watchful, his eyes not on the impending lash but on the face of the man who wielded it.

"Wait a minute, Bert," put in one of the other riders. "This kid ain't so simple as he seems. Let's hear how he can explain things to us!"

"Explain? What explanation could there be?" cried Ingram. "But I don't mind. We're losing time, but I'd like to hear what the young liar has got to say for himself."

"That's right," said the other. "What's your name?"

"Leicester Tarron."

"Les, just you up and tell us how the tracks of that horse told you that he was brown and that he had a white patch in his tail, and that he was a big horse?"

"He must have stopped beside the fence here," said Tarron, "and rubbed against it."

He tapped the outside of the fence, where a tiny patch of brown hair could be observed.

"Say, but that's pretty thin, kid!" exclaimed Ingram. "However, we'll let that go. You've got enough behind it

27

that I might want to hear explained. The white patch in his tail, for instance?"

Les pointed toward the shrubbery at some distance.

"There's a white hair tangled yonder," he said.

"Hello! Where?"

"Right there."

"Go' look, Charlie."

The delegate returned with a hair almost a yard long, which he was winding around his forefinger.

"The kid's right. He's got uncommon sharp eyes, though. Uncommon queer. But you've only started, kid. You said that this here horse was tired out."

"Sure he was tired out. Right here where he rubbed against the fence, he stopped and staggered. Look at where those tracks are doubled."

He pointed down.

"Where?" asked Ingram. "I don't see—wait a minute. By heavens, I think the kid is right!"

"A horse don't stagger for fun," said Tarron calmly.

"You're right he don't. But, go ahead! You said that the man was fagged out and hurt."

"There's his trail on this side, closest to the fence. Look at his steps. By the way that the heel-marks show, he's a big man; but his stride is short, and in some places it's a lot shorter than in others. He's a big man, and he's able to step out and walk fast, but something holds him back and ties him up, and what could that be except that he's been hurt and weakened inside so's he's not himself?"

The five regarded the youth as if he were a sort of minor prophet. The sneering smile had left even the face of Bert Ingram who, dismounting, crawled along the ground upon his hands and knees and scrutinized the marks with a careful eye. Others of the troop followed his example, and there were frequent murmurings.

"And he seen that without even bending over!" exclaimed the man called Charlie, as he stood up. "Is there any Indian in you, kid?"

"I don't know," said Tarron.

"No," said Charlie, "I reckon that you ain't interested, either."

He wagged his head, as though this remark concealed some profound meaning.

"Go straight ahead with your yarn," ordered Ingram. "I'll swallow most of the rest of your bunk, but I want to know about this stuff of the double-barreled shotgun! Just lemme hear how you knew that! By the way he limped on his right foot?"

And he grinned with a curious malice.

"Now," said Tarron, "there's nothing queer about that. You see the moss along this streak of the fence, don't you? Well, that takes an impression pretty easy. And look here!"

He indicated two tiny indentations, each a little curve, very difficult to see.

"When the horse stopped for a minute, the man stopped too, and he leaned his shotgun against the fence here."

"Hang it," shouted Ingram, "he's got his answer all pat for everything! But, just the same, I'd like to know one last thing, and if he can build us an answer out of the trail, I'll eat half of my hat. Look here, kid, didn't you tell us that the horse of this gent—the second horse, I mean—had dropped dead in the other valley?"

"Yes, I said so."

"And how did you know that?"

"I didn't *know* it. But the buzzard that was sailing over that spot has dropped, and there come the rest of the buzzard family, traipsing up this way!"

He indicated the specks sailing through the heavens.

"That valley," Les continued, "ain't nothing more'n a bowl of rocks and sand. Nothing living goes through it except men, so far as I know; and only men in a terrible, desperate hurry, at that. The buzzard dropped because there was some dead thing in the valley floor. What dead thing would be there? Not likely a man. More likely a horse. And that's the only thing that was behind my guess."

He paused and yawned broadly, as though already tired by his unusual exertions.

"It's good," pronounced Bert Ingram, staring fixedly at the young mountaineer. "I hate to say that I'm beat by any man, and especially by any kid, but this kid beats me. I'd like to see the faces of his ma and pa. There's something queer somewhere!"

"Sure there is," agreed one of the troop. "But what a heap of use this kid would be to us if we had him along on the trail!"

"Aye," agreed the leader, with much unction. "And why shouldn't he come? Look here, son, there's a dollar and a half in it for you."

"No," said Les Tarron.

"Why not?"

"I can't go without that horse of mine, there."

"Well, take your horse along, kid. Why not?"

"I don't own him."

"You don't own your horse? Then who does?"

"My father."

"Wait a minute. You don't own him, but your father—well, what do I see in this?"

"Make me a present of that horse and I'll do what I can for you."

The leader whistled softly.

"How much?" he asked.

"Dad turned down a hundred and fifty for that colt the other day."

"Aye, it's a likely looking piece of horseflesh. I pay you a couple of hundred dollars for a couple of hours' work?"

"That gent that you're trailing," said Les Tarron, "has so much nerve that it's worth spending a little money to catch him."

"You know that much about him, do you?"

"Yes, anybody that's willing to tackle the valley yonder with a fagged horse, has got a lot of nerve. Most folks are afraid to try it even with a fresh one."

Ingram again whistled softly.

"You'll do what? Bring us up in sight of that fellow?"

"Yes."

"And if you fail to do that?"

"Then you take the horse for yourself—and I walk home!"

"This gets better and better," said the leader. "Did I say that this kid was simple?"

He added sharply: "Suppose that there was a brush along the way and that we needed another fighting man.

Would we have to take care of you, or could you take care of yourself?"

"I don't know," said Tarron quietly.

"I mean—can you shoot?"

"I got a gun."

"Let's see it!"

Bert Ingram took the revolver and chuckled over it.

"Kind of loose," he estimated. "Rattles in the head and shaky in the heel and wore out in the teeth—well, fifty years old, ain't it?"

"I dunno," said Les Tarron. "My granddad owned it."

There was a burst of laughter.

"Give him a good gun, chief, if you're going to try him," advised Charlie, who seemed to be a second in command, a sort of lieutenant to Ingram.

"Let him try his hand with his own gun," decreed Ingram sternly. "Hit this!"

He waited until Tarron, unabashed by the ridicule, dropped the revolver back into his pocket; then, scooping up a piece of gray slate three or four inches in diameter, he tossed it into the air.

"Hit it, kid!" he ordered, as the stone sailed through space.

Young Tarron stood with his fine head thrown back, his dull, vacant eyes apparently lost in a study of the blue heavens above him. As for the spinning stone—surely nothing so near and so small could arrest his attention!

But just as the stone reached the crest of its rise and poised for the fall, the Colt flashed in Tarron's hand. There was a loud explosion; a puff of old-fashioned black powder smoke.

But the piece of slate had disappeared.

It had been snuffed out in mid-air. In the brush near by, an instant later, there was a light rattling, as though a handful of sand had been thrown upon the foliage.

Mr. Ingram, for some reason, dropped his quirt on the ground and trod upon it. And he flushed redly. Could it be that he was remembering how he had raised his whip, and how the mild, blank eye of this handsome boy had watched indifferently the impending stroke?

Mr. Ingram winced—as though it was his own soul he had heard rattle like a handful of sand against the foliage.

Chapter V

Across the Hills

Mr. Tarron, Sr., coming slowly in from the plow, saw a little cavalcade advancing to the house, his son among them, riding the gray colt. He forgot the service which Les had rendered that morning. As a matter of fact, it was his habit to be angry first, and to think afterward, and truly this boy of his had given him ample provocation.

So he shouted: "Les!"

"Aye?"

"What do you mean by leaving the cow pasture?"

"These gents want to buy the gray," explained Les quietly.

It put only a slightly better face upon the matter, however. No mountaineer could refrain from a horse sale or a horse exchange, to be sure; but Mr. Tarron had great expectations for the colt.

"I ain't selling him," he said to the leader of the riders. "I'm keeping him for a while till he gets more mature. Then I'll try him."

"I'll make allowances for him being young," replied the leader. "And the man who's to ride him ain't a heavyweight. Come on! Let me have a price on him, will you?"

He turned his head a little and looked frowningly toward the crowded peaks of the range, amid which the lamed, weary, wounded fugitive was struggling.

Yet, with all a Westerner's love of a good horse trade, the big man would not allow his impatience to show; for there is no better way of losing all advantage in a sale than by letting it appear that one is in a hurry.

"I'll tell you something," said the farmer, with an expectant grin. "There was a fool the other day that offered me only a hundred and fifty dollars for that horse!"

Bert Ingram drew a long face.

"A hundred and fifty?" said he. "Why, man, that's a lot of money."

"A lot of money it is, and I ain't denying it," said the farmer. "Yes, sir," he added darkly, "I never paid that much for a horse myself in my whole life."

"Then," snapped Ingram, "tell me how you happened to have such a colt as that foaled on your place?"

"There's a story behind everything," said Tarron, rubbing his chin with pleasure as he thought back to that older day. "I had a fine gray mare. She was the best thing that I ever had in horseflesh. And once I drove her down into the valley—they was having the races there, y'understand—I seen that the big stallion that had been shipped in from the East and that had won the main race and a whole fortune in betting—why, I seen that that horse was pastured out in a five-acre lot—and the fence around that lot was particularly shaky—and, tell me, partner, what harm was there in putting the gray mare to pasture near the weakest part of the fence?"

He laughed joyously as he remembered the trick, and even Ingram could not help laughing also.

"You paid no fee, and you got yourself a good colt," he said.

"Yes," said the farmer, "and a lot better horse than ever his father was in his palmiest day, and that father won lots of good races."

"Hold on," said Ingram, "it's a good thing to see a man admire a horse, but I dunno about this colt. His legs are a trifle short for real speed."

"Are they?" snorted Tarron. "Mind you, I ain't showing him off in the hopes of selling him. His price is too high for most. But what makes his legs look short is because his hocks is let down so far, and because he's got something in his shoulder. Hold on! Seeing is better than hearing. Just let that partner of yours on the brown take a spin up the road, and back, and my boy will catch him on the gray."

"The brown has made quite a march today," said Ingram craftily. "It ought to get a handicap."

"Well, I ain't particular about that," declared Tarron. "Run to that white tree and around it and back. And you can have a start of from here to that black stone."

Ingram was surprised.

"Hello!" said he. "D'you mean to say that the colt could beat the brown in that distance with such a start?"

Tarron bit his lip nervously.

"The brown is a good one, I see," said he. "Well, I'll stick by what I said, though. And if the gray feels like galloping today, you'll see him run right over your horse."

"I have fifty dollars," said Ingram, "that says he won't."

Mr. Tarron's face turned actually gray.

"Fifty dollars?" he echoed huskily, for very little hard cash really passed through his hands in the course of a year.

Then he remembered a sock filled with savings that was hidden away in the house against some great crisis in their life.

"Wipe out that handicap," he said, "and I'll take your bet."

"You've got a fresh horse against a tired one," insisted Ingram.

"Then, damn it, I'll take your bet as it stands!" cried Tarron. "Go on, Les, and if you ever woke up in your life, wake up now!"

Les Tarron was already on the gray. A surcingle furnished him with a seat, and for a bridle there was a light bitless halter on the colt's head.

"Get in place, Harry," said Ingram to his man, "and ride that brown out like the wind. You know what she can do. Look to it that you get all the possibilities out of her!"

Harry needed no more encouragement.

He glanced rather contemptuously at Les, hunched ungracefully on the gray stallion. He looked at the rather coltish body of her gray. Then gathering his reins, he shouted over his shoulder: "I'll win this, and I'll win it without a handicap, too!"

"Do your talking afterward," said Ingram. "Are you both ready?"

"Ready!" they called.

"I'll shoot twice to start you. If there's only one shot, keep on your mark. Understand?"

"Yes."

"Around that birch. Now—go!"

He saw that at this moment Les Tarron had turned his horse to the side, and as he spoke, he fired twice.

The brown was off in a flash. The gray started floundering behind him.

"It's no race!" screamed Tarron. "It's crooked, and I won't pay. Jim didn't get a fair start—that fool boy— I'll skin him alive for this!"

"Go it, Harry! Go it, you little brown devil!" shouted Ingram, entranced by the success of his trick.

The brown mare was already far in the head, and to the white birch and back was, after all, only a short race.

It seemed as though the brown was gaining, under the flogging whip of her rider. But expertly as Harry jerked the cow pony around that birch and started her back, the gray gained wonderfully in the maneuver, and as the animal straightened out for the home run, the watchers could see Les Tarron, lying along the back of the gray, laughing contentedly.

"By heavens," cried Ingram, "the kid thinks that he can win still!"

"He will!" shouted the father. "The lad never makes mistakes about horses. He'll win, too!"

There was not the slightest doubt of it. In half a dozen long bounds, Jim was up with the mare and went by her with his ears pricking, perfectly in hand. Les Tarron was easing his mount at the finish. And Harry came by well to the rear, eating the dust of the gray.

"She went lame!" yelled Harry, furious and bewildered. "She stopped for nothing, after she got around the tree."

"No," answered the leader, "she ran her race, and she got beat by a better horse. That's all. Now, Tarron, what's the price of this stallion?"

"Name something," said Tarron, grinning. "You've seen him run!"

"Wait a minute. Is he trained for cutting?"

"He's a young horse," said the other defensively.

"Good with a rope, then?"

"Young to train," said Tarron gloomily. "I'll sell a horse. Him that gets my colt can train him."

"Thanks," grinned Ingram. "You got a horse here that can't cut a calf, and that can't work with a rope, and you're asking—how much?"

"When I seen that gray foaled," said Tarron, narrowing his eyes, "I went back into the house and I told my old woman that we was five hundred dollars richer than when the day was an hour younger."

"Hello!" cried Ingram. "Five hundred dollars?" And he whistled.

"That's what my wife done when I told her," said Tarron. "But I've stuck by it even since. And I've laughed at them that offered me less."

Ingram turned his head once more toward the distant mountains, and back again toward Les Tarron, whose services were now placed at such a high figure. But he had had proof enough of the value of both youth and horse, and now he was eager to finish the transaction and carry the pair off with him.

From an inner pocket he drew a fat wallet, and out of that counted five crisp, new, hundred-dollar bills. He placed these in the hands of the astonished farmer and then called: "Get ready, Les. We start now!"

"Hey—what! I ain't through!" cried Tarron, who began to suspect that he could have obtained a thousand dollars from this affluent stranger with as much ease as he had drawn five hundred. "And what d'you mean about Les? Les, what're you doing?"

Les had come from the shed carrying a battered old wreck of a saddle, which he now strapped on the gray's back.

"I'm leaving," said Les Tarron.

"Leaving?" cried his father. "Les, d'you know anything

about this man that wants to take you, and where he wants to take you?"

"I only know that he's taking me away," answered Les Tarron. "And any place over the hills is good enough for me."

He was already in the saddle.

"Hold on!" cried Tarron in genuine alarm. "I ain't gunna let you go. Your ma— Why, Les!"

"Lemme be," answered Les. "I been a fool at home all my life and now I want to see if I can't be something better on the other side, across the hills."

Chapter VI

Like a Gallon of Water

MR. TARRON WOULD not have ended his protests here. He was a comparatively slow man, but now, as he realized that his son was on the verge of riding away with strangers, his voice and his temper rose to a high pitch.

The huge form of Bert Ingram rode in before him.

"Get under weight, Les," he commanded. "I'll handle your father."

"I'm coming back, Dad," said Les Tarron. "I'm coming back to put everything right for you and Ma. Goodbye!"

"Les!" cried the father. "And you," he added to Ingram, "who are *you?* Where are you going? What work do you want Les for?"

"Work that'll keep him warm enough," replied the other. And he grinned gloomily at the farmer. "I've bought your horse, and I've bought your boy; be glad that I ain't touched a match to what's left of your family. So long!"

He turned the head of his horse, and rode instantly in pursuit of his companions.

They had turned the shoulder of the mountain, when he came up to them, and Les Tarron on the gray was in the lead. The others, having seen the matchless trail craft of the boy, were quite willing to give him precedence now, unchallenged.

He rode along at a swinging gallop until he reached the place where the trail near the cow pasture forked into two branches.

There he dismounted, and examined the ground with some care.

"He hasn't gone fast," said Tarron, in answer to the anxious question of Ingram. "And he took the upper trail here. That was foolish, because the rough ground will kill off his tired horse. And we'll surely have that horse before it's gone a mile and a half."

"If we have the horse, we have the man!" exclaimed Ingram. "Scatter out a little, boys. Let the kid work out the trail, because he can make a better job of it than all the rest of us put together. Scatter out, and keep to cover as much as you can. If I thought that the trail would be so short, we'd never have lost so much time on the getting of the gray horse. Scatter out, and go careful, because the man that Dorn sees is a dead man, as you all ought to know by this time!"

Under these instructions the men spread out, and so they advanced up the gorge, always slipping cautiously from tree to tree or from rock to rock, and sweeping every atom of the country before them.

"The kid said a mile and a half, and we've already gone a mile," said Charlie to Ingram.

"Wait a minute," chuckled the leader. "He ain't a prophet. He's only a queer kid, working out a hard trail. What does he find on those rocks, will you tell me?"

"He's got microscopes for eyes," declared Charlie. "Now tell me if *he* wouldn't be a hard one to follow and catch, particularly since he's got that gray under him?"

"As soon as this here trail is over, Charlie," asked the leader, "how long is the kid to keep the gray?"

"I thought that was his price?"

"He said he couldn't go with us unless he had the gray to carry him. That was all."

"I see." Charlie grinned. "And then he can walk back, after we've found Dorn?"

"When Dorn is dead, the kid can find his trail home

39

without a horse," said the leader. "I've an idea that I could make use of that gray. It would carry my weight in another six months."

He added, as though some explanation were needed even to this ruffian follower of his:

"The kid was sassy when I first talked to him. Now he'll have to pay to learn good manners—with me for the teacher!"

In the meantime, the gorge along which they had been working narrowed and narrowed, and finally pinched away and came out on the side of the mountain.

The whole surface was dented with abandoned pits where miners in older days had sunk their shafts in search for precious metals. And, still surviving from the old time, a cable stretched across the sharpsided canyon to the farther slope. Along that opposite slope a roadway had been hewed roughly, and there the mule trains received the ore and carted it down to the smelter far away.

A very clumsy arrangement, but one which had turned hundreds of thousands of dollars' worth of metal into coin.

Now there was a sudden shout in advance:

"There's the horse!"

They could see the exhausted brute standing, head down, beside a trickling stream of water. The saddle had been torn from the animal's back by its master before deserting his mount; and now it was standing, with glazed eyes, intent on the difficult business of breathing and trying to keep erect on its trembling legs.

Whether it would live or die was a problem.

"And Dorn is somewhere yonder," exclaimed Ingram. "Now, go like cats. He ain't far off. The kid has been right about everything else—even when he said that we'd get the horse within a mile and a half. You would think that he knew the mind of a horse, wouldn't you? Go slow, now. Even if Dorn is hurt and sick, he'll still fight like a devil, won't he?"

These cautions did not seem exactly necessary, for the four riders who followed Ingram were stealing along like cats, keen for the hunt, but careful not to expose themselves.

There was another sudden shout ahead, followed by a humming, rumbling sound. At the same moment, the old ore car, which had not traveled across the line of the cable to the far side of the valley for half a generation, perhaps, came surging out upon the line and swayed with quickening speed along the wire.

"It's that devil Dorn!" growled Ingram. "Confound him, he's side-stepping us again! Plague take him and his tricks! Stop that ore truck! Who'll stop that truck? There's five thousands dollars for him that'll stop the truck and—"

His words died suddenly. From the racing ore car there was a spurt of flame, and, with a yell of terror, one of Ingram's men jerked his horse to one side.

The next instant all were in close covert, while five steady rifles opened on the speeding car. From its metal sides came back a rapid tattoo. But would soft-nosed rifle bullets pierce the stout old sides of that truck? And if they did, would the body of the fugitive be found within?

It seemed very doubtful, and even while he reloaded and fired, big Ingram was cursing steadily to himself.

In the meantime, however, another element began to work against the fugitive.

The ore car, which had run down the cable rapidly enough at first, quickly lost pace, and now, sweeping toward the farther wall of the ravine, it had to ascend along the slack of the ancient cable. The moment this point was reached, therefore, the way of the car decreased. It swung and staggered to and fro in the air, and a strong vibration could be seen running through the old cable across the gorge.

That brought a yell of expectant triumph from the watchers. Another moment, and the car came to a halt while it was still a full twenty or thirty paces from the end of its journey.

There hung the car suspended, and the man within was powerless to move his vehicle.

A figure came quietly up and sat down beside big Ingram, who was in a frenzy of joy and excitement.

"Kid," said he, "I ain't forgetting how much of this I owe to you. I ain't forgetting. It's the end of Dorn. It's the absolute end of him, and may he burn forever!"

He looked round at his young companion and found that Les Tarron, far from showing the slightest interest in his words, had turned up his face to observe the rapid flight of a hawk which, having gone to shelter in a tree-top during the shooting, now took advantage of the lull in the firing to flash across the gully and high up into the blue of the sky at a pace which made the eye move rapidly to follow.

"Horses are pretty good," declared the boy. "But no horse can move like that. Not even Jim!" he added softly.

"I'm talking about Dorn," said the leader grimly. "Look here, kid, d'you mean to say that you're not giving a rap what happens to him? Ain't you even got any care for a man that has to hang out there and starve to death, unless he takes it into his head to throw himself out of the car and break his fool neck on the rocks under him, yonder? By heaven, I hate Dorn and I've let the whole world know that I hate him, but I've never seen a fellow in such a dirty corner as that; I can tell you! I'm sorry for him—almost. And I should think that a kid like you would feel your blood run cold!"

"Cold blood? Run cold? Never heard of that," said Les Tarron as he shied a pebble accurately, and splintered it against the face of a small rock twenty feet away.

"You don't care whether he lives or dies, eh?"

"Why should I care?" said Les Tarron. "What's he to me? Did he ever gimme a meal? Did he ever hand me a piece of good advice. Nope, he's nothing to me, dead or alive! Unless he should do something pretty fine, and it don't really look like he would."

The curiosity of the leader had become intense.

"What do you mean by that?" said Ingram. "What do you mean by 'Something pretty fine?'"

"I'll tell you now," replied the youngster. "When we was on this trail, I thought that this gent was holding out so well that maybe after I'd lived up to my contract with you and brought you into sight of him, I would just slip over and give him a hand to get away from you."

"You thought that, eh?" snarled the leader, his keen eyes narrowing.

"I thought that. But now I see him hanging out there in a bucket neither up the well or down, and such a fool as that don't deserve nothing except to be spilled out like a gallon of water!"

Chapter VII

"Something Pretty Fine"

It reminded Ingram very much of the attitude of a wild beast—of a wolf, say, which has regard only for the things which it may prey up, and those which it may not. So it was with this youth. There were in this world certain things to be feared. The first were of account, the others were worthless.

In what other manner would a beast of the forest think, and how else would it act?

There was only one sharp point of divergence. It seemed that one capable of a "fine" performance would gain the hearty respect, almost the friendship, of this singular youth.

"Just tell me, kid," said Ingram, "just lemme know how this here Dorn could have done anything finer than he worked while scooting up the valley ahead of us. What else could he have tried?"

"I'm willing to tell you that," responded young Tarron. "In the first place, he would have left his horse a way back and hid him in the trees."

"Would that have puzzled you any?"

"No, but it would have puzzled you. And he don't know

that I'm on his trail. He don't even know that there's a fellow like me in the world. He should have hid his horse to hold you up. Then he should have hiked along up the valley, and at this point, maybe where there's plenty of water and good shade and berries to be had—he should have laid down; then he should have washed his wound, and rested, and waited for you to show yourselves. And when he got a chance he should have killed at least one of you."

"Supposing that he could!" cut in Ingram, who was nevertheless intensely interested in the recital of possibilities.

"He could have done it, well enough," answered Les Tarron. "He has the steady nerves, and he ain't unused to shooting at folks it seems."

"That would have left five of us to surround him!"

"No, he couldn't know about me. For all that he know, there was only five of you. He kills one. Maybe he wounds another. Anyway, at the most, that would leave only four of you. You have to circle around through the rocks. There ain't any place from which you could fire down on him, and there ain't any place from which he couldn't fire down on you. That would have made a good deal of difference."

"While we sent one of us to hunt chuck, and the other three watched him, and he starved to death here!"

"You think so? No, he could live for a couple of weeks on the roots of these here, and on the berries. Dry 'em on the rocks in the sun, and grind 'em up, and they're thick with seeds and stay your belly almost as good as bread."

Ingram frowned a little and bit his lip. He felt that he knew wilderness men and wilderness ways, but this youth was introducing him to a stratum of knowledge far beyond his ken. Far below it, too, perhaps.

He said finally, with a shrug of his shoulders: "He's badly wounded. That would have made it impossible for him."

"Not so badly hurt that he couldn't keep you all busy following him—and not catching him so very fast, after all. He could have stayed up here for days, until his wounds got better and he was all rested. And, in the meantime, you four would be having your dead man to bury and your own chuck to rustle, and you'd be pretty miserable after a while, because gents like you ain't very good for that kind of work."

"Just what kind of work? Fighting?"

"No, watching. The cat sits by the gopher hole. You know what I mean? You want excitement. That's where you're pretty weak. I would have laid up here and never made a sound. Finally one of you would have had to come up closer. You couldn't help it. You'd say: 'Maybe he's died of his wounds. Maybe he's dug a hole for himself and got away. Maybe he's asleep.' You would have thought like that, and felt pretty bad, and finally one of you would have come sneaking up to see. And after that," concluded Les Tarron, "there would have been only three of you to watch this here place, and that three would have been feeling pretty sick, and beginning to think about home, and bacon and eggs!"

"It's easy to kill men in daydreams," said Ingram.

"And in fact, too," said the boy.

"Did you ever kill a man, kid?"

"Oh, no. I never wanted to. But I could, easy enough."

"You got no doubt about yourself?"

"Nope. You see, it's easier for me to shoot straight at a living thing than it is at a dead one. I'm not so dead certain shooting at a rock. But a bird on the wing—I like to shoot at that!"

He nodded and laughed a little, rubbing his strong young hands together.

"I believe you with all my heart," said Ingram. "I believe that some day you'll be wanted. I believe that some day you'll be chased by a thousand men. Well, when that time comes, good luck to you! And if—hey—what in damnation!"

He broke off thus suddenly because of a shout from Charlie followed by a rapid firing of rifles.

A voice was crying at them from near by: "Wake up, chief. Dorn has left the ore car, and he's hauling himself toward land hand over hand!"

It was evident at once that this was exactly what had happened and that the man in the car had not the slightest intention of hanging in the air like a bucket of water to evaporate. Rather, he would leave the car and trust to the strength of his weary arms, hauling himself hand over hand toward the farthest side of the ravine.

The ore car, in the meantime, released from his weight, began to swing from side to side and to bounce up and down on the cable, not rapidly, but with sufficient vibration to make it extremely difficult, no doubt, for Dorn to keep on his way.

However, the oscillations of the car served one good purpose with Dorn. For at the very moment when a rifle was trained upon him, the ore car was sure to swing between him and the muzzle and the bullet sped not into his flesh but into the metal sides of the car.

Instead of having a certain prize in his hands, big Ingram now was confronted with the danger of losing his man altogether; for if Dorn could reach the farther side he would have gained valuable headway over his pursuers—so impracticable would be an attempt to cross that ravine.

Ingram's fury and impatience boiled over.

"Scatter to the sides, you fools!" he screamed at his men. "Scatter to the sides, and then you can plant a bullet in the hide of that—"

A wild stream of profanity followed. The men hastily scattered to this side and to the other, rifle in hand, until they could see before them the almost naked body of the fugitive flashing in the sun; for Dorn, in his last terrible effort to escape, had as a matter of course, stripped off practically all of his clothing. He dangled from the cable, swinging himself along with rhythmic sweeps of his arms, and in this crystal-clear mountain air, one could even see the play of the sunlight upon the gigantic muscles which covered his back and shoulders.

Big Ingram shouted suddenly: "Hold back, all of you! By heaven, nobody's to have the pleasure of killing that swine except me! Don't nobody fire a shot, you hear?"

They heard, and they stayed their eager hands.

"Dorn!" shouted Ingram. "Dorn! It's me! It's the fool kid and blockhead that's got a gun trained on you. Will you turn around to take the bullet in the breast?"

Another half dozen efforts and Dorn would have been at least close enough to the edge of the ravine wall to have thrown himself toward the brush which lined its slopes and trusted to chance.

Now that voice of enmity stabbed him and all at once he hung limp, dangling at the full length of his arms. The heart had gone out of him, and Ingram, sighting down his rifle, laughed with a black exultation, for of all the sweets in the world, there is none so entrancing as the knowledge that your foeman confesses your conquering hand before he dies.

Spirit was snatched from Dorn, it seemed, after his long and daring struggle for life, and yet, no—he could still make another effort. Gathering himself with all his might, he flung back to Ingram a defiant shout, and swayed his heavy, sun-polished body on toward the ravine wall.

That shout seemed to find an audible echo on the nearer shoulder of the mountain. There was a ringing cry of admiration, shrill and high, and the next instant Ingram's hat was lifted from his head, and, caught by a passing gust, whirled away over the liquid shadows of the ravine.

He started back with a cry of terror.

"Who—what—" he began, when another bullet sang through the air not an inch from his nose.

He asked no more questions; but his wild eyes, sweeping his men, saw them scattering hastily for the rocks, and shelter. He himself leaped for protection, and at the same moment his thundering voice announced: "It's that devil-born brat—it's that young hound, Les Tarron! He's betrayed me! Oh, send him through fire and back again!"

Thus wailed big Ingram, as though sure that this sudden flank attack would give his foeman safety.

Taking shelter under the lee of a rock, he pitched the rifle to his shoulder. Yonder was Dorn, still struggling toward safety with weary, heaving shoulders; but as Ingram curled his trigger finger ready to launch the bullet, he saw his target suddenly drop downward.

Dorn had tumbled into a mass of shrubbery against the farther wall, and five rapid-fire rifles poured a hasty hail of lead at the spot where he had disappeared. There was still at least one good chance out of two that they would nail him.

But Ingram was too furious, for his part, to aim straight. A black mist of fury kept swirling across his eyes.

"May I get 'em both!" he sobbed, in the ecstasy of his anger. "May I get 'em both! *Charlie!*"

"Yes?"

"Did the kid really get the gray colt, too?"

"I don't see the gray anywhere."

"Ten thousand damnations!" shouted big Ingram. "That gives us ten times as much work for getting him!"

Chapter VIII

A Drifting Log

LES TARRON, among the rocks, was amusing himself to the top of his bent. Five men were attempting to force their way across the mountainside toward him, but he had in his hand Charlie's Winchester, an excellent and new gun, and around his hips was the cartridge belt of another of Ingram's riders. So that he was supplied with a gun and with ammunition.

He was not shooting to kill; he was not even shooting to wound. For this appeared to Les Tarron only a game— a complicated and dangerous game, to be sure—but, nevertheless, one to be mightily enjoyed.

He had three problems before him, while retreating. In the first place, he must keep under cover. In the second place, he must break that cover to observe his advancing enemies. In the third place, he must break that cover to fire upon them.

He managed it with the greatest possible adroitness. The gray colt, Jimmy, had been sent on ahead, and like an obedient dog the fine horse wandered in the lead, now and then tossing up its head with a snort as bullets whined through the air close by. Behind the horse came the master. He was never in one spot long and, shifting constantly to one side or another, or drawing back, he never showed himself twice in the same spot.

49

All that was to be seen of him at the best was a mere flash of face at the corner of a shrub or a stone, and in a single instant he had seen what he wished to see. Or else there was a single flash of rifle or revolver, and a bullet sped down the mountainside to clip within half an inch of a head, or to cut through the sleeve of a man who hardly dreamed that he was exposed.

The five men, infuriated by this tantalizing fire, and never dreaming that these bullets were not intended to kill, grew hotter and hotter for their work and in their eagerness to close with the foe, for each of them felt that he had escaped death at least once by the merest hair's breadth. Yet they had learned caution, and not one of them dared to advance except on hands and knees from shelter to shelter, or even like snakes, wriggling forward.

Whenever the faintest chance offered, they sent a hail of lead at the fugitive. But they scored no hits, and they knew it; for ahead of them, time and again, they heard a burst of half-manly, half-boyish laughter, as Les Tarron slipped away before them.

Who has not felt the joy of a game of tag, and the thrill of passing just under the tips of another's fingers? But Les Tarron was to be tagged with a slug of lead from a Colt .45, or a large caliber Winchester.

When he was halfway down the slope, he suddenly increased his rate of retreat. He caught the gray colt, sprang to his back, and sent him scampering to the rear. It was a singular thing to see Jimmy running like a mountain goat along the steeply angled hillside; but he had been raised among the mountains, and he had learned to jump from rock to rock and hold his footing by turning up his toes and letting the spongy frog of the hoof do the gripping.

So Jimmy carried his young master lightly down the hillside and before Ingram had the slightest idea of what was happening there was a rattling of stones toward the bottom of the ravine. Then, spying down among the shadows, he saw a bright, fleeting glimpse of Jimmy as the good horse passed into the densely sheltering thicket of the river bottom.

In the meantime, what had become of Dorn?

Unless he had been pierced by one of the bullets that

were showered at the point where he disappeared into the brush, he by now had had a fine respite, and it might well be that he had moved on. But in what direction? Had he gone on over the ridge, or had he turned back and wandered up the headwaters of the creek? Or had he simply blundered feebly downstream?

But there had been no question of further walking with Dorn. He had been thoroughly exhausted already, and the strain of swinging himself along the cable by hand had completed the wreck of his forces.

He had rolled down through the thicket more like a log than a man; then he had lain on his back and, while gasping in his breath, had looked up through a gap in the treetops and watched the spitting guns on the hill above him—five guns against one!

What mysterious enemy had arisen against his pursuers then?

He was too enfeebled even to think. When he could rise, he staggered to the edge of the water, not because he had any plan, but simply because it was downhill.

There he saw a half-rotted log stuck against the shore. It gave him a thought. He thrust it from the bank and lay face down upon it, embracing it loosely with his nerveless arms. In that fashion he floated down the stream.

Had the water been swifter, it would have spun this natural raft like a top. Had it been shallower, he would quickly have grounded on any one of a hundred banks. But the water that day was neither too high nor too low, and kind gods who had watched the persecution of Dorn now came to succor him.

He thought neither of gods nor men. He thought not at all. Utter exhaustion had blanked his mind, and now he relaxed like one who has been pierced by a bullet.

Pierced he had been, but no wound he had received could compare with the dreadful drain of his fatigue.

His eyes closed. He slept, with his hand trailing into the snow water and growing frozen, and with the sun burning into his back. He slept, and every breath during his sleep was a deep moan of relief.

And, in his sleep, he only knew that he was constantly drifting on and on. It was no longer the legs of an exhausted horse to which he had to trust. It was no longer

to his own failing power that he had to commit himself.
The river at its own pleasure carried him softly on and
left his enemies, if it pleased God, far behind him.

Such was the sleeping mind of the fugitive, when it
seemed to him that the sun passed behind a cloud, and
the motion of the river ceased.

All that had kept him unconscious during that hour of
drifting had been the sense of motion. Now, as that sense
was lost, he roused himself suddenly and sat up on the
log.

It threatened to roll over with him. The trees wavered
before his eyes. And then he saw that before him there
was a new enemy—a man sitting on a rock at the verge
of the stream, while a gray horse stood near by, picking
at the green, tender tips of the shrubs and watching the
shining face of the water and every shadow that dappled
its surface.

Dorn rallied himself.

He had slept for only an hour, but with what an
incalculable value had been invested that brief time of
rest! For now he could think and feel. Life, which had
hardly been more than a blurred mist, was now a desirable
thing. The taste for it had come back. Yes, with a violent
passion he saw that he loved life as he had never loved it
before.

And, having slipped through the hands of the terrible
Ingram and his band, he was now confronted by a youth
of less than twenty, surely.

Here was something hardly to be feared. Rather was
it not in the nature of a gesture from heaven itself? This
man had been sent across his way to provide him with
clothes, weapons, ammunition, with everything that he
had thrown from him when he made the attempt to leave
the car and get to the valley wall.

So Dorn, lifting his bearded face from the boy, smiled
at the stranger.

"Hey—hello!" said he. "It looks as though I've been
asleep."

"Aye, it looks that way."

"Have you been sitting here watching me long?"

"Not more'n half an hour."

"What? Half an hour?"

"Yes, about that long. You started to wake up as soon as you got into the shadow. But it took you a long time to come around."

"Half an hour here?" echoed Dorn.

He stretched out his naked arms. One could see, then, the strength which had defied Ingram through the long pursuit. Dorn was not a young man; he was all of forty. But at that age, when some men grow soft and flabby, others grow mightier than ever. The head is a little slower and the step a little heavier. But the eye is more steady, and the hand has an enormous weight which it lacked in younger and more athletic years.

So it was with Dorn. He had been a mighty man in his youth. He was a mightier man now. If he had not quite the lightning foot and hand which the boxer needs, he had the cunning and the vast weight of power which the wrestler requires.

And now Dorn schemed only how he might be able to lay his grip upon this young man. That was all! Once that grip was established, he would master the youngster, strip him of those possessions which were necessary to his own existence, and then he would pass on, leading that gray horse over the rough, and riding it over the smooth. If only that horse had looked a little more powerful!

In the meantime, was this boy simply a country yokel, or was he a member of the Ingram gang, keeping post here, while Ingram and the rest rushed up to close in their arch enemy?

He would not ask questions. With that resolution, Dorn worked his way to the end of the log until his bare feet touched the muddy bottom; then he waded for the shore.

When Dorn stood up, he looked larger than ever, for he stood several inches over six feet, and thirty or forty pounds more than two hundred were distributed on his magnificent frame. He had been hurt, too, and one could see in his bare side the half crimson, half purple gash which a bullet had made in raking his ribs. But one hardly thought of such an injury seriously enfeebling him. For so great were his strength and his bulk that such scratches were merely like small indentations on the broad trunk of an oak.

Chapter IX

Slippery Shores

ONE LONG STRIDE brought Dorn to the shore. There he
slipped a little in the slime and the mud and staggered.
The youngster on the bank instantly extended a hand
which Dorn grasped, and, drawing himself up, he changed
his grip from that hand to the body of his assistant and
flung himself with all his power upon the smaller and
younger man.

He saw a hand flash down toward a gun, and he seized
the forearm and began to twist the arm with all his might.
In just such a manner, taking a clever purchase, he had
once broken a strong man's arm. But now he felt muscles
leap out like steel ridges beneath the covering skin. The
arm twisted out of his grasp. He threw his whole might
into a bear-hug that should have fairly broken the back
of the smaller man. Instead, the comparatively slender
body of Les Tarron swelled with prodigious power, and
then—

Dorn could never exactly understand how it had been
done. But all at once he was lifted and whirled; then he
lay upon the ground.

Over him leaned a face as cold as iron, and eyes like

the eyes of a tiger blazed down at him. A clawlike hand closed over his throat—

Then he was raised swiftly and lightly to his feet.

"I guess I understand," said the youth. "You didn't have much, and you thought that you might help yourself to what I've got. Was that it?"

Dorn smiled suddenly and frankly.

"You've taught me a lesson, lad," said he. "I came down this creek nearer dead than living, and I acted as other desperate men might have acted. The fact is that I'm more than half starved, pretty badly hurt, nearly naked, as you can see for yourself; and behind me are five fighting men, all well mounted, and wanting nothing so much as my scalp. Now, if I haven't made an enemy out of you, too, I want to know what you'll do for me? Have you anything to say? Anything, I mean, beyond the fact that I've tried to treat you like a snake?"

"Get on that horse," said the youngster. "He'll take you along; you can't travel overland with bare feet, you see."

With a foot already in the stirrup, Dorn asked almost fiercely: "Will you trust me with this horse, lad, after what—"

"It's not much of a trust, as a matter of fact," Tarron smiled. "You simply couldn't ride Jimmy away if you tried."

"Hello! And why not?"

"Because he'd come back to me if I called to him."

"Even if I used a whip to him?"

"That would only make him buck you off. Come here, Jimmy!"

Dorn pulled back on the reins with all his might, but the stallion shook his head and trotted up to his master.

"The confoundedest thing that I've ever seen," said Dorn, panting with his effort. "And now what do we do?"

"Ingram is coming down the valley," said Tarron. "But he's still a half mile away. That gives us time. You ride Jimmy in the water there where the water's shallow and the sand is firm. You can tell by the clean face of the sand and the way that it shines back at the sun, like gold."

Dorn obeyed without a word. And, combing his thick

55

beard with his fingers, he found himself being carried down the course of the stream smoothly and easily, while his young guardian followed on the bank.

"They must be coming close!" cried Dorn at last, growing tense with impatience.

"Listen!" said the boy.

He raised his hand, and Dorn, straining his ears, could hear the crashing of the brush farther up the valley.

"They're coming," gasped Dorn. "And if—"

"Don't do it," said the boy. "I've got a rifle and a revolver, as you see, and I could kill you easy with either of them. And I'd do it, too, as sure as I'm standing here. You understand?"

Dorn stared into the calm, quiet face, and nodded.

"I understand," he said gloomily. "But what are we to do?"

"They'll slow up pretty soon when the trail goes out."

"They're the very devil in following hard trails. I know by experience, my lad. They may cast straight ahead and so come on us here!"

"I don't think that they will, though. Ingram is too hot to kill you, and he won't take chances of overrunning your trail. You can depend upon that!"

"You know Ingram?"

"I know him today. I know that he wants your scalp!"

"Aye, and he does, though," said Dorn. And he added through his teeth: "But he'll never have it. He's chased me and hounded me for a long time, but he's never had me. And he never will have me—only what's to be done now? Something quick! Something quick! Let me just give this good horse his head—"

"No," said the boy firmly.

"Wait!" said Dorn. "I'll buy him from you."

"There was five hundred dollars paid down for that horse today in hard cash," said Les Tarron.

"What's your name?"

"Tarron—Les Tarron."

"Tarron, I'll give you a thousand! Take it out of this wallet and if you help yourself to an extra hundred or so, it will do no harm—but this horse has got to be mine!"

The wallet was not taken.

"I won't sell," Les said calmly.

56

"Rent him, then!"

There was a sound of horses breaking through the underbrush along the stream. It threw Dorn into a panic.

"Tarron," he cried, "rent the horse to me! Take the thousand, take two thousand if you like, and let me go with him."

"You don't mean that much to me," said Tarron coldly. "I want you to win, and I'm taking my chances with you. But I won't let you take the gray. And if you try to make a break—I tell you, I can shoot straight!"

One last frantic glance was cast at him by Dorn, and then the latter surrendered.

"Have it your own way. Whatever you decide on, I've got to do; but remember that if Ingram finds you with me, you're the deadest lad in these mountains."

"Ingram find *me?*" said Les Tarron. He laughed.

"No," he said, "whatever happens, Ingram won't find me! Ingram is pretty blind, you know."

"Ingram blind—a poor trailer, you mean? Well, young man, let me see what you do. I have my own opinion about what that fiend of an Ingram can do at working out trail puzzles."

"Here we are," said the youngster, as they came to a point where a slender rivulet wandered down into the main creek. "Turn Jimmy up here and keep him going."

Dorn hesitated only an instant, then he rode the horse up the little run of water.

"We're hemming ourselves in against the wall of the valley," he complained. "There's no way out if they catch us here."

"They won't catch us. They're too hot on the trail."

"But if they miss me, they'll still have your footprints on the bank."

"No," said Tarron. "Because I'm leaving no footprints that they can read."

Dorn, glancing askance at him to see if this were a joke, noticed that as a matter of fact the boy's foot never fell on the sand. Where grass grew short and compact, there he stepped with wonderful lightness; or on stones, or on fallen tree trunks. Sometimes he had to bound from one place to another; but the older man began to understand how it was that even a keen eye would hardly be able to decipher the trail which he left.

A scant hundred yards from the start, the rivulet was found to tumble down the sheer wall of the canyon.

"Now?" inquired Dorn.

"We'll stop here and rest," said Tarron.

"Stop here, right under their noses?"

"I hope that they ain't going to find us. For their own sakes I hope that!"

"Five to two!" said Dorn. And he added: "One of us hasn't a gun!"

"Are you straight with a rifle?" asked the boy.

"I've done a great deal of shooting."

"Favor your left hand a little," said Tarron. And he passed the rifle to his companion. "It shoots a trifle to the left. If you try anything over a couple of hundred yards, allow about two inches to the left. But shorter than that, it hardly matters much, unless you're trying for the head."

Dorn swallowed hard.

"That leaves you what?" he asked.

"This," said Tarron. And he drew out a Colt. "Take Jimmy out of the water," he ordered.

Dorn obeyed. Then, dismounting, he watched the horse take position behind its master.

They were in a little bracken of tall ferns and short shrubs. The trees before them made a thin screen, but anyone who advanced within fifty yards of them was sure to see the horse, at least. No; a word from the boy made the stallion lie down. And now Dorn began to breathe a little more freely.

After all, there seemed good reason to hope that the party would pass on down the stream. But if they turned aside, with odds of five to two—

He hardly cared to think about that.

In the meantime, the horses and the voices of the pursuers were passing down the canyon. Another moment, and they were at the mouth of the runlet. There, instead of passing on, they paused.

Dorn cast an anxious eye at young Tarron, but the latter smiled back blithely.

"It may be a party, after all," he said.

Dorn gaped. A party! Was that the opinion of this youth concerning a battle of two half-armed men against five fully equipped with weapons?

Then they heard the ringing voice of Ingram shouting: "Scatter and hunt!"

Chapter X

Five Riders Searching

ALMOST INSTANTLY THEY could hear the sound of horses turning toward them.

"They've got us cornered here!" gasped Dorn. "And if they sight us, how can we get away?"

"That's why they'll never look too close in here," said Les Tarron. "Lie low. And keep your rifle ready. If you'll take one, I'll take the other. And always remember that if two come together, you take the right hand man. If only one shows us, I'll take him!"

He snapped out these orders like one accustomed to command; and although Dorn was a fellow who had been through many a bitter fight, still he accepted the orders unquestioningly, with the instinctive subservience of a man who realizes that a superior authority is present.

They lay in the ferns. The gray colt was stretched out like a dog in the grass, his eyes glistening and his ears sharply pricked, as though this were a great game to him.

Glancing aside at young Tarron's face, Dorn saw that there was an equal joy in his eyes, and all the while he was smiling a little to himself. It made Dorn shake his head in wonder, but it also helped to steady his battered nerves. A companion who looked upon battle with a sort of hungry joy was just the man for an emergency such as this!

Then through the brush ahead of them, and not twenty steps away, loomed a rider.

Dorn set his teeth, expecting his companions' gun to bark at once, but there was no sound. He glanced at Les Tarron and saw that his face was suffused with blood and that the triangular muscle at the base of his jaw worked rapidly in and out. Plainly he wanted to send a bullet into yonder fierce rider, and also plainly he was holding himself in check with all his power of will.

Another shape came shadowy through the trees. It was Ingram—Ingram in person, turning his stern eye here and there in quest of his quarry.

"They'll never be here," said the first rider.

"Why not?" snapped Ingram, in high bad humor.

"Why, it's a regular pocket; not even a fly could climb that wall of the mountain. And Dorn wouldn't be fool enough to try to hide in such a place."

"It ain't Dorn that I think about," said Ingram. "I've finished chiefly with him—for a while."

"What? Finished with Dorn?" gasped the companion.

"Aye," said Ingram.

"Finished with Dorn, and the belt that he wears?"

Dorn's hand instinctively went down to his belt, which circled his body above the hips and against the skin. But young Tarron had not seemed to hear.

"I'll have the belt in the end," said Ingram. "But before we can ever get Dorn, we'll have to tag the kid with a slug of lead."

"That won't be hard," replied the other. "He's a smart kid on a trail, but he's too young to amount to much."

"Too young, you say!" snarled Ingram, and he added: "I'll tell you this, bo. Some gents get old in one way, and keep young in others. I've seen a lot of men that was wise and old in their own front parlors and was worse'n infants in the wilderness; and I've seen gents what was fools in town that was Solomon himself in the mountains. And this kid may be one of them!"

"You rate him high," said the other carelessly. "But one slug of lead would finish him."

"And five slugs would finish us," declared Ingram. "And maybe the kid is the one to shoot 'em!"

"Anyway," said the other, "two men can't ride one horse—when one of the men is the size of Dorn!"

"Aye, and I thank God for that! We got 'em in our hand. If only we can find how to close our fingers over 'em! But the worst day's work that we ever done was when we took the kid along to help us on the trail."

"It was," admitted the other.

"It'll take a lot of undoing, that job will. Go ahead, there, and ride through that shrubbery."

"All right."

Ingram's companion started forward; but, at that moment, there was a sudden series of shots and a yell farther down the stream. The riders whirled about and spurred their horses hotly in the direction of the noise.

Dorn relaxed on the ground with a gasp.

"I thought that we were gone just then!" he admitted.

"Did you think so? *They* were nearly gone, though. And, look here! If you hate Ingram so much, and if you need to get rid of him as bad as he needs to get rid of you, why not take a chance and kill him out of hand?"

"And let the law into this game, my young friend? No, no, I've dodged the law so far and I intend to keep on dodging it!"

"Seems to me," said Tarron, "that you'd have a pretty good proof of self-defense."

"What good would that do me? If they could bring a charge and get me arrested, that would hold me quiet and steady. And then a bullet through the jail window, or when I was being brought into the courtroom to the judge—why, those things could be handled so easily by them that they would ask for nothing better!" He added bitterly: "Besides, what difference would it make to me if I were to kill Ingram. He's only a unit. There are others. And the one at the top could hire twenty men as good as Ingram. They know that he's headed me off, so far. And that's the only reason that they keep him in command. But if he were dead, maybe there'd be a dozen they could get that would run me harder than even Ingram has done!"

He said this with an utter conviction that could not be

gainsaid. Then he went on: "What's happened to call Ingram away from this spot?"

"Luck!" said the boy. "We're getting them puzzled. They don't know what to make of us, quite. And they're beginning to be nervous. That's why they started shooting. One of them thought he saw a shadow move like a man, I suppose. He began to use his gun. Listen to them chasing down the canyon! Him that started the shooting is ashamed to admit that he didn't have anything real to shoot at. And now all that we have to do is to go up the back trail for a ways."

"Leave the shelter here?" asked Dorn.

"Aye, leave the shelter. You can't win any sort of a game by sitting still, you know!"

"Yes, I know that, of course. I'll go if you say the word, Tarron!"

Forth they went, but new ideas were beginning to form in the mind of Les Tarron. He knew the face of Dorn and the face of Ingram. He knew that they were trying to kill one another. But their motives were all obscured utterly. He could tell that Ingram hated Dorn, but it might very well be that there was no foundation for the hatred other than the fact that he was trailing the man.

In the meantime, other items had been added to Les Tarron's stock of information concerning this singular affair.

In the first place, there was a motive for the hunt in something contained in the belt which surrounded the hips of Dorn. In the second place, there was a power behind Ingram which thrust him on along the trail. So much so that if Ingram fell Dorn declared that a dozen others could be hired to take his place. In the background, undiscerned and distant, there were powers which pulled the strings that caused Ingram to ride with his four stanch fighting men. Who and what were those powers? Who were "they"?

However, these ideas did not trouble Les Tarron's mind a great deal. They merely occupied him more and more. He had lived in a dreamy world of little meaning. Now he had been brought out into the real world, and that first contact with danger and excitement was like the taste of fresh air to stifled lungs. And he was utterly contented.

He did not care where the trail led. It was sufficient to him that he was actually on the way!

Now he turned down the little rivulet, which masked the trail of Jimmy, as it had masked the trail before. They went straight up the margin of the creek for another hundred yards or so, and then Tarron at last gave the word to the big man to ride his horse up on the firm bank.

Behind them, Ingram and his followers had at last made up their minds that there was little to be gained by continuing the hunt downstream. They had turned back, and the noise of their horses could be plainly discerned to the rear. For all sounds were magnified and made much of and wonderfully prolonged in the echoing heart of this canyon.

"Let him jog along," said Les Tarron. "I'll follow along behind you.

Dorn, accordingly, loosed the rein and the stallion broke into a long, freely striding trot. It seemed to Dorn that he had never been conscious of more delicious motion than that which carried him with such fluid ease away from Ingram and his men. And when he glanced behind him, he saw Les Tarron running lightly in the rear, not at all embarrassed by the speed or by the grade up which they were climbing.

Such a man hardly needed a horse to help him!

So thought Dorn, and shook his head again. For the whole affair of this day was beginning to look more and more miraculous. It was as though the heavens had opened in his time of greatest need and sent this rescuer to help him. It looked, indeed, like the very hand of Fate.

Dorn began to relax all through his spirit, and, sitting back in the saddle, he abandoned himself to the superior guidance of this creature of the wilds.

In the meantime, they were coursing swiftly up the valley. They climbed past the point at which the cable and the old ore car crossed the ravine; and they could see the car dangling above their heads, now trundled a little from side to side in the rising wind. They climbed still higher. And then the ravine melted away and came to

64

a point where the stream which had carved it joined the side of the mountain.

There the two fugitives paused. They looked behind them down the valley, and when Dorn raised his glasses to his eyes, he could make out in a clearing of the woods, five riders searching slowly for their prey.

And it seemed to Dorn a miracle that he was not down there still, and in the shadow of their danger!

Chapter XI

For The Lost Cause

LES TARRON STOOD on the top of a hill where the last
light of day was clinging, though the valley at his feet
was deeply drenched in shadows. And through those
shadows he watched the glimmering lights of a town begin
to shine in greater and greater numbers, like golden bees
coming forth to taste the sweetness of the night.

He turned back to the huddled heap of manhood; Dorn,
lost in a profound sleep. For the brief slumber of the
afternoon had not appeased the enormous fatigue of the
big man. It had simply given him the little added strength
which was necessary before he could be able to make the
final effort to escape. All through the afternoon he had
been failing, and a dozen times he had nearly fallen out
of the saddle, so deep was his slumber. Now he lay
prone and nothing would wake him. It seemed to the
boy safe enough to leave his companion.

When the black waves of slumber were about to over-
whelm Dorn, he had roused himself for a last moment
and unbuckled a belt from about his hips. He passed it
to his youthful companion.

"If anything happens to this," he had said, "I'm worse

than done for. I'm a ruined man. I'm too exhausted to keep my eyes open, and I'm going to ask you to take care of it for me until I wake up again. Will you do that?"

Les Tarron nodded.

"Mind you," continued Dorn, "there are fellows in this world who would shoot you down like a dog if they knew you had that belt in your possession."

Tarron nodded.

"Ingram and his men would forget all about me, if they knew that you had it. They would turn off my trail and never take it up again so long as they thought that you had the belt and what's in it!"

"I'll believe that," said Les Tarron, "but when I was with Ingram last he seemed tolerable keen to have your scalp."

"You were with Ingram then?"

"Yes."

"When?"

"Today. I helped him to work out your trail up the valley."

There was a faint shout of amazement from Dorn.

"Aye, aye! I thought that he was following me very close—for him! I thought that he had taken a new set of wits. And it was you, lad! But how did you ever happen to work for him?"

"For the fun of it—and the price of the gray."

"What? Jimmy? Did he give you Jimmy?"

"He bought him for me."

"But what made you leave him?"

"I told him that I'd bring him in sight of you, and I did it. I didn't tell him that I'd help him to capture you. And when I seen you swing out of the ore bucket and start for the valley wall along the cable—why, I seen that you was worth saving. So I just slipped off to the side among the rocks with Jimmy, and I cut loose at them with the rifle that I'd borrowed from them. That made them hunt cover. And before they could open up on you again, you'd dropped for the brush."

"God be with me! God be with me!" murmured Dorn. "I see how it came about. I see it and I understand it! I could almost have sworn that heaven had sent you down to me, lad. But I see, as a matter of fact, that it was only your own sporting sense of fair play that made you fight for me. Am I right?"

"Call it what you please," said Les Tarron. "I seen that it would be a better game helping you to get away from five men, than helping five men to get you. That was all there was to it!"

"Aye, lad," murmured Dorn. "Some day, when I'm out of this, I'll have a chance to thank you. I'll have a chance to tell you——"

But Les Tarron held up his hand. In his heart of hearts he was strangely bothered by such talk as this. He was not at all accustomed to it, for at his home whatever he could be forced into doing, was taken as a matter of fact and course. There was never any gratitude spared for him. And when big Ingram came along he bought the services of Les Tarron for a price.

This, however, was something very far different. For here was a man overwhelming him with thanks, and in a deeply moved voice, like one who means more than he can find words for. And Tarron felt a new sense of pain that hurt him more deeply than anything that had ever happened to him.

He said: "Don't talk like this. I don't want to hear how——"

He paused. He felt that he had spoken with a too brutal abruptness. But Dorn seemed to understand and added: "I understand, old man. We'll let it go, then! Only, I see how decent you are; and, after all, the decent fellows are always on our side of the matter. They hardly ever start with the others; but even if they do, they switch over to us, and stay with us to the finish—— God help them!"

He added with a sudden burst of frankness: "Give back the belt, Tarron!"

He fairly snatched it, and added: "I was a hound ever to let you have your hands on it. So far as I know, they may have marked you down already, just because you've been with me this long and have been helping me. Because all of us that work—we've been marked down by them, and one by one they get us!"

These words sank deep into the heart of Les Tarron. He guessed at some enormous mystery, but what it was lay far beyond his understanding. It was a cause which good men supported.

"Then it ain't you that they're chasing?" he said to Dorn. It's something behind you?"

"Me?" laughed Dorn. "Chasing *me?* No, I'm only the tool. I'm a mighty small thing, lad! But better and stronger and finer men have tried to do the thing that I'm trying to do now, and they've all failed! Ah, I've known a few of them, and I've known what's happened! People thought it was a little odd when poor Chivveley was burned in the barn. A man like Civveley! But the two doors of that barn were locked, and oil was scattered to make the fire spread! Poor Chivveley—a hero, and yet he went out like that! And it was a queer thing, too, that Rogers should have fallen out of the big boat and drowned! I knew Rogers. He wasn't the sort to fall out of a boat, and he could swim like a water rat. I knew Barrister, too. Barrister grew dizzy on the edge of a cliff and fell and was smashed to a pulp. Another accident! Accidents will happen, you say? Three accidents, then. But odd that all three men should have been doing the big work that I'm doing now. Very odd, I have to admit! But it was no accident that stabbed Lucas. Suicide? He was the brightest-souled man in the world. Suicide? I always laughed at the idea. But I never could laugh when they said that Margent had been a suicide also. Margent of all the men in the world! Margent! Would he have taken poison, if he had wanted to end the thing? No, no, Margent had heart enough to use a gun and leave word behind him that the thing was his doing, so that no innocent man could be blamed. But they all knew—they all chose to risk their lives in the great work—and they all went down. And I suppose that I'll go down, too! Today should have seen the last of me!"

Les Tarron was tingling to the tips of his fingers.

"But why not let me know?" he asked. "Why not let me know? I've wanted some sort of work—that wasn't work. I've wanted something that wasn't roping cows and cutting firewood. Something sort of bigger and better and harder—y'understand?"

The big man smiled sadly, and kindly and wisely, too. "I understand," said he. "I was in such a mood when

69 ·

I undertook the thing. And I'm a dog to have talked to you so much about it now. As a matter of fact, the thing will never be done. But men will still try to do it, just because it's impossible! That's what makes it attractive—knowing that it cannot be done! And if I were to open my mind to you and tell you what I know and ask you to join, I can tell by the fire in your eye that you would. You're the meat that feeds the tiger—volunteers for the lost cause. No cause is great that isn't lost. Nothing is worth doing that can be done. Nothing is worth having that can be had. So we shoot at the star. Any star. The one that we see first, when our hearts are big. Your heart is big now. You want to try this way up the mountain. But I tell you, keep the humor. Find something else. Something that'll bring you glory, even if it kills you young. But in this work, you died—by accident. And people forget who you were and where you fell—"

He paused, his gaze fixed far above him, as though in fact he were staring at some distant star in the heavens.

And Les Tarron actually turned his head and stared in the same direction.

Those who knew Tarron in the after days felt that nothing could have made him tremble. And yet trembling he certainly was at that moment. He hardly knew what the thing was which had taken possession of him. It was an ache of the heart and a blindness of the eye and a fierce, determined eagerness.

"You think I'm just a kid," said he. "Well, I am just a kid, I admit that. But I can do things. I don't know much—except about the mountains. But I'll take my chances like a man, I think. If you give me leave!"

"I've said too much," retorted Dorn aloud, and he nodded. "I should never have said so much as this. Never! But—what is it you want?"

"To help you guard the belt, for one thing."

"You really want it?"

"Yes, tonight—while you sleep. You'll be a dead man till morning!"

Dorn covered his eyes with his hand. Then he extended the belt again with a sudden gesture.

"After all," he said, "why not? Who am I to do the picking and the choosing? They would take you and use you, if they could see. And they're better and wiser than I am! Take it, Tarron—and God help you, and forgive me!"

That was what had happened, and five minutes afterward Dorn was asleep on the top of the hill, leaving his young companion to clutch the belt in his hands and turn it back and forth, and squint at it curiously, and fumble the little buckled compartments which composed it from end to end.

Strange things were passing through the mind of Tarron, and a roll call of names hummed through his ears: Chivveley, Rogers, Barrister, Lucas, Margent had died by poison, the knife, a fall, a drowning, and fire. They had passed away mysteriously—men who had devoted their lives to the service of "them." They had been destroyed by the long arms of the other "them" to whose service Ingram and many another man were committed. And was it all for the sake of this old money belt which had been given to him by Dorn?

Tarron, determined, on the instant, to examine that belt and see what it contained!

Chapter XII

A Belted Knight

WHEN I THINK of Tarron on the crest of the mountain, examining the money belt by covert matchlight, other pictures come into my mind; and I see the young new-made knight watching all night over his arms—the shield which is to defend him and all who are defenseless, the sword which he is never to draw, save in a faultless cause, and the spurs which bid him never to sleep upon the trail of his duties. That is what I see, for I know what was passing in the heart of Les Tarron, sanctifying him, subduing him.

As he opened each pouch of the belt, a shudder of mysterious horror and dread and delight passed through him. There was no sense of guilt, for he had not been told to leave the belt alone. It had been placed in his hands to guard with his life, and had he not the right at least to see that for which he was willing to fight to the last drop of blood in his body?

Aye, and he felt that he was giving himself not for a moment, merely, but for all of the days of his life; accepting peril, devoting himself to some distant cause, great and good. Later, in the fullness of time, enough would be explained to him—all that he deserved to know, at least!

So thought Les Tarron, as he went through the pouch slowly, reverently, but with his heart on fire. And at every moment he lifted his head sharply and looked about him across the darkness of the valley beneath and to the darkness of the mountains above.

But no foes crept in upon him. And there was only the gray body of Jimmy, glistening by starlight through the gloom.

What did he find in the money belt?

In the first compartment, he discovered nothing more than a minutely folded letter of Dorn's mother to him, complaining because he was away so long, and begging him to return soon to his home and to her and to his wife and his children. It sobered young Tarron to read this, and to realize how full was the background of this man who now lay stretched in full exhaustion so complete that he drew every breath with a slight groan.

In the next compartment of the belt there were a few of the more delicate working parts of a Colt revolver—a wise precaution to bring them, to replace any that might be damaged. Next he found some silver money—not more than three dollars in all. After that came a rough sketch, which appeared to be a map, and Tarron was beginning to feel that he had utterly wasted his time in this matter when, in the last compartment of all, he found something of much greater value.

There was half a handful of uncut stones, green and red, and though Les Tarron knew nothing about jewels, yet he felt certain that these were gems of great price. If they were cut and polished—better still, if they were genuine rubies and emeralds—they would be worth a huge fortune, for each one was of considerable size.

What they might be worth, he could not guess even remotely. He poured them into his hand. There were eleven of them altogether—six red and five green; and he felt sure that the smallest of them, once put into a remarkable condition, would bring at least five thousand dollars.

This was the rudest sort of a guess. And in his heart

he thought that he must have far underestimated the value of the whole.

He felt that he had the explanation of the mystery now in his hand. This was a fortune large enough to cause many men to risk their lives. On the one hand, there were people to whom these jewels belonged and who hired brave men to transport them; on the other hand, were people who coveted the stones, and who hired others to intercept the convoy.

Yet this explanation made the very soul of Les Tarron shrink. For a great cause he had been willing to risk himself. But for the sake of mere money—why, that was a very different matter!

However, when he reflected on the thing, he decided that what had been enough to command the services of such a man as Dorn must surely be worthy of all his strength also. And then there were those others—Chivveley, Rogers, Margent, Lucas, Barrister—all of them had given up their lives. And even though it were only for money, yet perhaps it was for money which was to be used in some great and mysterious good cause.

Tarron rebuckled the compartment flaps and belted the thing about his hips. Then he considered the problem that lay before him.

If he left Dorn, danger might come upon the sleeper. If he did not leave Dorn, they would find themselves in the morning very short of provisions, with the necessity of shooting game; and guns made a fatal noise in this empty wilderness. Moreover, they would have to continue their march with a single horse, and that would be out of the question.

The lights of the town, by this time, had reached their full number and their full brilliance. Complete darkness covered the sky, and the handful of little yellow stars huddled in the valley beneath promised to the boy everything which he and his companion could need. Les gave a final look to Dorn, made sure that the big man was absolutely unconscious; then he started down the slope, mounted the gray stallion, and galloped rapidly for the town.

It unrolled before him, in the starlight, into a handsome little village, with the rush of a mountain stream through the midst of it keeping the air in a tremor of sound throughout the central ravine.

Les Tarron left the gray in a cluster of trees, and, making the stallion lie down—assured that the animal would stay there without moving until he returned—the boy started for the village.

He did not go at once to the main street. He preferred to slip along through back yards, growled at by a dog now and then, but never betrayed. At kitchen windows and beside back porches he listened to fragments of talk, until he was sure that the fight and the escape in the valley across the mountains had not been reported in this place as yet. Otherwise, some reference to it would surely have been on the tongues of some of the people upon whom he eavesdropped.

In the meantime, he needed a horse above all other things. And he had that fat wallet which Dorn had entrusted to him and never asked back.

He went boldly to the hotel veranda, which he knew would be the established gathering place of all of the gossips in the town.

A fat, coatless man, in the doorway, with a cigar in his mouth, Les took to be the proprietor, and he went up to him.

"My dad is back up the valley with a wagon," he said. "We busted down. Our sorrel mare, she turned dead lame. Dad told me to go on ahead and see if I could buy or hire a horse to get us into town."

"Hello!" said the fat man. "It's kind of queer that he wouldn't have come in to do the buying himself!"

"Yes," said Tarron, "but he stayed out there to rub the sorrel down with liniment. He says that it's a strained muscle in her leg."

"What kind of a horse do you want?" asked the proprietor.

"A biggish sort of a horse," said Tarron. "And if—"

"Can't hire a horse to you, son," said the fat man. "I dunno that I ever laid eyes on you before. And if you got the horse, maybe I'd never lay eyes on you again."

"Well," said Tarron, "I'd buy a horse if I had to—a goodish sort of a horse, y'understand, if I have to buy it."

"I got some horses in my corral," said the fat man, "but I ain't got a thing under eighty-five dollars."

"That's all right," said Tarron, "what I want couldn't be bought for that price."

He was led out behind the hotel, and a little group of men followed to watch the transaction.

Lanterns were bought. A full dozen of horses lifted their heads and their bright eyes glistened out of the darkness toward the light.

"I'll tell you what I'll do, kid," said the proprietor. "You stand up there on the fence and take your choice. My own horse is in that lot—my special riding horse. But if you can pick him out—why, I'll sell him to you!"

"All right," said Les Tarron. "But what's the price?"

"We'll settle that later on."

"I pick the horse, and then you ask whatever you want for it? That's a good bargain for you!"

"Come on, Jeff," said one of the bystanders. "If you want to see if the kid knows horses, you got to give him a chance. Give him a shot at a bargain, because there ain't much chance that he'd pick out your Monte!"

The proprietor writhed.

"Well—three hundred dollars, kid!"

"Hold on!" cried Tarron. "Three hundred for the horse that I pick out?"

"Mine is worth twice that, kid!"

"Three hundred for the horse I pick if it's the wrong one. But if I pick your Monte a—hundred and fifty."

"What?" yelled the fat man. "Not in a thousand years, I tell you!"

"The chances are twelve to one against me," said Tarron.

"That's true," spoke up an outsider.

The proprietor turned the matter over slowly in his mind.

"I feel kind of creepy," he said at last, with an embarrassed laugh, "at the idea of losing my Monte for a hundred and fifty dollars. But I ain't a four-flushin' cheap sport. I'll take the chance with you. You stand to bust three hundred dollars open if you don't get the right one."

"That'll do for me."

"Go ahead, then, and make your guess."

"Gimme a lantern, first, and I'll go have a look at them."

"All right! Here you are. Careful, though, because they're a wild bunch!"

"I'll risk it. If I can get close enough to talk to 'em!"

And he climbed through the bars, lantern in hand, and approached the little herd.

They swept together in alarm at his approach, throwing their heads high, their nostrils quivering.

Les stretched out his left hand, palm up, and then went gently toward them.

The horses quivered, they shrank, but they did not scatter and flee.

"Look, Jeff," said someone. "You better begin to shake. This kid has handled horses!"

Chapter XIII

A Way with Horses

FOR LES TARRON went among the horses with perfect ease, and those high-spirited mustangs which would run like deer if a man dared to enter the corral gate now quieted themselves and let him pass among them.

"What's he doing?"

"Looking at their backs."

"What the devil can he tell by their backs?"

"And looking at their feet, too."

"Yes, look at him handling the hoofs of that roan!"

"I see it! What does he expect to learn by that?"

"I dunno, but it looks as though he's got some system."

"Well, here he comes."

Les stepped out from the herd of mustangs and came back toward the corral fence.

"Well, kid," said the fat man, "have you come up for air and a second start?"

"No," said Les Tarron, "I've made my choice."

"You've made it?"

"Yes."

There was a breathless silence.

"You mean, kid, that you think you've picked out my Monte?"

"Yes. You say that Monte is in that caviya?"

"Yes, he's in there."

"Then I've found him."

"You have!" gasped Jeff in consternation. "Which one do you pick?"

"It's the mouse-colored gelding."

Silence fell upon the crowd, and then an impatient bark from Jeff: "Some one of you hounds done me dirt and told him!"

"Nobody told me, mister."

"Then how could you know so sure?"

"Why—"

"Monte ain't nothing to look at much."

"I didn't pick out a horse for looks," said Tarron. "I just picked out *your* horse."

"Go on, kid. You're getting kind of mysterious."

"No, I can prove that I had reason behind what I done."

"Prove it, then."

"You ain't a lightweight, mister?"

"No, not since I was a lad. What about that?"

"Well, a heavy man in a range saddle sometimes rakes a good deal of hair off the back of a pony."

"Yes, that's pretty true."

"Another thing—most fat men don't ride a lot."

"That's right," said one of the bystanders. "They hate to tuck their stomachs inside of a pommel, even a high one."

"So, naturally," said Les Tarron, "I just went out to see if I could find a horse with heavy saddle marks on his back, and shoes that hadn't had much work. And there was the mouse-colored gelding, with white spots all over his saddle, and his hoofs growed out long over shoes that ain't been changed in a long time."

"By the Lord," said the fat man, "I thought that there was something queer about it, at first. But now you can all see that there wasn't nothing to it."

He added, to show the direction in which his thoughts were drifting: "You can't expect me to give up my horse for a fake like that! A measly hundred and fifty dollars for a nag that's worth a thousand?"

"Wait a minute," said another, "there's a lot of things that look pretty simple after they've been done, but they're hard enough until the way has been showed. And I figure that this kid has a head on his shoulders. Let me see any of the rest of you make them nags stand while you paw them over and lift up their heels like you was their granddaddy!"

This remark seemed to have a great deal of effect, and Jeff, with a reluctant groan, had to nod his assent.

In the meantime, above the heads of the crowd, young Les Tarron heard a sudden sharp voice exclaiming: "It's him!"

He thought that that voice was more than vaguely familiar to him, and he would have hunted for the speaker at once, at any other time. However, he had the matter of the mouse-colored horse on his hands at the moment, and the price had not yet been paid down. He merely scanned the faces in the crowd, and recognized none of them.

He paid down a hundred and fifty dollars for the gelding; and an additional thirty for a secondhand bridle and saddle, with a saddle blanket thrown in for good luck.

"Where did you say that you hailed from, kid?" asked big Jeff, mournfully eyeing the gelding which was about to depart from his ken.

"From over Buxton way."

"Did you know Chris Buckley?"

"I've heard about him."

This questioning did not please Les Tarron. He knew where Buxton lay, and that it was in the direction from which he must pretend that he had come with his fictitious father.

But as for people in that town, he hardly could connect a single name with it.

"But the father of Chris was the great old boy. You knew him, I guess?"

"Oh, sure."

"And the way that he used to crack his jokes about his wife?"

"Of course," said Les Tarron, strapping the saddle on the back of the gelding.

"Folks used to say that he would have been a pretty dull man if he hadn't been hitched up to a patient woman like her that was too deaf to hear his talk."

"I've heard that," said Les Tarron.

"All right, sheriff," said Jeff in a tone of greatest satisfaction.

At that moment, having jerked the bridle over the head of the mouse-colored mustang, Tarron turned to swing into the saddle and ride from the town, for he had decided that there was no use wasting time in this place in buying provisions. It was much too dangerous. Too much talk. Too many questions.

So thought Les Tarron, and was prepared to leave straightway. But, as he swung about, he saw a little wide-shouldered man standing with his feet well apart, a brace of Colts in his capable hands.

This sawed-off cross-section of Hercules called out: "Just shove 'em up, kid!"

"Hello!" said Les Tarron, looking over his shoulder. "Who's wanted?"

"You are," said the sheriff, smiling grimly. "You dunno why, I suppose?"

"I got no idea in the world."

"Put your hands up over your head and maybe I can tell you about yourself."

Tarron's hands rose reluctantly as high as his hips.

"Up, up! Get 'em up!" said the sheriff angrily.

Very slowly, Tarron's hands crept toward his shoulders and hung there, twitching nervous.

"He don't like to get them up," said the sheriff, calling the attention of the bystanders to the obvious mental struggle through which the boy was passing. "I'd say that there was something of the nacheral gun fighter about this kid, by the way of his hands. Get those mitts up above your head!"

The last was delivered in a savage roar, and as he spoke, the sheriff took a long stride toward Les Tarron.

The latter submitted to the inevitable and hoisted his hands slowly to a level with his ears.

"Up higher!" commanded the sheriff.

But there the hands of Tarron stuck, as though it was beyond his power to budge them farther.

In the meantime, directed by the sheriff, the willing hands of the fat hotel proprietor relieved Tarron of his Colt.

"Pat his pockets," said the sheriff, unwilling to give over the search so quickly. "And frisk him thoroughly. That kid has an ugly way with him, and we don't want to take chances!"

The fat man was wonderfully thorough. He brought out at last a formidable hunting knife, but there his researches ended without a further profit.

"I want to know why I'm stopped here!" exclaimed Tarron.

"You'll have a chance to tell everything to the judge," said the sheriff.

"I want a fair chance," said Tarron. "There's my father up the trail—"

The sheriff cut in briskly: "Your father? We've had your father on the wire on the other side of the mountains. It ain't likely that he's flown over here in the last few seconds, is it?"

That retort caused a stir through the listeners, and a sudden widening of eyes. The crowd gave back before the prisoner and his captor.

"What's the charge, sheriff?" asked someone.

"Charge?" said the sheriff. "Oh, it's bad enough. You'd think that such a young kid wouldn't have the nerve for it. But this one did. Horse stealing, boys! Rank horse stealing, at that!"

And Les Tarron saw surprise and sympathy fade out of all faces and instead, hard sneers of anger and of contempt appear.

Horse stealing? Of all the crimes in the world, he and his whole kind considered this the meanest and the most detestable vice. Horse stealing?

"Aye," someone remarked, "I could believe that. He's got a way with horses, and we've all seen him use it. Don't let him get through your fingers, old-timer!"

The sheriff laughed at this exhortation.

"I'd rather let a murderer slip than a horse thief," he said. "Keep back and give me room and don't bother

82

me none. I'll handle this kid and I'll handle him without gloves!"

And Les Tarron knew that the man of the law meant what he said.

They approached a low, squat building, and as Tarron noted the steel bars which crossed the windows, he knew that it was the jail.

At the same time, the sheriff called: "Here he is, Bert. And I think that was a good tip that you passed to me. I've got him, you see!"

And Tarron, glancing quickly to the side, saw the harsh face of Bert Ingram, now wreathed with broadest smiles of triumph.

Chapter XIV

A Cornered Wild Cat

Now THOSE TWO things together might have stunned an older man than Tarron—the appearance of Ingram and that charge of horse stealing. But Les Tarron remained perfectly calm.

Clap your hands at a wild cat and it may flee a mile. Corner it, and it will fight as though possessed by ten devils. And Tarron was cornered.

At the door of the jail he said: "Will you tell me what the charge is, sheriff?"

"I'll tell you when I get you locked up safe. I understand that it ain't exactly wise to take chances with you, kid, and I never was fool enough to play anything but a safe game with crooks like you."

"I ain't a crook till I'm proved a crook," said the boy.

"Kid," said the sheriff, "I dunno but what you've got the law against me on that point. But I've never yet heard about a gent being accused of being a horse thief if there wasn't some sort of fire behind the smoke. Ain't that right, in your own experience?"

He brought Les Tarron into the interior of the jail.

The sheriff had been a busy man. He was always a

busy man. But nevertheless, there were cobwebs in the corners of the jail's room. For the work of the good sheriff, like that of many another Western supporter of the law, was too often performed across the wide face of the desert, and the chase ended in a gun fight that brought death to the fugitive. Or else, the man of no law escaped from the man of the law and wandered off into the inaccessible deeps of the mountains, while the sheriff turned back to wait for a better chance and a fairer time. So that the work of his hands rarely had brought home a harvest to the jail.

Cobwebs gathered, then, and yet that jail was to be known among other things more for the fame of having held this same young unknown lad, Tarron, than for having such a sheriff as he who really brought the victim in.

However, that was a matter to be established in the future; and for the present the sheriff regarded his companion with a mixture of hatred, disgust, and wonder.

"You don't look like a snake," he confided to Tarron, after the latter had been locked behind the bars of a cell. "You don't look like a snake and you don't particularly act like one. But a snake you are, young feller, and if I had my way about it, there would be only one way of punishing a horse thief, and I'll tell you what that would be, if you would like to hear."

"I'd like to hear," admitted the boy.

"Well, kid, I'd take that there horse thief, and I'd take the clothes offn' him, and I'd tie him hand and foot, and then I'd lay him out an I'd stake him down where he couldn't budge too much; and after I'd done that, I'd lay a trail of molasses from him and smeared all over him to the nearest ant heap, and then I'd go off and I'd wait and watch. And pretty soon, when he came to be black all over with the ants, and when they was wandering into his eyes and out again, and into his mouth and out again, and into his nose and out again, then I'd holler out and I'd ask him what could I do for him? And when he told me what he wanted, I'd tell him that hell would be a lot more miserable for a skunk like him than the place that had been laid out for him there. Because I'll tell you this, kid, that God, sure hates a hoss thief worse'n He

85

hates the old devil himself. Because a hoss thief, he's more ornerier and meaner and lower and sneakier, and blacker, too, by heaven!"

He said this with a ring of honest enthusiasm that might have made Les Tarron smile had he been a little older; but young men are serious men, and Les Tarron was very, very young.

Besides, he had been jailed for horse thieving in a section of the world where it was considered the best of good sport and fair play to take a horse thief from a jail and hang him up to a limb of a near-by cottonwood.

Les thought of this, and he said: "Sheriff, I want to tell you something."

"Go ahead, kid. I guess I don't have to warn one of your kind that everything that you say now can be used again' you!"

"You don't have to warn me of that," said Les Tarron, "only I'd like to say to you that I've never stole a horse in my whole life, and that I wouldn't want to begin now."

The sheriff merely smiled.

"It's all right, kid," said he. "I can see that you're young, but you've already got the hang of things. You've got the face for it. I understand."

Young Tarron leaped to his feet and strode to the bars and pressed his face against them.

"I swear to God," said he, "that I never stole no horse!"

The sheriff pushed back the hat from his head. He scratched that head, regardless of the hat falling upon the floor.

"You never stole no horse?"

"Never!"

"Why would Ingram tell me that, then?"

"Ingram? Why, I'd tell a man that that ain't very hard to guess straight through to the end. Ingram? He hates my innards worse'n if I was a snake. He hates me that bad!"

"Why should he, you being a kid?"

"Because I beat him out of capturing or killing the man that he hated most in the world—hated most until he run up to me!"

The sheriff waited. But no more was said. There was no

fierce or tremulous outpouring of emotion from Tarron. Instead, there was a controlled and patient endurance in his face and such bright, keen eyes were fixed upon those of the sheriff as he had never seen before.

"I think you mean something, kid," he said at last. "I'll tell you what. I'll give you a chance to meet this here Ingram and have a talk with him in front of me."

"I'd like nothing better," said the boy.

The sheriff left.

Les Tarron did not wait for the return of the man of the law; instead, he looked hastily and carefully about him. He tried everything in the room. A strong wrench at the cot, which was bolted down, brought one end of it up with a creak. A tug at the other end, and it was clear.

Tarron nodded with a short, gasping breath of satisfaction.

What did the looseness of that bed mean? Nothing, except that he had matched his strength against the strength of things in that jail, and he proved that he was the stronger—in one respect at least.

He stepped in some eagerness and confidence to the bars, and tried his strength on them. But there was not so much as a creak of protest from them. He tried his shoulder, prying against the bars with all the might of his body.

The faintest of creaks answered him.

But that was not enough. For the present, at least, he would have to admit that the cell was stronger than he. But something might be evolved later on for beating even the strength of those steel bars. So he stepped back, rubbing the coiled pad of shoulder muscles which had been pressing against the bar.

A moment later the sheriff came back, with the long form of Ingram striding beside him.

"Where's the kid?" asked Ingram.

"In here."

Before the cell the tall man took his stance.

He raised his long arm and pointed.

"Kid, where did you put my gray hoss?"

"Your gray—whose gray?"

"Listen, sheriff, he don't seem to me to be in a very

87

fancy lying mood tonight. Is that the best that you can do, kid? I suppose now you'll say that the horse don't belong to me?"

"It don't!" cried Tarron hotly.

"All right! All right!" said the other. "I ask you—did I pay down five hundred dollars to your father yesterday?"

"You done that," admitted the boy.

"And did he give me the horse at that price?"

"Yes, he done that, too. I know that as well as you do."

"You admit it, do you?" asked Ingram. "Dog-gone me if I didn't think that you'd try to disprove that; because if you don't, where does the rest of your case lie? You admit that you seen me pay five hundred for that horse, and that I took the horse. Wait a minute. Maybe you think that I got five hundred back from this kid, sheriff?"

He turned to the man of the law, but the latter shook his head, bewildered.

"He just don't talk like a liar, though," said he.

"He's got brass. I ain't denying that," said Ingram. "Oh, he's got enough brass to furnish an army of beggars with, that kid has. That was why I give him the run."

"You gave me the run, did you?" asked Les Tarron.

"I took him along for a chore boy, y'understand, sheriff?" explained Ingram. "And dog-gone me if the kid didn't slip away with the gray horse that I had bought from his father. Done a clean and neat get-away."

"What's your story, lad?" asked the sheriff.

"He wanted me to help him on the trail. I wouldn't leave home without I had my Jimmy horse with me, and so he bought Jimmy, and told me that if I brung him in sight of the other gent, I should have the horse."

"Hold on," said the sheriff. "Sight of what gent?"

"One that was pegging up the valley on a spent horse. But his trail was near lost in the rocks. I got an eye for trails, and when I spotted this one, Ingram said that he wanted me and wanted me bad."

"By Gad," burst out Ingram, "it sort of riles me, sheriff, to hear the little runt talk as if I could ever have had any need of him. If it wasn't that you got him under your wing, I'd give him a lesson! But he knows that the bars protect him!"

Tarron sprang against the bars.

"You dead-eating buzzard!" he shouted. "Open the door of this here cell, sheriff, and let him and me have it out with bare hands, and I'll show you how much I'm scared of him! Or with guns or knives or any way that he dares to fight me!"

Ingram switched suddenly to a new track.

"There's your young, innocent kid that couldn't have the nerve to steal a horse!" he said. "Look at the face of him, sheriff, and look at the hell in his eyes."

The sheriff whistled.

"Aye," said he. "It's a picture that would sort of scare even his ma!"

Chapter XV

Vain Search

THE SHERIFF BEGAN: "You claim that Ingram needed you on the trail? Shut up, Bert, and let me handle this."

"Yes," said the boy, "I claim that very thing."

"And he offered you the horse if you was to bring him in sight of the gent that was ahead of him?"

"I claim that."

"I've knowed Bert Ingram for a long spell," said the sheriff. "And I would say that he's as handy on the trail as any man that I ever come up again' in my whole life!"

He paused, and Les Tarron made no answer.

"What become of the man that was being chased?" asked the sheriff suddenly.

"He's off in the mountains with the gray."

"How come that?"

"He was fagged out and wore out. He had to sleep. And I come down here to get another horse, if I could."

"And then there ain't anything in your yarn about your pa being down in the valley?"

"No."

"Then you admit that you lied about that?"

"I admit that I lied about that."

"And where did you get the money to buy 'Fatty's' horse?"

"The gent give it to me."

"He's kind of large and freehanded, ain't he?"

"You ask me all of the questions, but just ask Ingram what did he offer me to go with him?"

"What *did* you offer the kid?" asked the sheriff.

"What would you offer him, sheriff? I offered him three dollars a week and keep for coming along with us and doing the fire building and the dish cleaning, and such, when we made camp. Besides, he said that he wanted to go south with us."

The sheriff nodded.

"That's all pretty reasonable."

He turned to Tarron. "Anything else that you want me to ask him?"

"Yes, ask him what he was doing with his four fighting men in the hills?"

"I don't mind telling you," said Ingram. "We got tired of Montana falls and winters, and when the nights begun to get a snap in them, we decided that we'd head south and try for a place along the—Alcazar."

There was just a trace of hesitation before this word.

"Sure!" said the sheriff amiably. "I know what it is to get tired of the long snows. Well, kid, are you talked out?"

"I've finished," said Les Tarron.

"As if," chuckled Ingram, "I would offer that kid a five-hundred-dollar horse to help *me* work out a trail!"

The sheriff laughed loud and long.

"And see the face of him," he said. "Dog-gone me if he ain't a sassy one! I got to go downtown, Bert. Will you come along?"

"I'd rather stay here," said Bert, "and have a chat with this kid. I dunno. Maybe he ain't so bad. I'd like to find out just what sort of a kid he is. Because maybe—why, maybe I wouldn't press the charge against him, that is, if there was any decency in him."

"That's talking like a white man, Bert," agreed the sheriff. "Every young fellow is a young fool in lots a ways. But they can mostly use a second chance pretty good. Take this key. Let yourself into the cell and sit down and have a chat with him, will you?"

"Thanks," said Bert Ingram.

The sheriff departed, and Ingram lighted a cigarette and leaned against the bars, smiled at the prisoner.

"You see how it is, kid?" remarked the tall man. "You got a sort of brains, but not enough to stand up again' a real man."

The prisoner was silent, watching and waiting.

"The jug would cool you down a bit," remarked Ingram. "It would probably do you a lot of good. Be a sort of college education in patience for you. But I hate to cut too deep. You're young. And if you'll gimme that belt that you got around you, I might call it quits."

Les Tarron blinked once, as a cat blinks at a sudden blinding light; then he continued to stare calmly at his enemy. Under that gaze Ingram grew restless.

"You know what it would mean, I suppose?" said he.

"What what would mean?"

"A jail term for horse stealing?"

"I dunno."

"About ten or twelve years. The judges in this part of the world are pretty hard on that sort of a deal."

"I didn't steal the horse. I done what I said I would do. I brought you into sight of Dorn."

"And then you quit me like a skunk and went over to him?"

"I had a right to do that."

"You got a right to stay in jail, too!" declared Bert Ingram.

"You don't scare me," said the boy. "I ain't going to give you the belt."

"You admit that you got it, then?"

Again Tarron blinked. Then his teeth clicked shut. Ingram laughed contentedly.

"Hard to keep from talking, ain't it?" he remarked. "Mighty hard, I'd say, when you got a man that knows how to draw out the words. But lemme have that belt and I'll call off the jail business."

"You can't bluff me," said Tarron.

"Bluff? Does this here look like a bluff?"

"It takes time to push through a thing like this," said

the boy. "You got to have lots of time. Have to be a witness against me when the trial comes off—have to stay around here. And you won't stay around here. You're afraid to."

"Why am I afraid?"

"Because if you stay put they'd find you, and that would be the finish of Ingram."

"Who would find me?"

"You know what I mean, I guess."

"Lord!" breathed Ingram, "that fool Dorn has talked to you—to a kid like you!"

He seemed partly wrathful and partly amazed.

Tarron was silent.

"There's nothing for it," said the tall man. "I've got to come in and talk to you!"

He opened the door and stepped inside, holding a naked Colt.

"I'll have that belt, son," said he.

"You will?" asked Tarron calmly.

"I'll have it or sink you, son!"

"It won't work," said young Tarron. "You ain't going to leave a dead man behind you."

The tall man set his jaw and glanced hurriedly over his shoulder.

"I don't want to do it," he said soberly. "I hate to do it, as a matter of fact. But if you make me, there's nothing left. Don't fool yourself into thinking that I won't, if the pinch comes. The sheriff's gone. He won't be back for a long time. I put a bullet through your head, and then I cut loose and take my horse outside the jail and ride off. How'll they get me? Inside of two days I'll be where no man in the world can put a hand on me!"

He laughed sneeringly.

Tarron studied his face. Suddenly he nodded.

"You get the belt," he said.

"That's sense," said the tall man. "Unbuckle it, will you?"

Slowly, his eyes upon the door as though he hoped that the sheriff might return, Tarron unbuckled the belt. He handed it to Ingram. After all, it was better to live and try to get back the belt than it was to die and lose life and belt also. Even Dorn would agree that this policy was the correct one.

Ingram, in the meantime, had backed to the door, as though eager to leave. But impatience overcame him. He could not wait. He had turned pale. His eyes had grown wonderfully brilliant, and his face glistened with moisture.

Rapidly he unbuckled the compartments of the belt, took out the contents—and suddenly dashed the belt upon the floor.

"It ain't here!" he snarled. "You little rat, it ain't here! Hand it over before I—before I rip it out of you!"

Tarron closed his eyes and opened them again.

He could not help smiling at the thought of the apparent candor and frankness with which Dorn had given him his belt to guard. But now it seemed that that had been a mockery. No, the jewels, if they were real, were certainly something. But the treasure which was of such interest to "they" was vastly more important—so much more important that Ingram did not think the loot in the belt worth another glance. Not even Ingram, a man keen for money!

The secret cause for which Dorn and all the others had fought, and which Ingram and his peers had attacked, was now elevated once more to a position of commanding importance. It was once more a vast mystery, and the blood of young Tarron leaped.

He laughed in the face of the furious Ingram.

"I ain't got it," he declared.

"Why, you little fool," said Ingram, "do you think that a lie like that is enough to bamboozle me? No, no! Come out with it! I got no time to fool away over you! No time at all! Come out with it, or I'll find it for myself!"

"I'll never hand it to you," said Tarron suddenly. "If you want it, take it with your own hands. I'll never have Dorn say that I gave it to you!"

"All right!" nodded Ingram, as though this were a reasonable point of honor. "I'll tell them that want to know that you done your best to guard it. But lemme know—what pocket is it in?"

"The inside pocket of my coat."

"Stand fast—take off your coat—no, never mind. But stand still while I get it, or I'll finish you, kid, at the first twitch that you make!"

As he spoke, he came close, and ramming the muzzle of his Colt into the prisoner's stomach, he thrust his long fingers into his inside coat pocket.

"Golly," Ingram muttered, "this day'll make me a great man and—where is it?"

He reached deeper.

Les Tarron struck at that instant.

Ingram's Colt knocked away from his body. At the same instant it exploded and sent a bullet scorching along Tarron's side. But the shot had missed; by a miracle it had missed. Or was it rather the unreasonable stiffness of that trigger?

Chapter XVI

Breakfast for Two

INGRAM, WITH A moan of rage and fear, jerked at the gun to bring it into position for another shot, but he found his hand caught in a crushing grip, whose like he had never known before. At that moment a fist like a club of steel smote him beneath the heart. Darkness exploded across his brain—darkness lit by red, tearing flashes. Ingram dropped upon his face and lay writhing feebly.

Tarron paused to scoop up the fallen gun. He had no time for anything else but that and the rescue of the belt, for outside the jail he heard excited voices.

He leaped through the cell door and raced for the entrance. Crouching beside it, he heard hurrying footfalls and the voices of two men, one of whom was the sheriff.

They strode in.

"Bert!" cried the sheriff, hurrying on. "Bert—what in—"

A shadow rose from against the wall just behind them and sprang through the doorway swiftly and silently. Yet it did not fail to catch the attention of the sheriff.

He whirled on his heel, with two guns working before he was really facing his mark, and sent three slugs, not through human flesh, but through the stout oak of the door, which had been slammed as the fugitive darted through. Slammed—and locked with swift, deft fingers.

The yell of the honest sheriff was like the scream of a mountain lion in agony.

Outside, young Les Tarron was already in the saddle on the sheriff's own horse. He turned it down the street and hammered his heels into its ribs. It settled into a rapid gallop at once.

Straight down the street went Tarron, straight back toward the heart of the little town. He flung the horse through a tangled crowd of cowpunchers who were mounting in front of the hotel. He leaped from the saddle and confronted the fat proprietor.

"What are you doing here?" shouted that worthy, his face purple with surprise. "And on the sheriff's horse—"

"I've squared it with the sheriff. He sent me down here as fast as I could come—Ingram's trying to murder him in the jail—" Half a dozen shots in rapid succession and a roaring of voices in the distance seemed to reinforce his words.

"Help! Send him help!" yelled Les Tarron.

He did not need to urge haste. The cowpunchers who were idling on the veranda of the hotel had already gone for their horses when they heard the first shots. Now they swept up the street like a volley of arrows, with the fat proprietor and all other pedestrians sprinting to keep up and get to the scene of the tragedy as quickly as possible.

And young Tarron in the corral was busily throwing the saddle and bridle which he had scooped up in the shed upon the back of a rough-looking, mouse-colored horse!

For, after he had saved himself from Ingram, he had no wish to surrender the animal for which he had paid honest money earlier in the evening, and become a self-confessed horse thief by riding away on the sheriff's property.

The saddle was on and cinched. The bridle was on; the throatlatch drawn up, and now he heard hoofs pounding down the street again in the direction of the hotel, the half hysterical voice of one man dominating the rest— a man insane with fury.

Now the sheriff's voice was deep and harsh, ordinarily,

and this voice was the voice of a yelling baboon, yet young Tarron knew that it came from the lips of the maddened man of the law. It came from him, and he would have blood to repay him for the insult which his pride had endured on this night!

Tarron listened and understood; and then, slipping into the saddle, he galloped the mouse-colored horse to the back of the corral. He paused there to throw down the bars. And now, across the front of the hotel, a dust cloud rolled, with horses and men boiling out of it.

"He's there!"

"No, here!"

"Look yonder across the corral—by heavens, that's him!"

A living screen had formed behind Tarron as he galloped Monte through the gap in the fence. For the other horses in the corral, alarmed by the clamor in the street and glad of this opening for escape, now swept through the exit behind the fugitive. And, like any Indian brave, Tarron had thrown himself along the side of his racing pony. Bullets, to strike him, would have to drive through the bodies of half a dozen horses running behind him.

There were fences behind him to be cleared by the mounted crowd, and cow ponies are not fond of jumping. They have neither the legs for it nor the knack of it. Gates have to be opened for them, and bars let down before they can burst through. And a running horse covers a thousand yards in a minute!

Before the ponies were well away, there was only a cloud of dust far before them, Les Tarron doubtless riding in the midst of it. For that goal they set themselves, but Tarron was already out of their ken.

At the first draw the herd of stampeded horses crossed, Les turned Monte to the side and cantered him easily up the depression. He reached a group of trees and, pausing there, laughed joyously to himself as he saw the dust cloud of the horses and the dust cloud of the sheriff's pursuit rolling behind the other across the country, leaving a long pale stain of dust through the air behind each sweeping body.

He was contented. He was more than contented.

To an ordinary man, there had been enough excitement and action to last for the rest of his life; but to the slaves of the mysterious power which Dorn and others served, such an evening was as nothing at all. A mere commonplace!

Tarron was still laughing softly as he turned his mouse-colored gelding up toward the distant hills.

Now that he had gained one object, he had no mind to return without executing the rest of his proposed mission. So he swung from his straight course toward the lights of the first ranch house that he saw.

He left the gelding, with thrown reins, at a little distance and, stealing up to the house, he saw a Negro cook in the act of finishing the evening dishes.

Five minutes later, the cook left a darkened kitchen, and Tarron entered to take what prizes he could.

A side of bacon, flour, salt, baking powder, some tinned jam, matches, and such incidentals as a great mince pie and a few other decorative details made up his plunder.

He slipped out a side window. Then, sitting beneath the trees, with the mouse-colored horse grazing near by, Les ate the pie with infinite relish, watched the lights in the house go out, and saw the stars gleam brighter and brighter in the central sky.

He was very contented. He had no flaws to find in this world or in the entire starry universe which the Creator had planned, as it seemed to him, so that brave men might ride abroad and win joy and mince pie at the risk of their precious necks. Such were the reflections of Tarron.

Then he mounted and continued on his way toward the rendezvous where Dorn must be waiting. Waiting and sleeping!

Prone on his back, his arms thrown out sideways, it seemed to the boy, at first, that Dorn was a dead man; and he leaned over him, half in fear, expecting to see the dark splotch where the knife had been driven home.

But Dorn was not dead. He slept the sleep of perfect exhaustion, however.

Tarron, curling himself into a knot, like a cat in cold weather, presently slumbered in turn; but he wakened at the first touch of gray in the sky, perfectly refreshed, perfectly alert, perfectly rejoiced with the work which might lie before him in the service of that mystery which Dorn followed.

And Dorn himself still slept, and continued to sleep while the boy prepared breakfast for them; and slept on until the eastern sky was a red blaze of glory, and the strong, sharp scent of boiling coffee attacked his nostrils.

Then he roused himself with a groan, and at the sight of Tarron, automatically grasped his rifle.

He recovered himself at once.

"Tarron!" he said. "God bless me, if I hadn't forgotten about you while I slept—and such a sleep! Such a sleep!"

Tarron grinned at his companion.

"All's well?"

"Yes."

Dorn's brain was still befogged. He staggered to a runlet of water that trickled out of the slope a little farther down, and bathed his face and hands. When he came back, his eyes were clear and bright.

"Where did you get this stuff, lad?" he asked, pointing to the food.

"They give away chuck to hungry people in this part of the world," said the boy.

Dorn cast a sharp glance at him and smiled in turn. He sat down to his meal without another word. But presently he cried: "Hello, there! Did that horse stray in here?"

"Strayed in," said young Tarron. He lowered his eyes to his coffee. "Strayed in and took his saddle off and made himself at home."

There was another keen glance from Dorn, but still he would not commit himself.

He finished his breakfast. Then he asked quietly:

"You have the belt, son?"

"Here."

Les handed it to the owner.

"Look inside," insisted Tarron, as he saw Dorn hesitate.

"Thanks," said the latter. "I will."

He examined the little series of pouches carefully and then looked with a smile at his companion.

"It's all right," he said. "I guessed that it would be, and it is!"

"And here's your wallet that you gave me."

Tarron handed it over, adding: "There's a hundred and fifty dollars out of that."

"Hello! Lost it?"

"On the horse, yonder."

"You went where?"

"To the town, yonder."

Les waved toward it. In the morning mists of the valley below, it looked a great deal farther away than it had during the night when the lights were shining from it so brightly.

"You went down there?"

"Yes."

"And got that horse for a hundred and fifty?"

"Yes."

"Is he a good one?"

"I made a bargain with the owner. Yes, it's a good horse. Not up to Jimmy, but strong enough to carry you; and fast enough to keep you away from trouble, I think."

"And you had no trouble?"

"Outside of Ingram, not much."

"What? Ingram?"

"He had me arrested for stealing Jimmy."

"The infernal—"

"The sheriff jailed me, but I managed to get away."

"Broke jail?"

"They left Ingram to guard me."

Les drew out the revolver which he had taken from Ingram and juggled it, a faint smile on his lips and a dreamy, far-off look in his eyes.

"On the way back, I picked up the chuck. I figured that it was owing to us, y'understand?"

"You killed Ingram!" gasped Dorn.

"No. Just pasted him and left while he was sleeping."

Dorn leaned back against a rock and whistled long and softly at the morning sky.

Chapter XVII

What Flies by Night

AFTERWARD HE SAID: "Lad, I'll tell you what I can do for you, and then I'll tell you what you can do for yourself. First of all I want to say that if I hadn't been sick and helpless with weariness and this wound in my side —why, I would never have let you tie yourself up with me for a moment. But now, I'll give you two thousand dollars that I have in this wallet. Never fear, it'll leave me still plenty of money for myself. After that, you can take your Jimmy horse—unless you'll sell him to me for a fat price, because God knows I'll need his speed—and ride for the nearest railroad. When you get to it, try for the first train that passes. Build a bonfire on the tracks. Do anything to flag it. And when you've managed that, get aboard and go wherever it will take you—north or south or east or west. Keep traveling until you come to the limit of this country; and when you get to Canada or Mexico don't stop there, but keep straight on. Keep flying. Put an ocean between you and the States. Change your name. Grow a mustache. Take up a new business. Change all your habits. Never mention the place you come from. And—if you do all of these things—you have a fair chance of living. But even then the chances won't be much more than even. They got Chandler in Java, and they killed poor Richards in the hills of Brazil. But it's worth your try. Life, Tarron, life is what you'd be flying for!"

"All right," murmured the boy. "If I run that way, which way will you run?"

"Ah," said Dorn, "I've committed myself. I've tasted the fire. It'll always burn in me until I do my work— or the work does for me. I can't give it up. I've gone too far. But you're only on the threshold."

"Well," said Les Tarron, thoughtfully, "there ain't any doubt that you mean what you say. You want me to pull out!"

"I want nothing more. I'd be haunted, youngster, if any harm came to you because I'd led you into this mess."

"I'll tell you about myself," said the boy. "I've been a lazy hound all my life. Never no good at anything. Nothing but a waste around the farm. But now I've hit something that I'm interested in. Peace, it don't interest me much. Money don't bother me none. Good chuck I can do without. But I been living all this while waiting for something to wake me up. And I think that you've brought the thing along with you. Because if it hadn't been for you, why, one of these days I would have got a gun and gone out hunting excitement on my own account."

His glittering eyes looked straight at Dorn.

"I've had thoughts of doing it often!" he added slowly.

Dorn, sitting bolt erect, frowning with interest, nodded.

"I don't ask no questions," said the boy. "You can use me for anything that you want me for. And I'll help to push you along your trail, wherever you want to go."

"La Paz."

"I dunno much about it."

"It's south and west, in the mountains."

"We'll head for that, then."

"Do you mean what you're saying?"

"Nobody ever meant nothing more!"

"Without even knowing what the trail is for, and what the thing is that I carry?"

"No."

"Whether in my hand or in my mind?"

"No."

"Then shake hands with me, Tarron!"

"I'm glad to do that."

"We'll finish the trail together?"

"We'll finish it together, Dorn."

"And in a day or so, when I know you better, I'll try to tell you what it's all about."

"I ain't impatient," said Tarron. "Things happen along this trail, and that's all that I'm interested in."

The sun still shone upon the mountains above the little town of Santa Trista. But the town was already in darkness, except for the mountain glow which was still reflected upon the big square bell tower of the church.

The town of the "sad saint," under the burden of the premature dimness, was preparing for the night. Dinners had been cooked and eaten. Men sat in the doorways with their cigarettes. Behind them, the women worked in their kitchens to clean the supper dishes. In the streets before them, dogs and children and rooting pigs worked through the dust, raised it in clouds, and filled the air with dirt and noisy merriment.

Into this town rode Dorn and Leicester Tarron. They threaded their way through the winding streets, with all the city turning dark around them, except for the still glimmering gilded cross above the church of the saint. They reached the hotel, and led their horses to the stable behind it. Water was pumped into a triangular wooden trough. The men stood side by side and watched their tired horses drink.

"How old it is, Les!" said Dorn. "Old, and sleepy, and forgotten by the world. A man could rest here. A man could rest here and forget even his sins, I think. Look! There are no electric wires for light or even for the telegraph. A century or two have slipped past them in this nook of the mountains. Perhaps they have heard strange tales of the other world which has managed to force its way up into the other valleys. Strangers like us have come in among them now and again. But I suppose they won't half believe what they hear. It becomes a fairy tale. There was a time, Les, when the horizons of men

104

were more limited. They could not see so far. They did not have such accurate maps. The world was still a big and strange place. Much was still to be discovered. Passes were inaccessible in winter. Electricity had not taken time by the throat. And everything that lay over the hill was a fairy tale, and a miracle. This is such a place, Les. Poor devils! you say. And it's true that such a place as this will breed a thousand fools. But at last it will put forth a wise man; and his wisdom will surpass all the work of the machine, all the efforts of steam and gas and electricity, and all the cleverness of the magazines and the newspapers. You would not have to tear down a forest and make it into paper in order to print all the thoughts that can be born in a village like this, but some few of those thoughts may be worth more than all the standing forest, and all the words that could be printed on the paper made out it! Do you believe that?"

"A bit less than half," said Les Tarron. "I dunno that I like the smell of this place."

Dorn laughed.

"That's true," he said. "There is one thing that time improves and sensitizes, and that is the human nose. The world is more fragant today that it ever was. But perhaps there are even better things than soap and water. You can wash the skin clean, you know, but what does the skin really matter. You remember that the old saints did not make a virtue of cleanliness. You may think they were fools. But perhaps they weren't. Perhaps they were a bit right in despising their bodies for the sake of something else."

"For the sake of what?" asked Tarron.

"I'm raving a bit, Les. Forgive me."

"It's all right," said Tarron. "When you get to talking like that, sometimes I understand a little bit of what you're saying. Like things that fly by you in the night, you can't tell whether it's a night hawk or an owl, y'understand? That's the way when you start in to talking the way you've been doing. But it's a quiet little town, all right, if that's what you mean."

The other hesitated.

"Yes," he said at last, "that's what I chiefly mean. And

tonight we'll have a chance to enjoy a meal cooked and served by the hands of others."

"Perhaps," said Tarron. "But if I was you, I'd prefer to stay out in the mountains. They're safer a lot!"

"Tush!" said Dorn. "There's a place for caution, and there's a place where chances have to be taken."

"I suppose that Chivveley took a chance, and so did Rogers?"

"No more of that. I say that we'll wash ourselves with good hot water and soap, even if the soap is only home-made; and then we'll have roasted kid for supper. And, after that, we'll each have a separate room, and a fine large bed to sleep in."

"I hope that we'll not wake up with a knife in the back," said Tarron.

Chapter XVIII

What the Moonlight Showed

LIKE A LOVER of the sun, long imprisoned in the arctics, and newly returned to the southland, Dorn expanded and relaxed under the influence of this quiet little town.

He was so gay and cheerful during dinner that Tarron could not help smiling and laughing in his turn. But all the while, the younger man was observing certain precautions, such as keeping his back to a corner of the room, and his revolvers ready at his belt; for by this time he and Dorn were both armed to the teeth with the finest and newest models of firearms. Moreover, he watched everything that happened with the keenest of eyes; not a shadow crossed the window that opened onto a little narrow balcony without bringing a glance from Tarron; and when the fat waiter entered the room with a burden of roasted kid or another flask of wine, he was constantly under the attentive eye of the boy.

Dorn, noticing this, laughed long and largely.

"Do you think, lad," said he, "that the news of us can have come even to this place?"

"I'd take no chances," said Les Tarron.

"You're a young fox, lad," said the older man. "But

this is a place where you can curl up and sleep with both eyes closed. There are no dogs to chase you. Why, my son, they hardly know that there are steamers on the sea; they hardly know that trains are running on iron rails; and they're probably referring to powder and lead as new inventions. You don't know what these little Mexican mountain towns can be like. But I do. I tell you that when we topped the head of the trail yonder and dipped into this snug little valley, at that very moment we left the old world which we knew and our horses stepped across several centuries. We entered a region where there is only one dimension—that of space! Do you hear?"

"I hear you."

"Aye, you hear me, but all the while your eyes wander from door to window and from window to door. And you are even searching the ceiling and the floor. Now, what could be wrong with the ceiling, lad?"

"There are some little holes between the bricks."

"Certainly! And the good and sufficient reason for that is that the old house had settled a bit on one side and thereby has thrown everything out of kilter—the bricks have moved a bit. And so those chinks appeared. I noticed them as we came in."

Tarron was silent.

"Come, come!" said Dorn, tapping impatiently upon the table. "You mustn't be quite so gloomy. It's not fair, my son. This is our cheerful hour. Here, for a moment, we lie basking in the sun. Danger has left us. We are free and alone—"

"Alone," agreed Tarron, "unless some gent is lying up there watching us through a chink in those same bricks, or listening at them. He could hear every word we speak."

"A great deal of good would it do him," said the elder man. "I hope there *is* an eavesdropper. I'd be pleased to have some one listen to us and write down what we say. I took a trip to the Himalayas one year with a notebook fellow who always had his pencil out whenever—I say, Tarron, I wish you'd let that mangy dog go out of the room! What do you see in the starved, sneaking cur?"

Tarron, with a shrug, shredded away a portion of a tortilla from his plate and offered it to the ragged brute, and the dog's starved eyes melted with joy as he devoured it.

"You never can tell," said Tarron. "A dog can often be a lot of use to you!"

"Tush! I think you've given him a taste of everything that was on your plate!"

"Well," said Tarron, "make a friend of a dog, and the least he can do is die for you."

Dorn struck the table lightly with his fist.

"By the Lord!" he said, "this is a great deal too much! You think that some of this food may be poisoned, and you're trying it on the dog?"

Again Tarron shrugged.

"I don't mind wasting a little time," he declared. "And it makes things taste better."

"Well, let it go," said Dorn. "I won't argue the point with you—but pass me that platter of kid again."

So dinner went joyously to its close, and afterward they strolled through the narrow streets of the town and watched the moon rise, broad-faced and yellow, and cover the mountains with a soft, transfiguring light. Then, back to the inn, and to bed; Tarron in a little chamber on the ground floor, which he declared was plenty good enough for him, though it had only a single small window; and Dorn, in the room just above, which was large, comfortable, with an ample balcony stretching across its big window.

From that balcony, the scent of strong cigar smoke curled down to Tarron as he lay awake for a time watching the single star which hung before his window. But at last his eyes closed, and he slept.

It was a fitful sleep. For many nights, now, he had been sleeping out under the sky, with the four winds blowing across his face; and the stifling air in the little room half choked him, and he roused again and again with a thundering heart and a sense of oppressive fear.

The third or fourth time this happened Les remained awake, listening to a new sound that sent a chill through his body. A small, soft sound, that seemed to steal across his room and stand beside his bed.

No. It receded. It seemed to stand in the middle of the room—

Gun in hand, Tarron raised himself softly on one elbow and stared about him. His concentrated gaze gradually pierced the gloom. Bare walls on all sides of him— there was nothing in the chamber with him to be feared! And yet, the sound continued, more slowly. It was hardly like a footfall, but rather like the dropping of water, falling slower and slower.

He slipped from his bed and dressed. After this, he knew that he would not sleep again that night. Moving gradually forward, his left hand held before him, he felt a drop splash suddenly upon that extended hand.

He drew back hastily—and at that moment something stirred the handle of his door.

He sank upon one knee against the wall, a gun in either hand, this time, and waited. Very slowly the door opened. When it reached half its width, it remained motionless, and a faint radiance penetrated the room—as from a lamp burning at a distance.

A moment passed. The stealthy sound of dripping water was no longer heard in the room. Tarron began to slip toward the door. A snake could not have moved more stealthily. He reached the opening, peered cautiously around the corner of the door—

There was no one to be seen.

Perhaps standing in the hall, waiting to lure him past the doorway—

More stealthily and cautiously still, he peered farther out. But the hall was still and empty, and only a single candle smoked and burned dimly in a bracket some distance away. He chanced to look at the back of his left hand, and saw upon it a bright smear of crimson.

He touched the stain—it was blood!

He turned hurriedly and lighted a match. There in the center of the room was a little dark-red pool; it had dripped from the ceiling through a chink in the bricks.

And above him was the room of Dorn!

Now Les moved like lightning, but softly as a hunting cat. He left his chamber, not by the door, but by the window, small though it was. A moment later he drew himself lightly onto the balcony above.

Standing full in the moonshine, Tarron peered into

Dorn's room. A broad shaft of the silver light entered ahead of him and showed him what he had to see.

Dorn lay face downward on the floor, both hands curled above his head. Instantly Tarron kneeled beside him—turned him over—and saw his throat wide cut, from ear to ear, and dead, fishy eyes staring blankly up to him.

Dorn was dead! After his long, long trail! Big Dorn was gone, and all his high hopes with him. And the great work unaccomplished! The blow had been struck in this small, sleepy village, to which time was a stranger!

Instinctively, Tarron glanced over his shoulder. It seemed to him that a shadow had crossed the door to the balcony, but when he leaped noiselessly to it, he found the balcony empty; and before him lay the quiet valley, beautiful under the moon, and the sleeping houses, their windows glinting like black, living eyes.

He went back to Dorn, and lighted a match; because the moon's light made the dead man's face so dreadful to see. But the light of that match showed Les something which was worth a keener attention. Where the hand of Dorn had lain on the floor—the dead right hand—some words were written in a red smudge.

As he lay dying, he had written on the floor with his own blood, until death stopped the sentence. Then, falling forward, in his fall he had rubbed out most of what he had inscribed.

A few brief words remained.

"—tall and scar—"

All before and after was indecipherable.

"Tall and scar—"

What might that mean except a description of the murderer, as Dorn had seen him, his eyes unclosing from sleep, the steel already in his throat?

A tall man with a scarred face, then?

So much for the murderer. But what of the great work? Tarron reached for the belt which Dorn wore ever buckled about him, night and day. The belt was gone!

And so Dorn's life-work was undone forever!

Unless, indeed, this mountain-bred youngster who had joined forces with him could carry on the great battle!

Chapter XIX

Like a Gale of Wind

YOU MUST UNDERSTAND that there had been so little spare time on the farm of the elder Tarron, and every day had been so filled with labor, that no one had ever had a chance to teach young Leicester Tarron how to pray; but when he kneeled beside that fallen hero and looked through the open doorway past the balcony and the treetops to the moon-flooded heavens, God could never have misunderstood what was in his silent heart.

After that, Tarron went out to the stables and found, as he expected, that both the gray stallion and the mouse-colored gelding were gone.

He remained for a moment in thought; then he went back into the house and tested his landlord's door. It was fast—locked! However, he gave his shoulder to the door, the inside bolt was wrenched off by his strength; and at once he strode into the room and found the landlord standing in the middle of the floor, half dead with sleep and bewildered with fear and wonder.

Tarron took the rifle from the hands of this worthy man and pitched it through the window. Then he took him by the hair of the head and dragged him to the window.

"Merciful God! Merciful God!" moaned the landlord. "Spare my life! Spare my life!"

"I am not God. My name is Tarron," said the boy. "I brought you to the window to study your face, and I see that it is like a book with only one page. Tell me: Who was it that murdered my friend this night?"

There was a loud scream from the doorway. The wife of the landlord had crept like a ghost from her bed after her husband was attacked. But when she came to the threshold of safety, her terror escaped in a screech, and she fled away down the hall, crying out for help.

"Listen, senor," breathed the landlord, "you hear that woman! She will raise the entire town. They will tear you to pieces! Flee now, and I shall show you a safe way out of the house!"

"Do you swear that?"

"I do swear it."

"Good. Then tell me first the name of the murderer—"

"Kind saints! Murder! Murder? In my house?"

"You rat!" said Les Tarron. "You small-eyed rat!" He shook the landlord until the wretch's teeth rattled together.

"Tell me!" he commanded.

"Senor, senor! There is nothing that I can say. You cannot pour wine from an empty jug!"

"Suppose that I put in a little wine first—can't you make it grow into a jugful? Suppose I tell you of a tall man with a scarred face—"

The landlord ceased his wrigglings and his prayers. He hung motionless between the hands of the boy and gaped at him.

"Very well," said Tarron. "I have not said that I am going to kill you. I've asked you if you'll tell me the truth!"

"Listen!" cried the landlord. "They are gathering! Do you hear them running? They are coming in hundreds. In another moment, even *I* cannot save you, for my wife will have shown them how to block the secret way."

"Friend," said the boy, "you have spoken well. But you can speak much better."

He laid the keen point of his hunting knife against the hollow of the landlord's throat and moved the handle so that the moonlight flashed up and down the blade.

Men who know their weapons have a certain way with them; it was not hard for the landlord to tell that Les Tarron loved knife-work.

"Senor," he gasped, "how could I tell? I only knew that he commanded us to keep in our rooms and lock our doors upon us. I could not disobey!"

Tarron saw a cord hanging round the landlord's neck and, snatching it, he burst open a little knotted rag at the end of the string. Half a dozen broad pieces of gold fell out and rolled across the floor—the frantic eyes of the landlord strove vainly to follow the direction of each one.

"Justice of God!" moaned he. "They will drop into chinks between the stones! They will be lost forever! They will do no more good in the world!"

"They will murder no more men, you mean to say," said Tarron. "But I've waited too long. Have you a prayer to say before you die?"

"Senor! Kind and wise young senor! Hear me!"

"Speak quickly."

"Had it been any other man, I should have turned him away from my door. But who could refused Don Quexada?"

"Is he one who can command here?"

"Does an eagle command crows and pigeons? Senor, I begged him to do nothing in my house. But he commanded. I—I could not resist. I asked my wife. She agreed with me that there was nothing I could do but obey. So we went to bed at the appointed time—"

"Who stole the two horses?"

"Stole the two horses!"

"Speak, man! Do you *want* to die?"

"It was he!" breathed the landlord. "It was Don Quexada, again, so that if he did not manage to kill you both, neither of you could pursue him!"

"Good!" said the boy. "I begin to understand. Now come with me out of the house!"

"I shall show you the secret way. Go before me—

this way through the hall—then down that flight of steps—"

"Listen to me, friend. I am young, but I am not a fool. If my friend had been of my mind, he would be still alive. Walk before me, now. If you look to the right or the left, your wife can have a new husband."

The landlord said no more.

Down through a winding way he led. The clamor of rapidly approaching voices swarmed above them and then grew faint. The landlord began to ascend again. He pushed up a trapdoor, and they were in a field behind the stable.

"Tell the stable boy to catch and saddle two horses. No, the boy is gone. We will catch them ourselves. Mind that I watch you every instant. And my gun never misses, even by moonlight."

The landlord was far too exhausted by terror to object or to attempt to escape. Mutely he submitted. The two horses were caught and saddled just as a fresh clamor began in the tavern and spread outward like rings in a pool after a stone has been dropped into the water.

By this time they had mounted.

"Now, where?" gasped the landlord. "Where do you take me, kind young senor?"

"This Don Quexada has ridden off. Which way?"

"Up the valley, senor. Shall we not follow? Yes, this way!"

"We'll not follow. Which horse does he ride?"

"The mouse-colored gelding, senor."

"You saw him away, I see! Was there blood on his hands then?"

The landlord cringed as though his backbone had turned to paste.

"Now," said Tarron, "I'm gunna get up with Quexada. I dunno how. But you know. Maybe there's a short cut. I leave that to you. If you bring me up to him by dawn, you can ride back here to your home and forget that there was ever a man named Tarron or a man named Quexada. But if you don't show him to me by dawn, I'll kill you. I'll tie you up by the wrists and cut off little pieces of you and feed them to that mangy dog that wants to follow us!"

The landlord rolled his eyes at the dog, and moistened his fat, trembling lips.

"Brave and wise and good senor! I am to die, then?"

"As you choose!"

"But there is no way! I swear—by the sweet saint—"

"Hush!" said Tarron. "Maybe you can still pray your way out of hell, but not if you lie about this!"

"Come," said the landlord, setting his teeth. "We can never overtake him, because he rides like the wind. But I don't think he'll try the upper pass. Oh, God pity me! God pity me! It's only through the upper pass that we could stop him!"

The landlord waited no longer, but turned his horse's head down the valley, just opposite to the direction he had first suggested. He rated his pony at a good, hard gallop; and with set face he pointed their course at a cleft in the upper mountains that looked now like the tall ears of a mule, leaning away on either side from a dark and narrow gap.

Mile after mile they rode; not a word was said, until the landlord suddenly turned in the saddle to his companion, who was always a significant length behind him.

"Have no fear, amigo. Ride up beside me. I begin to wish that you win. I begin to wish that Quexada should die. I have seen the times when I've ridden that pass. No one else dared to try it, but I could do the thing. I was young then, and no Quexada would have dared to treat me like a dog, as he's treated me, and as he treats all of the rest of them!"

"*Bueno!*" said Tarron. "I see that time may have made your hands a little dirty, friend, but your heart is still clean."

"Clean as a bone," said the landlord, taking more heart, and raising his head to the fresh, sweet wind of the night. "I shall spend half of the gold Quexada gave me for Masses. In that way, I shall do good for the heathen soul of your dead friend, and I shall also save my own soul from danger. I shall not forget you, either."

"A little gold to spread out a long distance, it seems to me," said Tarron. "You've ridden this pass before?"

"When I was a boy, senor, I would have taken Quexada by the beard and laughed in his face. Look! I bought that big tavern with money that I made before I was twenty-five. Well, how is so much money made so early in life? Not by lying in bed at night, you guess? And you're right! Holla! I was abroad, and I rarely came home without something in my pockets. There are ways for brisk young men to push on in the world! Come on, and on! We'll go through the pass like a gale of wind— God willing! God willing!"

Chapter XX

In the Dust of the Trail

So WITH THIS villainous landlord to guide him, Tarron
entered the pass.

They had not climbed a mile into the back throat of it
before Les could understand why even fugitives would
not willingly use this pass. For a cold wind screamed
through the heart of it continually, and a stream had cut
a narrow ravine through the center of the gorge. Along
the edge of that stream they had to ride, and fifty times
they had to cross and recross the white water, never
knowing when one of their horses might lose footing and
go whirling down the torrent with his rider.

Nevertheless, Tarron was contented, for he guessed
that they were cutting across the neck of a long loop
around which this Quexada must be riding. What amazed
him most of all was the fine spirit with which the plump
landlord undertook the task. Never once did his heart
fail him, though twice his horse slipped and nearly cast
him into the boiling water.

But presently they reached the crest of the divide, and
from that moment the going began to be infinitely worse,
for the slope pitched down at a terrific angle. Rain was

falling. The stones were slimy and wet, and there was not a ghost of a trail to follow. Even now, the landlord kept on with a brave spirit. And as the wind howled, he howled and shook his fist back at it.

"We'll teach Quexada to murder men in their beds!" he shouted. "We'll let him know what happens when he dares to shame honest taverners and their taverns! This should be a day marked with red on the calendar. I shall do such a good deed that I shall not have to spend money in Masses for my soul. A good mark against a bad mark —and that strikes a balance! Holla! A fig for the wind and the rain! Are you there, senor? Shoulder to shoulder, brave heart, we'll win through together. We'll come down on Quexada like two thunderbolts. We'll strike him from the face of the earth! Oh, the midnight murderer!"

So trolled the tavern-keeper, passing into such a joyous ecstasy, that Tarron could not help smiling more than once in spite of the hardships of that wild passage of the mountains.

Drenched and cold and stiff, they came down from the upper pass; and as the dawn began, they saw before them the rolling hills, and the white road looped loosely across them.

"That is the place!" said the landlord. He drew rein and looked anxiously ahead of him, screening his eyes with his hands, though there was not yet light enough to dazzle even the eyes of an infant.

He had lost a great deal of his enthusiasm. And Tarron understood.

He said grimly: "Wait up here. I'm going down. There's Quexada now!"

He pointed, and plain in sight was a horseman, riding one animal and leading two. The silver flanks of Jimmy glistened in the early morning light.

"God be with you, senior," said the tavern-keeper. "And what becomes of the good horse of mine that you are riding?"

"I ought to take him," said the boy fiercely. "And I ought to take the one that's under you now. And I ought to turn you out of your clothes and send you back naked!"

"*Madre mia!*" gasped the other. "What a tiger you are!

At one word, you have your teeth in a man's throat! Forgive me, senor. Keep that horse. I make you a free present of him. I wish you joy of him."

But in spite of himself he could not help making a wry face.

"I don't want your horses," said Tarron. "I'm gunna head down there for Quexada. And after he dies, I might leave you this horse of yours and the horse that Quexada is riding, too. You can have them free of charge. But when you get back to your house, you see to it that the body of my friend Dorn is buried all right and proper. You hear me?"

"Senor, senor!" gasped the host. "You carry me away with your great kindness. You make me like dust under your feet."

"You're a liar and a scoundrel," said Tarron, "but I can't help laughing at you! I see that you ain't so sharp for getting at Quexada, now that he's in sight?"

"Senor," said the fat man, making a wide gesture with both hands, "you see how this thing is? I have not had guns in my hands for a long time. Besides, why should I go to help where no help is needed? Is it fit for a thing like me to take the credit from a hero like you?"

"Wait here," he said, "and keep yourself out of sight."

And he rode straight down the nearest draw that pointed toward the distant road.

Before he came to it, he entered a little grove; and, while he was under the shelter of the trees, he heard a distant sound of shooting coming from the direction of the pass.

Could it be that the treble traitor, the innkeeper, was striving to betray to Don Quexada the danger in which he was riding?

Tarron pushed suddenly out on the road and saw before him, not fifty yards away, the form of a tall rider mounted on Jimmy, with the other two animals in the lead.

It was Don Quexada, peering to the side toward the mouth of the pass, where the innkeeper was firing his gun rapidly to attract attention.

Quexada took the warning; he was in the act of reining his horse sharply to the right when Tarron's challenge met him from beneath. He whirled Jimmy back into the road. But the good gray had seen his master, and in an instant he had bolted to reach Tarron's side. The lead ropes snapped like twine, and a frantic buck, high in the air, flung Don Quexada out of the saddle and rolled him in the dust.

Before Quexada could rally himself an iron grip was on his throat and a Colt pressed against his temple.

"Will you lie still?" asked Tarron.

The latter nodded. And still as a stone he lay while Tarron took from him two Colts, and a long, murderous hunting knife. Even the cool nerves of Tarron could hardly endure the sight of it, with the faint blur of blood about its shaft. He tossed it into the long grass and went on with his work, which was to pinion the arms and the feet of his captive, and last of all, to remove from his hips the long belt.

Kneeling in the dust, with rapid fingers he went through the compartments of the belt, and found that all was there even as he had last seen it, except for the middle compartment at the back.

This had been empty when he examined it before. But now it was completely filled by a small steel box, black with age and covered with fine engraving. It was perhaps three eighths of an inch in thickness, and three inches long. The moment it lay in Tarron's hands, somehow he knew that the prize was in his grip.

It had been this little trifle that Dorn had abstracted from the belt before he dared entrust it to Tarron.

"Open it," said Quexada bitterly. "There is death in it. I looked within last night, and I die this morning!"

"Last night," said Tarron, "you murdered for it, eh?"

"Murdered?" repeated the Mexican, raising his brows. "Murder? Is not everything fair in this war?"

He spoke as though in perfect innocence.

"And do I reproach you," he said, "because I am to be murdered this morning?"

"I took you man to man, with the sun to show you what I intended to do," said Tarron.

"A horse bucked me off his back, young man," said the Don. "Or else you would be at the gates of hell now!"

"Good!" said Tarron.

He leaned back and rolled a cigarette.

"It looks to me," he said, "as though you have your share of nerve. I suppose that they would have given you a pretty stiff price for this job?"

"Ingram could not do the thing that I did," said the Mexican.

He had the air of a man who has performed some admirable deed. There was no trace of shame in him for the foul murder he had committed, and yet he had all the appearance of an intelligent human being. His forehead was high and well proportioned; his eyes big and well placed, and only the length of his mustache and the sharpness of his beard gave a sort of old-fashioned stiffness and fierceness to his aspect.

"Ingram couldn't do it," admitted Tarron.

"I followed him," said Quexada. "I followed where the tracks led, and where the tracks were not. I outguessed Dorn. I knew that he would never keep on the straight road to La Paz, no matter how hot he was to see her. And there he was—so near, and yet what a distance from her! What a distance! Ha! At the very time when he thought that he was ready to stretch out his hand to her, the knife ended him! And then the devil sent you to bring me bad luck!"

"Was it the devil?" asked Tarron. "However, all your work is nothing. Here am I to take the thing on to her."

"Do you think that you are as near to the end as he was? Then ride ahead! Try your best. You will soon see! You will soon see!"

His laughter was like the croaking of a raven in the boy's ears.

Two touches of a knife set Don Quexada free. One of his own Colts was tossed into his hands as he rose in wonder to his feet.

"I swore to myself that I would forget everything until I'd found you," said Tarron. "But I can't butcher you like a dog. There's a gun. Now fight for your life, Quexada!"

"*Madre de Dios! Madre de Dios!*" gasped the Mexican. "Do you give me the victory after all?" And almost before his eyes had been lowered from the sky, he notched up the muzzle of his gun and fired.

A neat shot, well-aimed; but Tarron had spun around sidewise like a top jerked by a string. The bullet humed past his head. His own shot struck fairly between the eyes of his opponent. He saw Don Quexada take three great strides toward him, and then fall headlong in the dust of the trail.

Chapter XXI

As Time Is Measured

WHAT PASSED IN the heart of Leicester Tarron when Quexada fell dead at his feet?

It was the first time he had actually aimed a shot at a human being. It was the first time that he had slain. And yet Tarron regarded the dead man with a calm unconcern. There was too much on his hands for him to waste time in sentimentalizing over death. First of all, he went through the clothes of Don Quexada with meticulous care. A well-filled wallet he appropriated without the slightest qualm of conscience. And the filled ammunition belt of the dead man he took also. He found nothing more of interest except, within the wallet, a letter which might well set him musing.

It was written in a clerk's fine, scholarly hand, rapid yet well formed:

My dear friend Quexada: When you receive this, you will know that the box is being brought into your territory by Dorn and a companion, a boy named Leicester Tarron. The box is actually carried by Dorn. You will take your measures accordingly. But by all means try to dispose of the boy also. Do not be deceived into soft-heartedness or neglect by his youth, because of the two he is the more important.

You have heard something of Dorn and his work. He has carried the box actually closer to the finish than any other man. He has worked like a hero, and he has given us more cause to worry than all the others combined. However, young Tarron is even more dangerous. At this time he knows very little about the box, even if he has heard of its existence. He has attached himself blindly to Dorn as an adventurer, and you may know that from such careless adventurers a great deal is to be feared. Therefore, do your best to destroy the boy if you wish to secure your retreat in safety. If you must leave him alive behind you, be sure that he will follow you, no matter how faint a trail you leave. If you leave him in your rear, ride by the shortest route, and kill your horse if you must. Tarron will be coming like a storm after you.

I give you this detailed warning because I feel that the matter is being placed in your hands more completely than it has ever been placed in the hands of any other person. It is now in your power, Quexada, to end this long struggle at a blow.

Do your best, and the matter will be over; and I shall see that you receive such a reward as even you cannot imagine easily.

Start instantly. Omit no care. Adios.

In place of a signature, there was a little impression of a seal. Beneath, was written hastily:

I open this letter in a hurry to impress upon your mind, finally, how vastly important it is that the boy should be disposed of.

With that, the missive ended.

There was enough in it to flatter the heart of young Tarron with a most pleasant warmth; but there was also enough to make him shake his head in concern. Here was proof positive that he had been marked down by the enemy and that they would spare no effort to cut him off.

But what interested Tarron more than all else was that "they" should have gathered so much information about him so quickly; unless, indeed, the tale of what he had done in escaping from the jail had been magnified in the report to the man whose seal was affixed to the letter. It showed him, on the whole, that he was face to face with a carefully elaborated system of spying. His enemies' informants were everywhere, and they made instant and copious reports. He could not help but be somewhat discouraged. For, when he had faced the great adventure, he felt that perhaps he would gain some advantage from his youth. Men do not expect great things of a boy as a rule. And he had hoped with all his heart to take "them" by surprise.

That was not to be. "They" had written him down at his full value, and perhaps something more than his full value. Yet it cannot altogether displease a young man to find himself regarded with dread by formidable foes.

Turning back to the consideration of the letter, he tried to make something of the seal. It looked to him at first like a wheel, but then he saw that what seemed the spokes were naked arms projecting from a common center; and what seemed the rim was composed of swords, hard gripped. A very curious thing as a seal. Tarron, knowing nothing of such matters, strove to make head or tail of it.

He could not decipher its meaning, except that it had been used in the place of a signature. It came, assuredly, from one of Dorn's enemies—one of his own enemies! Somewhere in the mysterious city of La Paz, man—or perhaps woman—had pressed that seal upon the paper, and the order had gone forth to destroy young Tarron.

It remained for Tarron to discover the whereabouts of that town, first of all; and, secondly, to learn who were the rightful owners of this little steel box which so many people had tried to deliver, and tried at such a dreadful cost.

In the meantime, his fingers had been constantly busy at that box, but it would not yield to his hand. Halfway down the side, he could make out the lips which joined in the closing of the box. But he could not pry them apart without using so much force that he feared to break the box.

And that might be a calamity! Whatever was in the box, mere exposure to the air might ruin it, and undo all the labor of having brought it so far and so cleverly.

Les did not fail to press every inch of the surface, in the hope of finding some secret spring; but he had no success.

When he studied the design engraved on the box, he had no better luck. It was covered with the most elaborate arabesques: except for a central frieze of tiny horses, men and dogs, chasing a stag. The work was done with such a delicate and admirable art that when he scrutinized the thing more closely, the more he saw of the vitality of the men, the straining of the horses, the fierceness of the dogs, and the terror of the stag at whose haunches the leaders were already leaping.

Altogether it was a dainty thing; but Tarron made up his mind that what the box contained was the important matter. He tested the weight. So far as he could judge, the steel was not very thick, and certainly there was nothing like gold within—the whole was much too light!

Never was a lad more thoroughly baffled than was young Tarron, and yet he almost rejoiced that his wits had not been able to penetrate to the heart of the puzzle. It left a greater work still before him. Drawing up the cinches on the gray stallion, Jimmy, Les swore to himself that he would never give up the trail until he had won; or until the enemy had crushed him, as Dorn and all the others had been crushed.

In the meantime, La Paz! He must find the city.

The dead man, Quexada, had said that the end of the quest had been comparatively near when Dorn and he were in the sleepy little mountain town where Dorn had been overtaken by the murderer's knife. Therefore, Tarron intended to ride in that general direction once more. Not that he meant to pass directly through the village again. That would have been too completely head-strong and foolish; but since La Paz lay yonder, in that way would he journey.

So he made all ready, looked his last upon the dead

man, and rode on down the valley. And it occurred to him that Quexada himself would have been hurrying back to reach La Paz and so bring the work to an end. Therefore, it was wisdom enough to ride down the valley.

A common goal for both the pursued and the pursuer!

Tarron marveled at this, but he had determined not to puzzle over seeming incongruities which might not be incongruous after all in the long run. In the end, all would be explained by a single word, no doubt!

He rode for perhaps two miles, and the sun was beginning to grow hot, when he passed a shepherd—a grizzly old man sucking at a black pipe, trudging slowly after his flock.

Tarron drew rein beside him.

"Good morning, father."

"Good morning, boy."

"I'm looking for the road to La Paz."

"La Paz?"

"Yes. Is this right?"

"This is right for Callahar and Santa Maria. La Paz? I never heard of that place."

"You've just come into this district, then?" said Tarron.

"Well, in a manner of speaking, I've not been here overlong."

"Is there any house near where I could learn?"

"No; nobody knows better than I do."

"What?"

"Well, why should they?"

"Man, man, you've just admitted that you haven't been in this district long."

"Boy, boy, that's as you want to measure time. But I've been around here longer than any of the rest."

"Very well, then. Let me know where La Paz is, will you?"

The other raised his skinny hand, uncertain and shaking with age, and pointed to the sky above him.

"It's there, and no other place!" said he.

"You like your joke," sighed Tarron.

"I'm too near that place to joke about it," said the shepherd. "Good luck, lad."

He pushed the sheep on, and went wearily along behind them.

But Tarron reined Jimmy back across his path.

"Listen to me, old-timer. You're making a lot of riddles for me, and I'm no hand at getting the truth out of such hard nuts. You say that you're traveling toward La Paz?"

"Toward La Paz. Yes, of course. And so does every sensible man that I ever heard tell about. But they never find it on this earth. The trail to it goes out in air, sooner or later, and you've got to die to live in La Paz!"

"You mean to say, then, that there is no such town as La Paz in these mountains?"

"I do."

"Then how long have you been here?"

"Only a matter of fifty-eight years, son!"

Chapter XXII

A Man with Three Horses

THE WAY TO Santa Maria and—what was the other town? Callahar?

Tarron stopped in his path. He let the shepherd who had known these hills and mountains for fifty-eight years go slowly down the road and out of sight around the bend. And then he watched the dust cloud which the sheep had raised hang long in the windless air, but at length dissipate.

This was not the way to La Paz. A man who had lived her for more than half a century had never heard of the name of such a town. As for the other two towns, he knew nothing of them.

Might it not be the name of some hacienda, then? At that thought, Tarron whirled Jimmy round, and with the two led horses galloping behind him, retraced his way at full speed.

He found the shepherd settling himself for a brief rest on a stump at the edge of the road, while the sheep scattered in search of the best grass.

"Look here," said Tarron, "there may be some other place that bears the same name—some house, some hacienda; even a river or a mountain—anything you know of that carries the name of La Paz?"

The old man shook his head, and yet he smiled kindly on the anxious enthusiasm of the youth.

"Set down and think," said he. "Thinking will get you farther than fast riding in this here world. Set down and think it over and take council. That's what our elders used to do."

Tarron, gaping at him, wondered what in all the world could be elder than this white-bearded grasshopper of a man.

"You've never heard of anything like that name?" he said.

"Nothing like La Paz," said the gray beard. "I know this here country better than a book. The doctor tells me that I'm gunna be plumb blind in another few years. God willing, I'm gunna be dead before my eyes die on me! But even if I have to go blind, I could still move about. I know every fence post inside of a hundred miles. I could walk blindfold over the worst of the mountain trails. So that it ain't likely that stream or mountain or town or hacienda could be called by any name that I really wouldn't know, is it?"

"No," said the boy sadly, "it ain't very likely, I suppose."

"Nor trail nor path nor pool," said the old man, "and some of the trees and the hills have their names, but nothing like La Paz. It ain't a name that would ever be popular around here. Why should it be, seeing that there ain't never been very much peace around these parts!"

Tarron, in his eagerness, had dismounted. Now he swung into the saddle again with a loud groan of vexation.

"It's no use, then," said he. "I've got to hunt some other way."

"Hunt any how you please," said the ancient, "you'll never find what you're hunting for. Not in this part of the world. Not peace in fact nor peace in name. It all looks dreamy and quiet, but there's all hell everywhere just under the surface."

So Tarron went on down the road again.

But he was tremendously ill at ease. Had there been even the shadow of a ghost of a trail for him to follow, he felt that he could have worked it out as well as any man under heaven, for he knew his powers, and recently they had been tested severely enough. But there was only a name which no man recognized.

How could he turn, then, and in what direction?

To go on vaguely and blindly might be to override the mark, and never know that he had passed it. And as he advanced, most certainly he would be advancing into danger—danger from men whom he did not know—antagonists to whom honor was a mere name, and who would shoot him from behind, or slash his throat in the night with no pangs of conscience.

Poor Leicester Tarron turned his problem back and forth and found no solution. But he felt that the shepherd must be wrong, in spite of all his fifty-eight years of experience.

Dead men do not dally with the truth except for a grim purpose, and Quexada, when he spoke of La Paz, had been no better than a dead man—death, according to his expectations, lay immediately before him. Therefore, he must have meant what he said when he declared that La Paz lay close to the little town in which Dorn had died.

Looking back up the slope toward the mouth of the dark pass, Tarron could see his host of the night before riding in desperate haste, leading behind him the pony which Tarron had borrowed and had turned loose for the sake of the better animals with Quexada.

There was an easy explanation for the actions of the innkeeper. The latter had felt his spirits mounting as they forced their way through the dangers of the mountain forge. But when they came out into the daylight, and when the familiar form of Quexada was in view, caution and policy had overcome the fat man's bravado. He had tried to give the Don warning, and he had almost succeeded.

However, Tarron thrust away such memories. He dared not dwell too much upon the past. It had all been so confused, so filled with terror, that to contemplate it was to make him despair of the future, and with despair no man can mate and win a game.

This knew Tarron, but as he wandered on down the valley, he felt like a rudderless ship.

The three horses were an embarrassment of riches. He could not manage them as well as he could manage two; and, for that matter, he half felt that it would be much better to dispose even of the mouse-colored gelding, and keep only the gray. In that manner he would be more free in his movements, and it was unlikely that any pursuit would tax the powers of Jimmy to the utmost.

There was only one thing that Tarron could do as he pursued this journey, and that was to keep wide awake to every possible ambuscade. And, in the meantime, he could map out the country in his mind, studying the face of each mountain as he approached and passed it. For land lies very differently to those who come and to those who go. If he retreated in haste through these valleys, he must know them as well as possible. And every creek he crossed must be jotted down in his memory as easily fordable, or difficult to cross, and its exact place remembered accurately. All of these details might become matters of life and death, later on.

It was not long after noon that he saw a slanting stream of smoke rising from behind a hill.

Instantly he reined his horse into the brush. For a smoke column was one of the oldest of signals, and might still be used in a region where the telegraph was strung only here and there, at wide intervals.

He made a semicircle around the base of the hill, and thus rode into view of a small house, tucked in a hollow of the slope, with a little garden of vegetables extending in brilliant green behind it. A broken-down horse cropped the scanty grass in the pasture; there was a pair of cows, and the cackle of geese and chicken came thickly on the air. But otherwise there was scant token of how a living might be eked out in this wilderness.

In front of the door sat an old man, with a silver beard that flowed down almost to his waist and flashed in the sun like metal.

Once more Les determined to dare the dangers of approach to a habitation. Information he must have, and quickly. And better a danger ventured here, than a greater danger risked later on. There had not been much time, perhaps the mountaineers had not all been warned against him. But before long the enemy would have spread a net for him everywhere. He knew it perfectly well, and therefore he rode up the slope with the sangfroid of desperation.

When he dismounted, he found that the old man's eyes were shut beneath a gray mist of brows. But as he spoke, the ancient one looked up.

"I, senor, am Pedro Gregorio. Put up your horse. Come to sit here in the shade for a while. Dinner will soon be ready. Lucia! Lucia! There is a friend to eat with us!"

"Friend?" cackled a voice within the house. "Friend? What one of your begging, worthless cronies is it this time?"

A stalwart woman of middle age came into the open doorway. Her formidable arms were brown and bare to the elbows, and there was a scowl on her brows. Yet she was a rather handsome creature, in a way, and perhaps not so fierce as she at first seemed, for a big, yellow cat came with her to the door and rubbed fondly against her dress.

"If you can spare me food," said Tarron, in her own Mexican tongue, "I am happy to pay for it, senora!"

"A man with three horses!" said the old man. "And you call him a beggar?"

The woman fell silent, staring at the new guest, and Tarron waited, hat in hand.

At length she started, as though out of a dream.

"No one ever comes here except some of his penny-clipping companions," she said by way of apology to Tarron. "You'll find crushed barley in the corner bin in the horse shed. Give some of that to your nags. And then come in. There'll be a dinner ready in ten minutes."

He gladly did as he was told. Grain for Jimmy was more priceless than gold just now, for the extra strength it gave his horse might be the saving of his master's life before the world was much older. Tarron brought his three animals to the stable, unsaddled them, rubbed them down with straw, gave them a generous feed of barley—wondering the while that such a place should possess such a luxury—and then, when he had added a portion of hay apiece, he came back to the house.

The old man had come hobbling back on a crutch and a cane to watch his guest wash face and hands at the spring, where the water slipped eternally out of the breast of the mountains and overflowed a little basin chipped in the rock.

"Keep your hands in the water above the wrists," said the old fellow. "That cools you off. After you have been soaking up this sunshine it needs water to soak it out of you again. Oh, and the back of the neck. Keep water on that, too, and it'll clear your eyes wonderfully."

Nothing pleases people so much as to see their advice followed, even in the smallest matters. It makes them patrons. They become straightway tender of the affairs of the veriest stranger. And Tarron was scrupulous in taking the directions of this tottering sage.

Chapter XXIII

Where Lies La Paz?

"WHAT BRINGS YOU through this part of the world, child?" asked the old man as they sat in the cool shadow of the pine tree before the house.

"I'm on the heels of an old yarn," said Tarron.

"Following a story?" The Mexican smiled genially. "I have followed them, too. I have had gold in every valley of these mountains!"

"You lie!" cried the woman from within. "Let me see some of it, then!"

"I've had the hope of gold," said the old man, after making a little pause so that the harsh echo of the woman's voice might die away. "Following the gold is better than having the gold, some say. If that's true, I haven't wasted my life."

"It's not true, though!" barked the woman.

The ancient sighed. But he did not look toward the door from which these ringing accents poured. He merely moved off a little farther. And Tarron replaced his stool for him on the farther side of the pine tree.

"But you're starting for the same thing?" asked the Mexican. "You're following gold, too? Ah, boy, you'll have years of happiness—and very little money, I suppose!"

"You've been here a long time?" asked Tarron.

"In one more year I shall be ninety."

Tarron breathed deep. He had never before seen a man so old. And never had he seen one who so perfectly filled the picture of what age should be—mellow, quiet, dignified, and wise, with all the bitterness of ignorant prejudices rubbed away.

Not all of these thoughts were formulated definitely in the mind of Tarron, but he felt them all, and he could not look at the old man without smiling, half-affectionately. Old men and children have little pride; therefore we may show that we love them. But most strong men had rather be feared than loved.

"Ninety years," said Tarron quietly. "Well, it's a grand thing to be that old!"

"Do you think so?" said the seer. "And why?"

"Why," said Tarron, "ain't it better to be a filled bucket than an empty one?"

This speech the other considered for a moment, stroking his beard placidly. And then he laughed, and his eyes shone blue and bright beneath the white brush of his brows.

"The pleasure's in the filling of the bucket," said he, "not in being where only a few more drops can be added!"

"Ninety years!" murmured Tarron. "And most of them spent on the mountains, here?"

"I've lived in a small way," said the other. "Small as people around here count distances. I've prospected over ten thousand square miles—a thousand square leagues, if you want to put it in another way. But I've never gone outside of the country that I was born to."

"You were born in the mountains, then?"

"Lad, my father built this house with his own hands. When I was eighteen, I chipped out that bowl in the rock beneath the spring."

"Ninety years in this place!" murmured Tarron. "That's a fine long time!"

"Fine and long or dreadful and long. There's two ways of looking at every day—or every thousand days.

What's done in them, or what's lived in them! Lucia thinks only of what is done."

He added suddenly: "You keep three horses?"

"Yes."

"And two saddles, too?"

Tarron was silent. He had not expected this sharp and sudden turn to the talk, and he could not help letting his eyes wander for a moment.

But when he glanced back, the old man had raised his hand.

"Don't explain," said he. "Never talk except about things that make you happy. We have long winters to make us remember the summer. I talk of summer in winter. And Lucia does not understand. But you will understand—with your extra saddle!"

And he smiled kindly, straight into the eyes of his guest. Yet Tarron had no doubt that, in this moment, he had been vitally weighed. He had been adjudged a fighter, a man-killer. And the empty saddle was, to Pedro Gregorio, the equivalent of a story of war and death. And yet the old man did not start or change color. His voice remained as even and as kind as ever, and Tarron could guess that it was not the first time that this mountaineer had had to do with deeds of death and those who dealt them.

"I'll tell you frankly what I've come for," said Tarron, with a burst of confidence. "If you'll not talk about it afterward?"

"Son," said Gregorio, "it is a kind thing to trust a stranger. And if you can trust me, I think that I can trust myself."

He added: "Tell me what you wish."

"Is there anything about these mountains that you don't know?" asked Les.

"Uncounted millions of things that I don't know. What makes that poplar grow twice as fast as the other? Why do the squirrels bury all their nuts beneath that tree and never beneath this pine? And a million other things I can only guess at."

"I don't mean about trees and squirrels, but about people."

"People? Yes, I have known a great many of them."

"And the towns?"

"Oh, yes. I have been in all the towns. Except the new towns on the San Jacinto. They were built only thirty-five years ago, and I haven't been there since then. My first son died in that valley," he added absently.

"You've heard of lost mines?" said Tarron.

"Many, many times. Are you on the trail of a lost mine?"

And he smiled gently, understandingly, pityingly on Tarron.

"No, no," said Tarron. "I'm on the trail of a harder thing."

"What can that be?"

"A lost city."

"Ah!" said the old man. "A lost city?"

Something in the idea seemed to interest him immensely.

"A lost city?" he repeated.

"A lost city," said Tarron, studying himself with a frown, as he saw that it sounded like nonsense. "I've heard of the place and when I asked for it, they told me that there was no such city."

"What was the name of it?"

"La Paz."

He waited, breathless, but the old man slowly shook his head.

"I never heard of that name," he said. "La Paz? No, there's no such name!"

Tarron could have groaned. Why had not Dorn, who had told him so much, not told him the vital bit more that he needed to know?

"I thought that it was hopeless," said he. "Because an old man who had lived here most of his life told me that there was no such thing. But when I saw you, I hoped that you might know better."

"Had he lived here long, then?"

"Wonderfully long. Fifty-eight years in this very country."

"So! Fifty-eight years?" said Gregorio rather contemptuously. "Well, that is not the age of a boy, to be sure! Fifty-eight years in this country—an old man, did you call him?"

"He is much older than that. He is a shepherd—"

"That would be young Gonzales."

"No, not young. He can barely totter with his years."

"I call him young, my son, because when he first came to this country he worked for me, and I taught him to shoot. But there was always a curtain across his eyes. He never could understand the hard things. And mountains are hard. Such a man could live all his life in a single room and not know the faces of the things that are in it!"

"I believe it," said Tarron gloomily, "but still he knows what I wanted to find out. There is no La Paz in the mountains!"

"Wait!" said the other. "If it is important, it is worth thinking back!"

He leaned against the trunk of the pine, half-closing his eyes.

"Our minds are like old junk heaps," he said. "We can sift and search in them for a long time. We pick up one little memory and then another. Turn it over. See that one side is twisted out of shape and the other quite strong and fresh. Perhaps I shall pick up something about this La Paz."

He closed his eyes again.

"Father!" shouted a strong voice.

Tarron turned with a start, and he saw that the woman was more than halfway down the path from the house to the tree.

"We are coming, child," said Gregorio. "I hope you'll have that good soup for him?"

"He'll get what he finds," said she ungraciously as ever.

"Ah, ah," said the gray beard, "a kind word is better than butter on dry bread. Well, Lucia, you are still young —God be praised!"

"If my soup were like your talk," said the daughter sourly, "it would be as thin as water!"

She turned her back on them and marched into the house.

Tarron was surprised to find everything neat within. His own mother was a meticulous housekeeper, but even she could not have improved upon the cleanliness of the rolled and swept dirt floor. All was in good order, and a meal for two was on the table. The yellow cat was curled beneath it, waiting for a portion.

"Where's Lorenzo?" said Gregorio. "Where's your boy?"

"Gone to the village with the goatskins this morning, as you very well know."

"Ah," apologized Gregorio, "it is that way with us old men. Tomorrow is clearer than today. There is always a mist over the present. And you, Lucia?"

"I have to get the cows in to water. I ate my share while I cooked."

"Time, time, time!" sighed Gregorio, taking his place before a bowl of bread and milk. "Well, since you worship time, may you surely have enough of it!"

"Here, Lady," said the woman at the door. "Come, come, you little fool!"

The yellow cat, as its mistress clapped her hands in fierce impatience, rose from beneath the table and stalked slowly to the door. There, as it paused to lick its whiskers and glance forlornly back at the steaming food on the table, Lucia reached down and swept up Lady, and marched away with her.

Chapter XXIV

The Pillars of Smoke

Now THAT THEY were left to themselves, Tarron saw that he had before him a plate of boiled beef, a sharp contrast with the bread and milk of his host.

And he said at once: "You've taken the wrong chair, father. That should be my place."

Gregorio smiled on him.

"This is enough for me, my friend. And when you are old, like me, you will soon forget your appetite. For an old man, meat in the stomach is like a day's labor laid on the shoulders. And I do not wish to be like some old people, having all their life in their bellies and no strength left for their brains."

"I understand," said Tarron, and he took his place.

The big, yellow cat, which must have slipped away from its mistress by some dexterous sleight, now ran into the room and leaped up into the third chair which stood by the table; and there she sat in all her feline gravity, the end of her long tail twitching with interest as she eyed Tarron's plate of meat.

"She's hungrier than I am," said Tarron, smiling.

And he gave her a piece of the meat.

It was too large a piece for her to swallow at once. So she held it between her paws, very like a monkey, and ate it bit by bit, while Tarron watched her, delighted at her daintiness.

"I've never seen a cat like that!" he declared.

"Lucia has taught her tricks," said Pedro Gregorio. "If she would spend half the time on her son that she——"

He paused with a sigh. Then he added: "Your food is growing cold, senor."

Tarron prepared to eat, but at that moment some thought or memory occurred suddenly to Pedro Gregorio. He said: "La Paz! La Paz!"

And he closed his eyes and leaned back his head, as though the effort to clear his mind were very painful.

"It's lodged somewhere back in my mind," he said. "I don't know where, exactly. La Paz! Where have I heard it before?"

Then as Tarron, forgetful of his food, listened in intensest interest, his eyes glued upon the face of his host, the latter added with a sigh: "But that is the way with us old people! For so many things have been crowded into our minds that we hardly know how to distingush between what we know and what we think we know. We feel that every face has been seen before; every story has been heard before; and every name is one we know. It is the same with this La Paz, perhaps, and yet something tells me that I have heard it. Somewhere a long, long time ago! I wish that I could think back to the day and the place. That might help me to remember the facts."

He shook his head.

"There's no use forcing the memory," he said. "It is a servant, of course, but a very stubborn one. When it pleases, it will supply you with what you need. But it will take its own time and act in its own way. And you—you are not touching your food!"

There was a good appetite in Tarron, and now that his hopes were postponed by Gregorio, his knife and fork were instantly busy with the meat. He had not brought a bit of it to his lips, however, when the voice of Lucia was heard calling Lady, and calling her with such a stormy voice that it was plain the golden cat was a very disobedient truant.

"Where *is* the cat?" asked Gregorio.

"She was on this chair," said Tarron, politely beginning to search.

"No, continue your dinner. Poor boy, you haven't touched your food, between a talkative old man and a cat! I'm heartily ashamed. Let me look for Lady—"

There was no need to look. A pitiful moan came from the corner of the room at that moment, and peering into the shadows behind the stove, Tarron saw great, round, burning eyes look back at him.

Then Lady, hearing the voice of her mistress, crept out from her warm shelter.

She was much altered. Her tail lashed her sides, and every hair on her back stood erect. Halfway to the door she paused, stood stiff-legged, and then fell in a fit, biting at the air, biting her own body, and striking out in an agony with her unsheathed claws.

"Lucia! Lucia!" shouted Gregorio. "Lady is sick!"

Lucia's formidable bulk appeared suddenly in the doorway. She was panting with haste and anger and fear. When she saw the cat she pointed suddenly at Tarron.

"You devil, what have you done to her? What have you done to her?"

"Lucia, Lucia!" cried the father. "My friend was only kind to her. He's even fed her from his own plate—"

"Curse him!" cried Lucia.

Her face wrinkled in fury and hate, and she dropped on her knees beside the writhing cat. Regardless of striking claws and dangerous fangs, she gathered up Lady and carried her out into the sunshine.

"Colic," said the old man, shaking his feeble head. "But I've never seen a cat taken so quickly and so severely with it—"

"That kind of colic," said Tarron, "doesn't take long to work."

"It'll soon be over."

"Yes," said Tarron, "I think it will. It will soon be the finish of the cat."

"The finish, senor?"

144

"Don't you see, Senor Gregorio? This is poisoned meat!"

And he stood up and pointed to the boiled beef.

"*Madre de dios! Madre de dios!*" breathed the old Mexican. "How can I believe that? What devil could make Lucia think of such a thing? Oh, God defend her from—"

He paused, staring white-faced at his guest.

"There is no harm done except to the cat," said Leicester Tarron. "I'll do her no harm in return, for your sake, senor. But there *is* a devil in that woman!"

"Disappointment, hunger for money, love of easy living, envy of the successful—those are her curses," said the father; "but what special fiend could have pointed you out to her? Would she have murdered you for the sake of your three horses? God forbid!"

He added: "And yet—when she saw you she was suddenly kind—ah, what a soul is in her!"

He buried his face in his hands.

"Hush!" said Tarron. "She isn't so much to be blamed as the ones behind her, because you mustn't think that she determined on this murder of me without having it suggested to her in the first place! No, she knew that if she could kill me, she'd have whatever she wanted, up to thousands and thousands of dollars! I could tell you more than this. There's no reason why you shouldn't know, senor. But I'm trying with all my might to find this lost city of La Paz, and the others are trying to beat me back from it. And poison is pretty welcome to them, if it'll stop me. You understand?"

"I understand that you are attempting to do a dangerous thing in these mountains. Ah, son, where are your helpers?"

"My friend that rode with me is dead."

"And he didn't know La Paz, either?"

"He knew, but he hadn't told me. He still wasn't sure of me."

"How did he die?"

"A knife across his throat."

"That is his horse?"

"One of them is his horse."

"And the second spare horse?"

145

"That was ridden by the man who murdered Dorn in the night."

Pedro Gregorio closed his eyes. Then, as he opened them, he said:

"I was going to give you advice that would usually be wise—to leave these terrible mountains, son. I know them well enough to understand the perils that are in them. The rider who came to the house this morning and spoke to Lucia—he must have been spreading the alarm about you; and by this time every eye in the mountains is searching for you, or waiting for you, and knife, gun, and poison will be out against you. But I won't advise you to turn back. Heroes cannot give up an enterprise they have undertaken, and it's better that they shouldn't, for otherwise the common men would have nothing to steel their nerves—no great examples!"

He paused, and then added: "How heartily I wish to God that I could help you! *La Paz! La Paz!* Oh, lad, to ride through these dreadful mountains in the hunt for a lost city of peace! *La Paz! La Paz!*"

He seemed to have worked himself into a mild agony in his effort to remember. Sweat stood upon his forehead, and young Tarron, leaning across the table, stared hungrily, intently, into the face of the older man. He saw that face grow blank.

"Alas, alas, my boy, if you can wait, and if I can think of other things, then perhaps I shall be able to remember!"

"I'll wait," said Tarron resolutely.

He picked up a piece of dark bread and, walking to the door, he looked up and down the valley.

"I'll wait," said he. "I have to wait, because—"

Here he paused suddenly, for to the side and on the farther head of the hill he saw three thin pencil lines of smoke rising, and thickening each moment. And why should *three* smokes be going up side by side?

He broke off short and hurried from the house, went around the edge of the hill, and into sight of three small fires, which Lucia was even now covering with green leaves to make them smoke more heavily. On the ground beside her, limp and dead, lay the golden cat.

At sight of Tarron, she shrank away with a gasping

sound, like a great cat spitting. Fear and hate and malice distorted her face unbelievably, but Tarron had seen all that he wanted to know.

Somewhere, far off among the mountains, those three columns of smoke could surely be seen rising against the sky; and as they were seen, so surely were men swinging into the saddle and riding hotly toward this as a rallying point.

The word was out, and it was high time for him to be gone. Here and there through the mountains he would soon have to be fleeing like a frantic deer, and malice as fierce as that of this woman would be pursuing him.

Chapter XXV

The End of a Famous Man

IT WOULD BE pleasant to say of Tarron that, no matter how thoroughly he understood the malice of this woman, he still treated her as men should always treat the opposite sex; but the fact is that Tarron looked upon people in very broad categories—as friends or enemies, as young or old, but hardly as men and women. Women were not of much interest to him at this period of his life. And as he looked at Senora Lucia, her femininity was the only thing that kept him from killing her.

So he strode up to her. Realizing that she could not flee fast enough to escape from him if he cared to pursue, she shrank a little away, but laid a hand on the knife which was carried at her girdle, and prepared to stand her ground.

In spite of the knife, Tarron stalked up to her and laid a finger on her shoulder. That finger was like a heavy rod of steel, and she winced under its pressure.

"I've stopped," said Tarron, "long enough to tell you that I understand. That meat was for me, of course. The poor cat died by chance. And if the old man had taken some of the meat from my plate, you would not have cared a lot! The sooner he is dead the better, you think. It'd leave you free. I tell you, you she-devil, that I'm coming back this way; and when I come, I'll stop in here to see how things are, and when I call, I'll make it a point to find out how the old man's been treated. You understand?"

Her lips writhed back like the lips of a snarling dog, but she said not a word, and Tarron went back to the stables. There he left the fine horse which he had taken from Don Quexada. It was a swift and sturdy creature, but it seemed a little soft in flesh; and a soft, delicate animal would never do in the campaign which Tarron might now have to wage.

The mouse-colored gelding, Monte, was of proved worth, hardy as mustangs are apt to be. As for Jimmy, he was as tough as wire, could run twenty hours a day, and in the remaining four do his resting, and dine heartily on cactus and thistles, if nothing better were available. His appetite was not fastidious.

With Jimmy on a lead, to save his strength for a critical burst of speed, Tarron rode Monte to the house and found the old man beneath the tree, an expression of bewildered suffering still on his face.

"About the cat—and the rest," said Tarron, "don't you bother about that—just let it go. But if you could only remember about La Paz—why, that would do me a lot of good!"

Gregorio struck his fist against his forehead.

"I've been trying to remember," he said. "I've tried and tried, but the idea won't come back to me! I can't remember! But, every day, I'll attempt to remember. I'll keep it in my mind, and sooner or later I'll have the thing. Can you come back again?"

"I may come back," said Tarron, "if I can't learn in any other place. Goodbye, father."

"Goodbye, my son! God send you good fortune."

"Thanks for that."

"I shall remember you in my prayers."

And Tarron rode off, selecting for his course not the road out of the valley but the road straight into the mountains. For somewhere, yonder, lay La Paz, the mysterious, vanished city of La Paz!

You can understand, now, why Tarron gritted his teeth and scowled at the heavens. If he only knew what object he was to attain, he would risk his life to get to it; but

149

he was thrown into the playing field for a dangerous game without even knowing where his goal lay! What is the use of dogged persistence when one is ignorant of the object to be reached? Baffled, bewildered, tired, but grim as death, Tarron felt the spirit of battle rising higher in his breast the more perfectly he became convinced that he could never solve this riddle by his unaided wits.

He kept up the valley, then, until he saw straight before him a thin cloud of dust, moving rapidly across the tops of some trees. At that sight, he reined back and to the side and found shelter in a little ring-shaped copse. He had no sooner gained that shelter than four riders burst into view, with half a dozen led horses behind them. They were only range mustangs; but range mustangs, for the rough ups-and-downs of mountain work, are as good as the best mounts in the world, and these men rode as if they knew what spurs are meant for. They galloped past in silence, but their eyes searched the country before them and upon each side. And Tarron did not have to be told that they were riding in response to the triple column of smoke which had been raised. Three white hands of smoke clutching at the heart of the sky, saying in language which would be well understood: "The man is here! Come! Come fast, and guns in hands!" These four had rushed to answer the summons, and it was well that they had not gained an open view of their quarry!

Grim-faced, tight-lipped, Tarron watched them go. And he could not help fondling the butt of his Winchester. At this short range four well-placed shots—

But he pushed the idea away. Bulldog ferocity would not win his goal for him. There were more enemies in this range of mountains than he could ever destroy!

So decided the boy, growing months older with every moment of this desperate existence. He saw the horsemen dip out of view into the valley, and then himself rode forward on the trail with a rising hope that perhaps he would be able to slip through the cordon of his enemies by this very loophole which the four riders had made.

Yet he was far from any blind confidence, and as he swung down a sheltered slope his keen ears heard the pounding of hoofs on the opposite side of the narrow grove. Deep dust, perhaps, had muffled the sound from his ears; but he had not time to reenter the shelter and so escape detection before two more riders shot around the lower elbow of the woods. Take a wolf by surprise in broad day, or an owl on a moonlit night, but never hope to surprise a mountain-bred Mexican. His nerves react more quickly than the nerves of a cat to water, or of a bear to noise. And as the two riders shot into view, that instant their guns glittered in their hands.

It is harder to shoot downhill than it is up. Moreover, Tarron was trying to turn his pair into the forest. But, letting go the reins, he whipped a Colt into either hand.

His first shot beat either of their guns. Oh, welcome were those long hours of practice at the draw with which he had killed time at home in the days when his father raged and his mother wept because he would not work in the field. Make a plow horse and spoil a racer!

That first bullet, fired hip-high from Tarron's fanned weapon, hit the first rider and dropped him dead from the saddle. A hornet sang past Tarron's ear before he could plant a second bullet; and, as he fired, he saw the horse of the other rider rear. The broad frontlet passed across the line of the slug and the mustang, rearing higher, flung itself back with a human screech of pain and pinned its rider to the ground.

Tarron was on the spot in an instant. The dead man needed no attention, but when he had helped the second fellow from beneath the dead horse, he was glad to note that the man was not badly hurt, but shaken, shocked, and a good deal bewildered by the sudden ending of this battle.

Two excellent and time-hardened cavaliers mounted upon good horses and armed to the teeth, flash upon their single quarry as they make a turning in the road. And in two minutes all of their excellence comes to naught and they are laid along the road, one dead and one helpless. So unnerved was this wounded man that Tarron did not even tie his hands or his feet. He simply took two revolvers and a pair of deadly knives from the Mexican, and a wallet each from him and from his dead companion. Then, rolling a cigarette for himself, he tossed the makings to his new-found companion. The latter rolled his smoke with trembling hands to which the heavy dust of the road still clung.

There was no threatening with a pointed revolver. No, from time to time Tarron actually turned aside from the captive in order to examine more carefully the dead rider's mustang, standing in the near distance; or to note the signs up and down the valley—chiefly down, where the three thin columns of smoke were still rising in close pencil strokes against the sky.

"It was that, eh?" he said in Spanish.

"Yes, senor."

"And you and your friend came to answer it?"

"Yes."

"How are you called?"

"Venustio."

"And your friend, there, who had the bad luck?"

"Senor, that is a famous man. That is Silvio Oñate."

It is never well to make a man explain his superlatives.

"I have heard of him," said Tarron, lying politely.

"Of course! How he happened to fall, I cannot tell!" sighed Venustio, and he looked half angrily and half bewildered at Tarron. "He should not have failed. He never fails! To ride at the side of Oñate into a battle is as safe as to ride at the side of lightning. He blinds men. They fall down as soon as they see his face—and there—Lord! Has he gone?"

"He has gone," said Tarron soberly.

"How—and in what manner? But you were waiting for us—no, you were trying to turn into the trees—we had seen your horse through the woods—we were ready—and yet he failed. He was beaten. Your gun was quicker than his—and straighter—it is a world of many miracles! And you, senor! What is your name?"

"My name is Tarron!"

"Ha! Tarron!"

"Then you've heard about me, too?"

"Tarron! It was you, also!"

"Who did what?"

"It was you who murdered poor Quexada—poor Don Quexada! Murder me, too, but still you will never leave the mountains alive!"

Chapter XXVI

All the Money in the World

ODD THINGS AND exciting things and desperate things had happened to Tarron before this, but nothing quite so singular as being threatened with death by a man who was at that very moment helpless within his power. Moreover, there was the fire of fearless accusation in the eyes of the Mexican. He pinched out his cigarette and stamped it under his heel, as though even the tobacco which he had been tasting was poisoned, now that he knew the name of the man who had given it.

"I'm a devil, then?" asked Tarron.

"Yes!"

"I murdered Quexada?"

"Yes, yes!"

"How?"

"You stole behind him and shot him through the back."

"How does it come, then," said Tarron, "that the bullet hole was through the head, and that the bullet entered between the eyes?"

"It did not!"

"How do you know that?"

"The people of the mountains know the truth."

"Well," said Tarron, "you're talking like a fool. Maybe you want me to go ahead and murder you, eh?"

He could not resist flashing his revolver, but Venustio scowled back at him, unafraid.

"You have taken a better man than I shall ever be by your trickery this day," said he. "Why should I hesitate to follow? I do not hesitate. Hear me, Silvio!"

He raised a hand and looked upward—a wild fanatic —as though the dead Oñate's spirit, flown from earth to heaven, could lean down and hear his voice.

Tarron dropped his revolver back into the holster.

"Very well," said he. "I'll not live up to what you expect, then. I murdered Quexada by shooting him through the forehead, face to face, giving him the chance for his life after I had him in the road as helpless as you are. I murdered Silvio Oñate in the fashion that you saw. And if you wish to die honorably, there is a revolver, friend. Pick it up, and fight for your life! I will show you how I murder!"

He tossed a Colt to the feet of the other, but the Mexican did not regard it. He stood stiff and straight, frowning at the American, violently striving to readjust certain ideas which had been upset, or seemed likely to be upset.

He said at last: "Can it be that they have lied?"

Tarron broke in: "You did not know my name?"

"No."

"But you came to hunt me?"

"Why not?"

"What were you told?"

"To chase a scoundrel with at least three horses—one mouse colored, one a fine gray. And it *is* a fine one, I see."

His glance flashed appreciatively toward the colt.

"And the signal was three smokes?"

"By day, and three fires by night, of course."

"I hadn't thought about that. Tell me who gave you your orders?"

"I have talked enough. Perhaps I have talked too much. I am ready to die, senor. I am not ready to talk any more."

"If I tie you and gag you in the forest there," said

Tarron, "you'll starve to death, or a mountain lion will take you before the morning."

"Yes," said Venustio. "That's true. What of that?"

"But if you take that gun at your feet and fight me, that will be murder, too."

"Murder? I am not a child with a gun, Senor Tarron. I warn you of that!"

"I know," said Tarron, feeling suddenly too old and wise. "You're a good hand with a gun. But I know the way that they talk. You see?"

He smoothly tipped a Colt out of its holster. It spoke. There was a light crashing through the branches above, and the headless body of a squirrel dropped between them with a thud into the deep dust of the road and lay there already more than half buried.

Venustio opened his eyes.

"That," said Tarron, "is not a trick."

"Senor," said Venustio, "I see that I have been told lies. You do not need to murder from behind!"

"Then," said Tarron, working out the problem painfully, "what am I to do? If I tie you in the woods, you die horribly. If I fight you with a gun, it is worse than murder. And if I turn you loose, you ride up the valley and tell your friends where I have ridden. You bring them all after me!"

The Mexican frowned in thought. But he attempted no answer.

"Damnation on all of you!" cried Tarron suddenly. "Take that horse and go!"

The Mexican mounted the dead man's horse at once. But when he was in the saddle, he swung suddenly around on Tarron.

"Senor, I begin to believe that you mean it."

"Mean what?"

"To let me go."

"What else do I mean, man?"

"*Madre de Dios!*" said the Mexican, "after I have said such things to you? And tried to shoot you down?"

"Your bullet missed," said Tarron, "though it was a close thing. And the words didn't hurt, because they weren't true."

"Listen to me, brother," said the Mexican with a sudden burst of emotion. "I wish to serve you. Tell me how!"

"Do you wish to serve me?"

"With all my heart."

"Then tell me where is the thing that I wish to find."

"If I can."

"I am hunting for the city of La Paz."

"The city of peace?" murmured the other. "You are not joking, senor?"

"I'm in terrible earnest."

"La Paz! I've never heard of that name."

"You know these mountains?"

"I've ridden through every inch of them."

"Ah, well," said Tarron, "it can't be helped; there's nothing more that you could have done for me."

"Senor, think again. I have friends. I could send you through the mountains with a written word—"

"You would? No, Venustio. What good would it do? They'd sell me out in spite of you. And you'd be ruined, too. Only tell the others when they find you, that when I met you and your friend here I fought square. Will you do that?"

"Before God, senor!"

"And that the last you saw of me, I was riding up that rocky draw."

"I shall say all of that. And what more?"

"There's nothing more. Adios!"

"Adios!"

Venustio started his horse slowly up the valley, but paused and turned.

"Search your mind, senor. There is something more, perhaps, that I can tell you."

"Yes. How many more of you are riding to catch me?"

"I don't know. There may be two hundred men riding through the mountains on the search."

"Two hundred!"

"Yes."

"Where did you start from?"

"Santa Maria."

"Where is that place?"

"Straight through the pass, between the mountains, by the side of the lake of Santa Maria. You'll see the lake flashing like silver as you come through the pass."

"I'll remember."

"And there is much money promised. A hundred pesos to every man who sees you close enough to shoot. A thousand to the man who brings you down. A thousand to every man in that party!"

"Very good!" said Tarron. "And you know that you can trust the ones who promise that money?"

"Ah, why not?"

"I'm a fool," said Tarron. "I should have asked you before. Who are the people who promise the money?"

"Ah, but you know that!"

"On my honor."

"Well, senor, you wish to make a child of me."

"I swear to you, Venustio—"

"By your honor?"

"Yes, by that."

"I have to believe. But who would start riding a race when he knew not what roads to follow?"

"I can't help it if the thing seems strange."

"I'll tell you the name. It is Don Roberto."

"Don Roberto? Who is he?"

"Ah, my friend, you are surely laughing at me!"

"No, no."

"But the whole world knows about him!"

"I never heard of him."

"Not of Senor Langhorne?"

"Is that the rest of his name?"

"Roberto Langhorne!"

"A Mexican?"

"American."

"And he's offered the reward for me?"

"Yes."

"Now," said the boy, "make it all perfect by telling me where Langhorne lives."

"That's hard to tell. He has several places, but mostly he is at Santa Maria, in the old town house in the center of the town."

"Did you say the center?"

"Yes, you may see the trees of his place behind the church. Only the trees. The house is too old and low. It is covered by the trees."

"Thank you. Armed men around him?"

"A hundred, I suppose!"

"Rich?"

"He has almost all the money in the world."

"Good," said Tarron.

"And now," said the Mexican, waving his hand in farewell, "wherever else you may go, you will know enough not to try to go near the house of Don Roberto. He is greater than the devil!"

Chapter XXVII

Enter Juan Cordoba

WHEN VENUSTIO LEFT, Tarron rode straight down the road; but before he had gone a half mile he heard the telltale drum of horses' hoofs before him, and turned in haste into the wood.

A moment later—almost before, it seemed to him, the dust which his own horse had raised could have settled —a compact body of riders went by, eleven men on good cow ponies, all well armed. It took Tarron's breath to see such mustering of armed forces against him. He decided that he would wait until dusk gave a veil to his progress. Then riding deeper into the forest, he picked out a quiet place and rested there until the sun was down, and the shadows were thickening through the trees. After that, he worked his way quietly to the edge of the wood with the two horses.

It was still too bright to take any risk. So he delayed until he saw the stars begin to peer faintly from the sky. Then three level rays of red light struck down from a hill farther on in the pass—three rays close together. On a hill on the opposite side of the pass, there were three more in a close group. He understood as they flashed at him, three from each side. Three columns of smoke in the day and three shining fires by night were to give the signal. They were calling the men together to watch him in the throat of the pass.

Very greatly Tarron wanted to pass that line and get to the town of Santa Maria beyond it. He stared up at the high faces of the mountains on either side. There might be some way of cutting through them, and so avoiding the pass. Or, for that matter, he might be able to steal straight down the pass.

The enemy could hardly expect that he would attempt to press through there by night; they were simply gathering their forces to attempt to head him off the next day and spread the search for him.

Mighty was the power of this Robert Langhorne who could at will call up a small host. All the country swarmed with his creatures—dangerous fighting men, as Tarron had had a chance to learn. No wonder that even at a distance he had been able to make his hand felt through the campaigning of such resolute fellows as Ingram. And Ingram himself must be working up this trail as fast as horses could carry him and his associates. When he arrived, if he were not on the spot already, the trouble would thicken perceptibly.

And yet Tarron's heart did not shrink, but rather swelled to meet this emergency. He had weapons which were all that heart could ask. He had two chosen horses at his disposal. And he was willing to play the game even against such odds. If only he could have a little clearer knowledge of exactly what he could expect to do and where his hand should strike as he progressed. Armed with such knowledge as Dorn, for instance, had possessed, he felt that he could have worked out a reasonable campaign. But as it was, he only had learned that Robert Langhorne was an arch enemy, though perhaps even he was no more than an outpost of the main forces of the foeman.

Tarron formed this resolution: He would press on toward Santa Maria, attempt to get to the house of Langhorne, and, once there, he would leave everything to the spur of the moment, learn what he could, and then determine his future course from that point.

There was, however, one great difficulty. Jimmy's color made it very difficult to execute a secret night march through the midst of foes. His gray, even in starlight, became a glimmering and easy target. The eye could catch it, and what the eye could catch a bullet could strike. Monte, on the other hand, was a perfect color—neither too dark nor too light, one that would blend into the vague light of the open spaces. It was heart-breaking to leave the fine stallion behind him, but so fiercely eager was the boy's desire that he would not let even this sacrifice stand between him and his work.

He put Jimmy on a lead rope at the edge of a stream that trickled through the woods, where there was a plentiful growth of grass. Unless the horse betrayed his presence by whinnying when a searching party was near by, the chances were that he would go undiscovered in this place for a considerable time. Perhaps for several days he could live here untroubled, except for the saddle, which Tarron decided not to remove.

So Jimmy was left in the little forest, and Tarron issued from the woods on the mouse-colored gelding. Straight up the main road he went into the pass and had ridden two miles into the gorge, which became increasingly narrow, when a voice shouted from the ground before him:

"Who goes there?"

He answered in good Spanish: "Friend!"

"Friend to who?"

"Senor Langhorne."

"What are you doing here?"

"Who are you that asks?" replied Tarron with an imitation of honest heat.

"I've got a right to ask," said the man. "Stand up! This fellow wants proof!"

"We got proofs enough," said a second man, rising like a shadow out of the bush. He brandished his rifle in the dim starlight. "What are you doing here?"

"You're part of us, I suppose?" said Tarron, as though reluctant to admit their authority.

"Oh, there ain't any doubt about us, but what about you? Just cover this man, friend!"

The other leveled his gun instantly.

"I've been riding my horse into the ground all day," said Tarron. "I've been hunting that Tarron, and all that I'll have will be a fagged horse if I hunt for a month."

The guard hissed with the violence of his agreement.

"He turns into smoke," said he. "He turned into smoke, too, after he murdered Silvio Oñate."

"What! Did he kill Oñate?"

"Aye! You haven't heard that?"

"What chance have I had to hear things?"

"Well," said the guard who had spoken first, "he murdered Oñate."

"Shot Silvio through the back?"

"No. Through the head. But there must have been some trick about it."

"There was no witness, then?"

"Venustio. But poor Venustio's horse reared, and that coward of a Tarron killed the horse."

"Ha!" cried Tarron. "What a devil! Then he murdered Venustio, too?"

"No, Venustio cleverly pretended that he was killed in the fall; and when he got a chance he mounted Oñate's horse and came away safe with Tarron chasing him."

"But they say Tarron has a fast horse."

"Well, judge for yourself. Venustio galloped away from him safely enough."

Tarron smiled in the darkness. It was plain that Senor Venustio was equipped with an ample share of imagination. However, he could forgive the man for that. At the time of the battle, the Mexican had shown courage enough and good heart, also.

"Where did it happen?"

"At the mouth of the pass."

"Then Tarron must have turned back."

"That's what we think; but no, we have to stay here. Another man has come who hunted Tarron in the north, and he says that Tarron will always do exactly the opposite of what people expect. So we are kept here to guard the pass."

"Well, I'll go in and get food. Where?"

"Go straight up the pass. What is your name?"

"Juan Cordoba."

"Cordoba? Adios, Juan Cordoba."

Tarron rode on, very well pleased. He had passed through the first peril, but he was a little disturbed by the resolute manner in which these fellows had questioned him. Suppose that one of them had come close enough to discover that his horse was neither hot nor covered with the salt of a day's sweat?

But he was past the first cordon, at any rate; and he went on, very cautiously, scanning the brush on either side. Working away from the main road, he came to an obscure bridle trail through the brush, which he followed for a short distance; but even that was certain to be watched, and therefore he left it, and began to move gradually forward, taking his course from tree to tree and rock to rock. Monte worked at the game with a catlike eagerness, as though he understood exactly what was expected of him. Once three men loomed through the darkness. Tarron checked Monte in the shadow of a low tree, and the three went softly ahead, talking quietly to one another. When their voices faded, he moved forward again; and presently, with a feeling that he had crossed the second line of defense, he saw before him what was unquestionably the main danger.

Straight across the throat of the valley there was a string of small campfires, with the black shadows of men around every one. Beyond, the ground dipped away, and Tarron knew that from this point the pass declined and the valley widened. Here the forces of Langhorne were massed. If he could pass this critical point, he might easily win down to Santa Maria.

But to steal through that mass of men? He saw at once that it could not be done. Above him, to right and left, blazed the triple signal fires, still recalling to the pass all the outlying forces. An excellent system. And yet it seemed rather strange to Tarron that the enemy should have chosen to block him by main force away from gaining passage through that valley rather than to attempt to snare him here at its entrance.

He had not time to work out such riddles. He determined straightway upon his course. If he could not advance farther by stealth, he would attempt to go ahead by brazen boldness which will often win when caution and skill have failed.

He looked at revolver and rifle, to see that all was ready in case of emergency. Then he touched the mouse-colored horse with his heel and went forward at a brisk jog-trot. And he as rode, the better to mask himself, he called attention to his way with a cheerful whistle.

Chapter XXVIII

By Starlight and Firelight

TARRON AIMED HIS course at the space between the two campfires which threw the least light into the intervening space. And yet, all seemed terribly bright. He reassured himself by remembering that his eyes had been accustomed to the deeper darkness of the open night, and that to watchers who had been long near the fires the light would seem dim indeed. He went straight on, therefore, abating neither his whistle nor the pace of his horse.

He saw before him a half dozen men walking restlessly up and down, as though they were already tired of sentry duty. One of them called something to him which he did not understand, but he waved his hand to them and went on. His heart leaped. He saw himself already through the last line of watchers, when he was hailed brusquely from the side, not in Mexican, but in the clearest English: "*Who goes?*"

"Amigo!" called Tarron, waving his hand as he jogged along, and resuming his shrill whistling.

"Stop!" yelled the voice. "Stop when I holler, or I'll drill you clean!"

Tarron saw a leveled rifle, and he drew Monte to a walk.

"I don't mean a walking horse; I mean a stopped horse!" thundered the voice.

Tarron eyed the space before him. He could see no one. The light of the bonfires was dying out. Straight ahead there stretched a dark, deep, and empty region, with the valley widening at every stride. But that leveled rifle meant business, judging by the voice of the man who carried it. If his opponent had been a Mexican, Tarron told himself that he would have rushed ahead to force the lines. But he was not a Mexican. He was a white man, and a white man with a cold heart and an angry temper. Monte was brought to a reluctant halt.

"Well? Well?" snapped Tarron. "Do I have to make a speech to you?"

"He's only a greaser," said one of three men who now drew near. "Let him go."

"I'm gunna stop him and I'm gunna talk to him," said the first speaker. "He sasses me! I'm gunna teach him that no greaser can sass me!"

"Easy, Jerry!"

"Oh, leave me be! I know my business, old-timer. Leave me be with him. Hey, greaser, get off that horse and come talk to me!"

Tarron's gorge rose high, but he checked himself. Leveled rifles are wonderfully eloquent. He hesitated.

"Jump!" yelled the other. A bullet sang not an inch past the brim of Tarron's sombrero.

Jump he did, and landed on the ground by the side of the gelding's head. There was a loud yell of laughter from all three. This was apparently the sort of humor which they were able to enjoy to the full.

"It's only a kid," said one. "Let the greaser kid go, Jerry."

"That Tarron's only a kid, too. I'm gunna have a look at this one. Kid, step up here, will you!"

"Yes, senor!" said Tarron mildly.

"Listen to him, will you?" said the first speaker.

"He's left some of his sass behind him, ain't he? He's learning to talk pretty and polite already. Oh, it don't take long to teach 'em, if you can only catch 'em young. That's the main difficulty, y'understand?"

The others chuckled. Now that they were committed to this game of torment, they seemed to like it nearly as well as their leader.

"What's your name, kid?"

"Juan Cordoba, senor."

"Juan Cordoba, what are you doin' wandering around through the night like this here?"

"My mother sent me up here, senor."

"Up here to do what?"

"To find my father, senor."

"Who's your father?"

"Also Juan Cordoba, senor."

"Hey, he's simple minded, ain't he? Listen to what he talks like!"

The stern voice of Jerry broke in: "What was you to do for your father?"

"Bring him eleven pesos and some made cigarettes, senor."

There was a roar of laughter at this simple remark.

"How far did you ride from?"

"Twenty-two miles, senor."

"Leave the kid go, Jerry. You've pestered him enough."

"Wait a minute. I'm gunna talk till I'm tired of talking, and I don't give a hang what the rest of you say. I'm just gunna find out about a lot of things."

"About what?"

"Why does he pack a rifle if he's so simple and such a kid?"

He stepped beside Monte and dragged the rifle from its case.

"My mother told me to take the rifle, senor. She thought that my father's other gun might have been broken, if he fired it too fast in the first day's fighting."

There was a grim chuckle from Jerry.

"Look here! Your father is a kind of a hero, maybe?"

"Senor, he is the bravest man in the world!"

Another chuckle, which ended in a snort.

"He's brave enough to own a brand new Winchester —and in tiptop condition, too!"

"Hello!" said one of Jerry's companions. "I think that

it *is* in tiptop shape. Never knew a Mexican to take such fine care of a gun. Lemme have a squint at it. Bring it over to the fire, will you?"

"We'll all have a look at it."

"Bring the kid over, too, and his horse. There's something kind of queer about him."

And "Juan Cordoba" found himself led straight toward one of the big bonfires to the side, with the frieze of black silhouettes around it.

"Careful, senor, senor!" said he, as the carrier of the rifle swung it around. "It has a hair trigger."

"Why didn't the brat tell me that before?"

"He hoped that you'd put a bullet through yourself, that was all!"

Glancing to the side, Tarron saw far off down the valley the twinkling lights of the town of Santa Maria. If he could get to the gelding and make a break in that direction, perhaps he could escape a following fire of bullets. But even while the idea of making a frantic break in that direction came to him, he saw all hope of such a move snatched away.

A line of no fewer than twenty men came riding up from the heart of the broad valley of Santa Maria; and, as they came, their fresh horses pranced and danced beneath them, and their riders were shouting and singing like so many children.

There was no longer a possible retreat in that direction. Suddenly the brain of the boy reeled, as he saw himself completely shut off from all escape.

That confusion did not last long. A leveled gun clears the wits. And the extremity of the crisis braced Tarron at once.

"While you're looking at that gun," he said, "might I have something to eat?"

"The kid's a good kid. He's hungry," began one of the trio.

At that moment, the gelding snorted and shied at a white rock. There was an oath and a crash. He had sidled into one of the three men and sent him spinning to the ground. Tarron instantly leaped into the saddle.

"I'll quiet him," said Tarron.

"Leave the horse be," roared Jerry, swinging around,

Tarron's rifle in his hand. "I want to look at the gun and at you, too! What in—"

The gelding, goaded in the tenderest spot on his flank by Tarron's heel, leaped ahead. A fist with the weight of Tarron and the running horse behind it struck Jerry's nose and flattened it against his face, and, as he fell, the borrowed rifle was torn from his hand.

Two of the little party were down. The third had two Colts out by this time and blazed away at the target not twenty yards off. Nothing but chance could save Tarron —chance and upset nerves. And chance and upset nerves kept the bullets away.

As a roar of shouting and confusion rose behind him, he drove the gelding for the nearest cover, a little circular copse of trees. Flattened along Monte's back, Tarron raced into that covert. Heavy branches struck at him and tore his clothes. But now he was through. The stars flashed above him once more, and to left and right the red, triple eyes of the signal fires shone threateningly down at him.

"Who's there!"

Straight before him, rising from the ground, two figures start up, gun in the hand of each.

Les had shoved the rifle into its case as he plunged away in his first flight. Now in either hand he held a Colt, spouting fire. With knee and voice and sway of body, Tarron could guide the supple gelding easily, though he had not over this horse the absolute control that he possessed over the gray. He fired at those riding shadows from either hand. He saw them go down. And as he galloped onward, he heard one scream from beneath Monte's hoofs.

Bitter work—but if with rope or bullet they can catch Tarron, they will do worse to him than this! So he gives no thought to anything behind him. Let the proved speed of Monte answer the flying hoofs which are beginning to follow! His guns will take care of what lies ahead. And the God who directs the shining of those stars take care of him, and prosper the right!

Chapter XXIX

Goodbye Monte!

SUDDENLY THERE WAS a flash of silver water under Monte's nose. He had no time to dodge. Everything must be taken in full stride or not at all. A single swerve will throw him back into the teeth of the lion. So both heels cunningly wound the gelding, and Monte, frantic with pain, flings himself forward with a squeal. In mid-air, his hat whisked from his head by the wind of the gallop, Tarron sees the broad, metal face of the water shining beneath him. A spurt of red fire darts from the opposite bank and a bullet whispers in his ear, then follows the crash of the explosion. Another miss! The devil is confounding these marksmen in the service of Robert Langhorne and giving fortune to the bearing of the steel box! Down shot the gelding from the height of his great leap. The black shore rose up before him— he struck, staggered, then the ground gave way sickeningly.

On the verge of that sheer bank, Tarron hung for half a second looking ruin in the face. He thought of flinging himself clear of the saddle and abandoning the horse. Before that thought could be put into execution the gelding, scrambling like a tiger-cat, had clawed his way up to a firmer footing.

"It's Tarron! Shoot, for Heaven's sake!" a voice was yelling in perfectly good English. And three guns unlimbered on his left.

A red-hot finger flecked across Tarron's forehead, and the blood ran down his face. But that was nothing. Monte was already under way. He silenced the fire of the three marksmen with a shot that crumpled the central figure with a groan, and the other two scuttled for cover, yelling for help.

Tarron did not waste bullets. No matter how many lay dead behind him to attest his prowess, the living still in front of him down the threat of the pass—who must have heard this uproar of voices and guns, and who would be nerving themselves for the battle—it was they who counted! He sent Monte down the narrow gorge at furious speed.

"Good boy!" called Tarron.

His ears jerked forward in acknowledgment of the praise, Monte rushed on. The pursuers were coming fast and furious behind him. The swiftest horses in the mountains bore them. The water jump had weeded out of all except the most daring riders and the finest animals, and these, unembarrassed by crowding numbers, made every jump tell.

But before them Tarron rode like a jockey on a race course. He had come up this valley in the darkness, noting every feature of it. And that knowledge surely served him well enough now.

If only the race had been against those who were already in the rear! But there are many ahead! Tarron had only passed the first and second lines of Langhorne's men; the outposts were still to be overcome, they throng down to meet the fugitive.

Tarron entered a long and straight neck of the pass. Surely it would be lined with men! But not a gun spoke, and the trees lay silent and dead before him. Only for a moment!

Behind him he heard a triumphant yelling. He feared he had run into a trap, and as he turned to glance behind him, a voice shouted: "Now take him, boys! Don't shoot too high!"

And half a dozen rifles spoke.

But it was the same story. Try shooting at *any* target when there is nothing but starlight to direct your bullets. Then imagine shooting at a racing horse with a rider bent low, jockeying his mount over rough and smooth, and dodging among the obstacles of the trail. Tarron was not touched—and the blood was already stopping its flow down his forehead.

He turned the next winding of the path and saw suddenly the veritable trap into which he had put his head. The trees were hedged close together on either hand. Even an unmounted man would have found it hard to make way among them, and for a horseman the wood was impenetrable. Before him they had heaped up fallen trees and brush into a mighty mound.

Higher than his head, even as he sat the mustang, towered the mass; and the cries of triumph along either side of the way had certainly their meaning. He was bagged—unless he could turn back. Not even that, for the riders behind had entered the narrow way between the groves.

He swung back toward the mound. Now that he was closer, it seemed far more imposing than before; and solid enough, too, bristling as it did with the butt end of logs thrust forth from the mass. All but the central and the highest portion—for through that mass he could see the dim twinkling of firelight burning on the farther side of the barricade.

Well, one chance in a million is better than no chance at all! Riding for liberty and a ghost of hope, the blood of a man runs faster and his heart is stronger than at any other time.

So it was with Tarron. He had ridden hard at the water, but he had not had the chance to gather his horse beneath him and bring it gradually up to a mighty effort; but now he could settle down, hand riding the gallant gelding, and whipping it into its most desperate stride.

Twice Monte, seeing the obstacle before him, buck-jumped and shuddered with fear, as though his master were riding him at a wall of rock.

But then, whether because he, too, saw the light glimmering through the upper tiers of the center of the barricade, or because of confidence in his master and of glory in his own might and speed, Monte straightened true as an arrow for the barricade and flung himself high into the air. Never a hunter behind the pack of hounds leaped an obstacle more gallantly!

It was as though gigantic wings had thrust the mustang upward. Will he not go over? No, you cannot ask the impossible even of Monte. He strikes the upper part of the heap—but strikes it solidly, head on, without flinching—and before him, what had seemed solid, but was really merely a pile of brush, gave way. Head over heels pitched Monte, flinging Tarron from the saddle at the first impact. Down they smash, but down clear of the wreck of the barricade. Screams and shouts surround them; but as the gelding regains its feet, a little dizzy from the fall, Tarron vaults like a tiger to the saddle. The roar of guns behind and before—the hot tang of gunpowder burning his nostrils—and the gelding is once more into its stride.

Gallant Monte, undismayed and stanch of heart! Never a truer run than this! Let them search all the old tales of Arabs and of racers, they will find nothing finer. He was at his work at once, gathering his power, shaking his head, still half stunned by the fall. But the voice of the master is strength running into his heart, and down the reins the master's hand is sending electric power.

On goes Monte, sweeping through the trees ahead. Now more open country sweeps to right and left. No despair, now, but a real and burning hope with the knowledge that the worst is behind them. If they have done such gigantic and impossible things, never to be believed, can they not accomplish easily what lies before? Only a scattering of men and horses intervene between them and that spot in the forest where the peerless gray waits to take the weight of his master from the tired loins of the mouse-colored hero.

So away goes the fugitive. Never say that Monte did not feel the thrill of his master's call in that final spurt. Never had his heels flown so fast. And there was need. Through the gap in the barricade which their heroic leap had opened, the finest heroes and horses of the pursuit have leaped and followed without so much as breaking their stride; and therefore they are closer.

Tarron leaves the woods to the rear and flings into the open. Let the pursuers be cautious how they try to close that gap between them and their prey!

For Tarron rides with a Colt swinging in one hand, and his eyes are flecked with red.

A rifle flashed before him!

Another miss! All. misses! No! Rising out of the very ground a man shows down to the waist and fires.

Monte staggered.

It seemed to Tarron, that the hindquarters of the gallant mustang had fallen away beneath him. No, he gathers himself again, and lurches ahead. And, as he gallops, the red blur of fury and despair and grief clears from Tarron's eyes. Into the shadow he fires, and the half seen man bobs down. He whirls past. The man is seen from a new angle, trying to creep away.

No mercy, now, Tarron! Again, again, and again he fires, a devil in his heart! He sees the creeper stop; sees the poor fellow writhing on the ground. He sees that writhing stilled.

A wicked and a cruel thing, to be sure! But there is no sorrow or compassion, Tarron. Only a swelling, aching, bursting heart. For beneath him, running almost as true as ever, he knows that Monte is dying, and that every stride he takes is marked with heart's blood!

Chapter XXX

A Light Shining

THERE WAS NO staggering, no reeling, no blind pitching, mind you. But only, as the gallant mustang ran, a little faltering, showing that though his great heart was driving him forward as earnestly as ever, somehow the body was failing to give a perfect response.

Tarron looked back. He saw a wide semicircle of horsemen sweeping behind him, each a proven man, each on a proved horse, each worthy of being termed the pride of a country. No little Eastern county, but one of those vast Western kingdoms of the desert, few in men, great in manhood.

But Tarron felt no admiration. The man in him was down; the tiger up. A rifle jerked from its holster and closed against his shoulder. He fired instantly, and saw a fine animal in the center of the semicircle leap high into the air and come down a crumpled heap, its rider flung head over heels to the side. And he shouted with a savage satisfaction.

A wail came from the rest—a wail of wonder and dread. It is not often given to men so to shoot from the back of a galloping horse, at a moving target, and by night. But miracles, to the desperate soul and the iron hand of Tarron, were as trifles, now.

The followers checked their headlong pursuit. They were falling back, and the faltering gelding gained a little.

He gained, then staggered and almost fell, and a moment later swept into a strong and furious gallop.

Tarron felt that effort with a breaking heart, for he knew that it was Monte's dying struggle translated into terms of gallant speed and true running.

On they went, the ground flying back beneath them and the trees spinning past with a whirl and a rush. They reached the edge of a little wood where the gray had been left. Was he alive? Had the wolves found him tethered there and cut him down? Had men discovered his lurking place and captured him, and left a guard on the spot, in case the master should return for his priceless charger?

These were things to think about, but Tarron thought of none of them, for all his heart was occupied by the plight of Monte!

If there was a God who watched man, could there be a God who did not watch horses? Surely not! And what justice was there in this thing? What was the sin of Monte save in serving too faithfully!

They pressed on, wavering and faltering, and on the edge of the clearing where the gray waited and raised a ringing challenge, Monte fell.

Tarron, on his knees, his arms close around the sweating head, his voice calling into the ears, saw them flicker forward, felt the quivering of the nostrils, and then—

Monte had gone to whatever heaven waits for good horses and true. God keep them all!

Grief has its place and its time, but this was no place or time for Tarron to indulge his. He was on Jimmy's back with a bound. He dared not wait to slip on the bridle. He could not even wait to untie the lead rope by which the gray was tethered. A touch of the hunting knife and they were free.

And what a freedom! Monte had been fleet, but what was his fleetness compared to this? As the leap of a deer to the flight of a hawk. And every note of Tarron's voice, every pressure of his knee and sway of his body had a meaning for Jimmy. He had been raised by the hand of Tarron and the very thoughts of his master sank into the soul of the stallion. And he burst from the copse like a storm cloud into a calm sky.

Now, Jimmy, what speed is yours? For the foe comes on the left and on the right. They have lost the edge of their gait by their rush down the valley; but upon the left are four riders and upon the right are three, and every man of the seven is shooting as he comes. Chosen horses, and chosen men, the best in the mountains!

What speed Jimmy had, he showed at once, but in a strange direction, for Tarron swung the stallion straight around at the trio to the right. And he rode with a yell that would have done credit to some champion of the dreadful Cheyennes in the old days of glory on the plains. His knees gripping the sides of the gray, his feet loose in the stirrup, his body part of the racing horse, his hair blown back from his head, the broad band of crimson drying like paint on his brow. I wish that you could look with me upon that picture of Tarron, charging his foes!

And if you could see him, as he was, you would almost forget that each hand held a flaming Colt. For the three before him well-nigh forgot his weapons.

All that they saw was the terrible man on the silver horse dashing at them like personified death. And for half a moment only they stood their ground.

Then a bullet crashed through the head of the best and bravest warrior. And the remaining two scattered, one to right, one to left.

Tarron scorned to pursue them. He thrust the Colts into the holsters and held the stallion into an easy gallop. It would have been well-nigh a racing gait for an ordinary horse, and it was sufficient to leave behind him the men from the pass, fagged as their horses already were by the effort of following the wonderful run that Monte had made that night.

And having failed to capture Monte, how could they capture this silver ghost, this twinkling will-o'-the-wisp? There was little joy in Tarron at his reunion with Jimmy, however. It was of Monte that he thought constantly. And when he saw that the pursuit had died and scattered hopelessly behind him, he doubled back like a fox to the place where Monte lay dead. There he laid bare the face of a birch, and with a pencil he scrawled on the shining bark:

Here lies Monte, that was the finest and the truest of them all. You punchers, you pray for a horse like him, but you'll never get his like.

He felt better after he had written this. Then he remembered that he should sign his name, lest there be the slightest doubt as to the identity of the writer.

He then took from the case the rifle which he had left with the gelding and, remounting Jimmy, went on his way. He felt very much better now that he had paid proper tribute to the dead horse. And, he reflected, in what manner could Monte have died better?

There would be one more comfort for him in the future. He would find the owner of Monte, and would tell the fat man how gallantly Monte had made his last run and died.

Now Tarron came out from the shadow of the trees once more and checked the stallion in the light of the stars. Pursuit, for the moment, he no longer feared.

He had Jimmy beneath him, and he was willing at any time to stake his life upon the strength and blazing fleetness of foot of the gray.

But one thing had been demonstrated beyond all doubt. He could not cross the pass. And what else remained for him to do?

Yes, and could he even be sure that when he got through the pass he would gain any advantage by slipping into Santa Maria? Perhaps that had been merely a wild goose chase, from the beginning to the end.

La Paz! La Paz!

Where was the city of peace? What a name to give to a town that was to madden those who hunted for it through these solemn mountains! Must the hunt be in vain?

And, in the midst of his distress, he thought of the one man he had ever met who possessed invincible peace of mind and utter calmness. He thought of old Gregorio—and his tiger daughter.

Perhaps, by this time, the mist would have lifted from the memory of the Mexican, and he could tell Tarron definitely the whereabouts of the lost city. So, at least, Tarron would have something to do on the following day—and a sufficiently dangerous thing; for all along his trail he knew it was most likely that men would be watching for his reappearance. Particularly since the old Gregorio might well have remarked that the wanderer intended revisiting him to ask his question.

So he headed back up the valley, and across the hills, aiming his course for the dwelling of Gregorio.

As he rode, he began to wonder a little at himself.

How long was it since he had tasted food or drink? How long was it since he had slept? What matter? His body was not faint, his nerves were not shattered. His strength was as great as ever, and his heart was marvelously light.

He touched his face with his hand. It seemed to him that the outlines of his cheek were flattened and that he was sharper and leaner about the jaws. But he could never read by touch the real alteration that had come to him.

He had passed out of his boyhood at last. Far behind him lay another self which he had sloughed as a snake sloughs an old skin. A newer, cleaner, stronger, keener, better self was this of the man Tarron. So, as he faced toward the cabin of old Gregorio, what wonder that his self-confidence was brimming, and that a whistle trembled on his lips?

He had long arrears of living to make up, and he was living fast and gloriously.

Through the night, he maintained the stallion at a steady, sweeping dog-trot, covering the miles in the tireless manner of a wolf, until, rounding a headland that jutted down into the valley floor, he saw before and above him the house of old Gregorio, and in its window there was a light shining.

A light shining—yet the hour was late! It seemed proof positive to Tarron that something must be wrong in the house. So he left the gray behind him in the trees and started forward on foot to stalk the place.

Chapter XXXI

Brave Talk

TARRON COULD HEAR the sound of men's voices when he was still at a little distance. From that point his approach was more stealthy than the creeping of a wolf. By degrees he came near the door. He could see Lucia waiting upon four caballeros and giving them wine as they sat about the table. They had finished their dinner, but still drank and ate crusts of bread to fill up the crevices of their great appetites.

"Call the old man again," said one of them in Spanish.

"There's no use in that," said Lucia. "He's said all that can be drawn out of him, the fool!"

"Well, there are ways of getting more from him."

"You think so," said the woman. "But I know better. When he was a young man, he did enough to make stories which they still tell through these parts of the mountains. Once he followed a wounded wolf into a cave, and a mountain lion sprang on him in the darkness and knocked the rifle from his hand. That great white scar on his forehead is the result of her leap. He got out his knife and stabbed her to the heart. Then he went on, found the wolf, and came back with the pelts of both the animals."

"That was when he was young," said one of the men.

"Aye," replied Lucia. "But though his body is old, his heart is still stubborn. Oh, don't I know? He makes my life miserable. What can I do with him? Nothing!"

Then another voice spoke from the back of the hut, and Tarron started in alarm for it was the unmistakable deep bass of Ingram, speaking execrable Spanish:

"You told us that he said Tarron would come back. Didn't he say when?"

"No, he didn't say that. And he won't say that."

"Perhaps he doesn't know," remarked one of the others. "But the best thing is to lie low here and wait for him to show his head."

Ingram laughed.

There was such an ugly sound to that laughter that the others turned their heads perforce toward the big man.

"Why do you do that?" they asked.

"You think that this boy will walk into your trap?" asked Ingram with a sneer.

"Why not?"

"You sit here laughing and drinking. He could hear you a mile away. That lad has the ears of a wolf, I tell you! Besides, by an extra sense which he has he would know that there is danger here."

He added: "Probably he is now up the hill talking with the old man! And laughing when he hears our voices below him!"

"I'll go and see!"

A handsome young Mexican sprang into the doorway.

"Come back!" called another. "How could even he ride up here from the pass?"

"No, that's true. Not after the work that his horses have done. And not after the work that he's done himself. He'll be asleep somewhere in the woods! Lord, Lord, it would be a thing to find him asleep that way!"

"Yes," said another, "if you could shoot before he opened his eyes."

"Let me have my gun pointed at him, and I don't care when he opens his eyes. I'll finish him!"

"Your hand would shake like a baby's, Pedro! There is a devil in him, beyond question. Ask Lucia. She's a sensible woman, and she's seen him and talked to him, which is more than most of us have done. Just see what she says."

"That's true," said Lucia with an air of importance. "I've talked to a great many men, but I've never seen any like him. He's a devil. Ah! I shudder when I think about him! I wouldn't like to meet him again. When the darkness came tonight, I began to tremble. Don't laugh! I never trembled before for anything! He has the evil eye. When he looks at you, he turns your blood cold!"

"Ghosts, ghosts!" said another, laughing. "Let's tell ghost stories."

"He'll make a ghost of you, my boy," said Lucia sternly. "Well, laugh like fools. I don't care."

Said Ingram slowly: "You, Pedro, you had the telephone message. How many was it that died?"

"Four are dying, senor, and they think that a fifth man will die surely. And there are six wounded. Nothing like that fighting was ever done before!"

Said another: "He must have gone down through the pass like a starved lobo through a pack of strangling dogs. I would have liked to see that!"

"From a distance, Manuelo!"

"Well, from a distance. I'm not ashamed of that. It would take a madman or a fool to want to stand up to such a fellow!"

"That's true. There was never anyone who could fight like that. You can see that he could not do such things except that the devil points his guns."

"Nevertheless," said Ingram, "there has been much greater fighting than this."

"Tell us one man who ever did more!"

"I could tell a lot of them. I'll give you one example, though: When Wild Bill Hickok was in a shack, ten men went to kill him. They rushed the shack under fire, and he fought them hand to hand. When he was full of wounds, three men who were left alive ran out of the shack and tried to get away. Two of them did get away, both wounded; but the third man was shot off his horse by Wild Bill. Now tell me, was that a greater fight than this boy made?"

There was a moment of awed silence.

"Yes," said Pedro, "that was a wonderful thing, and a hard thing to believe!"

"That is the truth. Everyone knows that—everyone in Texas, I'd say."

"Well, I should like to have seen the face of the man that did that thing!"

"He wasn't like Tarron. Tarron looks like any boy, except that he's a handsome brat. Wild Bill looked like what he was. A king! Well every desperado looks tremendous until he goes down. And when I've caught this Tarron, you'll see that his claws are not so long!"

There was another moment of silence, and then the voice of Lucia asked coldly: "A great many brave men have tried to catch Tarron. You seem very sure of yourself, senor."

"I am," said Ingram. "I feel in my bones that I'm the man to corner him, one day. Besides, I have the horse that will do it."

"Your black horse is very fine, that is true. And he *may* run down the horse of Tarron."

"The finest thing that ever stepped, that black. And he cost a price! Arab blood and thoroughbred mixed. He has the flint of the Arab in his bone; and he has the size and the stretch of a thoroughbred, y'understand?"

"He is a grand horse to see."

"He moves like running water."

"What was the price?"

"There was twenty-five hundred dollars paid for that critter, my friends!"

A general shout of wonder came from the listeners.

"Oh, he could win on a race track," said Ingram proudly. "And besides he's been toughened all his life to mountain work. You will see something when he begins to run."

"Besides, the best horse of Tarron has died."

"No, the gray's better than the one that died."

"Better?"

"Aye, a marvelous horse. You'll see him run, one day. I hope that you'll have a chance to watch the black catch him, though."

"What do you call your horse?"

"Name of Benedict. I call him Ben for short."

"Where is the sheriff, Senor Ingram?"

"Which sheriff? There's two of them on the trail. They'll be working up different trails. They'll never catch him, because they'll be working too slow for him. But they all help. We've got these mountains filled with hornets, and one of 'em is sure to sting this dragon fly sooner or later."

"Dragon!" broke in Lucia. "That's a good word for him!"

"They have raised the reward," said another.

"To what?" snapped Ingram eagerly.

"It is eight thousand dollars, now, and more offered nearly every day."

"The little fool!" exclaimed Ingram exultantly. "To get the law on him like this!"

"For horse stealing. That was bad enough. Now for murder!"

Ingram whistled.

"We'll soon have an end to him. Oh, for one fair run at him with Benedict! Oh, for a fair chance!"

"Aye, senor, but suppose that your black horse should carry you too far ahead of your friends—"

The questioning voice stopped in the very pitch of malicious interrogation, and Ingram answered calmly: "I'll be ready for Tarron. I know that he's as brave as a lion and as secret as a snake. But something tells me that I'll down him. We'll have to wait and see!"

This remark was greeted with another silence, rather of wonder than of contempt, for it was plain that Ingram was speaking out of actual conviction rather than a mere empty boast.

"How did you come to hate him so much, senor?"

"Because the first time that I met him he made a fool of me and stole my horse—that same gray. And ever since, I've wanted to get at him. God's gonna turn him over to my hands!"

A sort of religious conviction thrilled in big Ingram's voice, and even Tarron, waiting and listening in the darkness, shuddered a little. He felt that, if possible, he would like to avoid an encounter with this man, because when a Western fighter feels that fate is on his side, he is apt to be invincible.

So it was with Ingram, now. He was not in an ecstasy of excitement. He was simply, calmly, bent upon his purpose. And a little rare chill of fear persisted in the heart of Tarron for a moment longer. He would decidedly like in some way to throw this big, grim fellow out of the chase. The power of Langhorne, the power of the law, the hundreds of free lance hunters for his head, they began to seem nothing to Tarron compared with the persistent malice of this enemy. Twenty-five hundred dollars for a single horse!

Chapter XXXII

Light Feet on the Mountains

Up on the hill he found a dark figure seated on a rock, and he could discern, even at a little distance, the glimmering silver beard of the old man.

"I shall not come in, friend," said Gregorio sternly, as he saw the boy approach. "I shall not come in. I am better here, and I have talked enough. Too much, perhaps, for the welfare of my poor young friend, Tarron."

"Ah, senor," said Tarron, "you need not be afraid that I'll ask you to go into that house!"

At that voice, Gregorio sprang up with a wonderful lightness and agility and coming in haste to Tarron he caught his arm with hands that trembled with excitement and with age.

"Dear heavens, my child," said Gregorio, "how have you come back here, so wonderfully?"

"I'm here, and I'm safe," said Tarron. "That's all. Don't worry about me."

"And the dead men who lie behind you?"

"Well," said Tarron, "they had almost conquered me. I had to fight back."

"God's will be done!" said Gregorio. "It has been a

glorious day for you, and after this, youths will stand straighter and have bigger hearts, remembering the great things that young Senor Tarron performed in the pass of Santa Maria!"

"But I haven't come back to boast, father."

"You have come back for what, child?"

"You can guess if you'll try, I think. For answer to the question that I asked you before I left."

"Questions? My poor old brain forgets nine tenths of the things that happen today. Only the old, dead years are clearly before my eyes."

"That may be true. But now, try to think. I'd asked you about La Paz. Where is there such a city in the mountains?"

And Gregorio answered slowly: *"Santa Maria de la Paz?"*

"Ha!" cried Tarron. "You have it! You've remembered it, then?" "The name of La Paz!"

"There has never been a city of that name."

"What was the name that you just used?"

"It came off the tip of my tongue by mistake, I suppose. Let me see—what did I call it?"

"Santa Maria de la Paz."

"Yes, yes, but—ah, now I remember! In the old days, men called it by the whole name—Santa Maria de la Paz! What was it!"

"Aye, and sometimes they shortened it to La Paz?"

"Yes, perhaps. In the very old days. I've almost forgotten. But somewhere—when I was a child—someone has told me, surely, of the days when it was called Santa Maria de la Paz."

"That's the place. That's what it must be. It's the only chance!"

"The only chance of what?"

"That I may find the lost city."

"Do you mean to go to Santa Maria de la Paz?"

"Yes, yes, if I can get there!"

"Ah, lad! Don't you understand what a thing it would be to cross those mountains where the head-hunters are waiting to snare you?"

"I understand. I've had a taste of them. But perhaps they won't be expecting me to try that way again."

"They will, they will! There is this tall devil of an American—this Senor Ingram. He seems to know beforehand just what you'll do, and he has been swearing that you'll try again to get through the pass."

"Ingram and I—" began the boy, and then he paused and left his sentence incompleted.

"He is the great enemy, is he not?" said Gregorio. "Ah, and there he sits with the rest of the bloodhounds, and they have drawn down the law on your head, lad!"

"I don't mind the law!"

"You think not, because you are very young. But the law never rests. And eventually it will win. Time is nothing to it. It waits ten years and then takes you while you sleep. It is a panther creeping through the dark and never stopping."

"Well," said Tarron, "but Santa Maria de la Paz is what I want to talk about."

"Only I know that, somewhere, I have heard that it was called at one time Santa Maria de la Paz. Some old man must have told me when I was a boy. That's all. What does that mean to you?"

"You can't remember that it was ever called only La Paz?"

"No."

"Then I'll have to run down this thread. Back to Santa Maria! Back to Santa Maria! Senor Gregorio, for the love of God tell me of some other way across the mountains—some way except the pass!"

"There is no way except where even a goat would be dizzy!"

"I'll try that way."

"No, no, lad! You could only cross it by foot. You would have to leave your horse."

"Then I'll leave the horse, and get another when I pass the mountains into the valley of Santa Maria."

"But the others will surely know about the pass, and they'll watch for you there."

"Perhaps they will; perhaps they won't, if it's a place where a horse can't go. I've got to take the chance."

"So, so, so!" sighed the old man. "I also was filled with

hot blood when I was young. But I was never quite like this. It is true that a young man cannot remain in his own front yard and conquer the world. But still—well—if you die you will be remembered. You have done enough this day, child!"

"The pass, the pass!" cried the boy. "Tell me how to get to it."

"You start straight for the pass of Santa Maria. And a mile from the mouth of the pass, you'll see a stream leaping down the face of the mountain to the right—"

"Yes."

"That is it."

"I remember that stream. What about it?"

"That, child, is the place where the pass of which I speak begins."

At that even Tarron paused, his breath gone.

"Has a man ever crossed that pass?" he asked.

"The Indians have a legend of a hero who once crossed it. That is why Langhorne may have the pass watched."

"I remember the spot," sighed Tarron. "And I thought that even a goat could never have got up it."

"No, it would be hard. But I've seen, with my own eyes, a goat climb the pass."

"Then I'll try it."

"Then may God be with you!"

"Senor Gregorio."

"Yes."

"I have one other thing to ask of you."

"Ask it, in God's name!"

"Senor Ingram came riding a fine black horse."

"Yes. It was a glorious animal to see."

"Where is it now?"

"Ah, ah! Must you do that, my son?"

"He is the devil on my trail," said Tarron gloomily. "I've no desire to murder a horse. But—I've got to stop Ingram. After I've done this job, then I'm willing to meet him and fight him. But until the work's finished, I want to keep away from him. My blood turns cold when I think about him!"

"It is always that way," murmured the old man. "The greatest and the bravest are always afraid of one thing.

189

There is one spot where they may be wounded. And with you, it is this Ingram?"

"Yes."

"Then you'll find the black horse in the little corral behind the shed. There is no other horse with him. He's a stallion and very savage."

"Well, so much the better. Father, good-by!"

"Good-by, child. Will you come back to me again?"

"Yes, if I live through the next ten days."

"You cannot tell me what takes you to Santa Maria?"

"No, because I hardly know myself."

"You hardly know!"

"Good-by!"

"Good-by, son. God grant you fortune!"

Tarron went hastily down to the rear of the stable, and there he saw the horse at once.

A lighthouse standing on the shore could hardly have been more conspicuous, even among the shadows of the night, that was this monster. He rose a full seventeen hands. His great eyes glistened in the starlight, the shaking of his mane in the wind was like a threat to Tarron.

Les stepped to the edge of the corral, and the big horse flattened his ears and lowered his head with a snaky and ominous movement.

"I'll have no advantage of you," said Tarron. "My knife only against your four hoofs, and we'll fight it out!"

He slipped through the bars of the corral, knife in hand, and had barely straightened when the black monster was upon him with a rush of hoofs. Had he been attacking an ordinary man, it would have been instant death, but Tarron was no ordinary man. His leap to the side enabled him to avoid the reaching teeth and the battering fore-hoofs.

He stood for an instant with poised weapon at the side of the monster. And then, lowering the weapon, Tarron whipped around and vaulted over the top rail of the corral. It had not been in his heart to take the life that was in this mighty king of beasts.

And the wicked devil raged up and down the bars of the corral, furious because this prey had been snatched away.

In the meantime, a voice, the familiar voice of Ingram, was calling:

"Who's out there? Who's bothering my horse?"

A footfall approached. Tarron hesitated. Now he could do the thing pat, waiting until the tall man's form loomed before him in the darkness. Taken by surprise, bewildered by the sudden challenge, big Ingram would be half beaten before he began to fight.

No, that was not the way. They were too magnificent a combination, taken together, for Tarron to wish to meet them except in the brightness of the day, man to man, hoof to hoof.

So he slipped into the shadow of the shed, and saw Ingram come to the bars and curse the huge stallion affectionately, and the stallion came and laid a head on the shoulder of his big master.

Chapter XXXIII

Over the Precipice

IT WAS A very strange thing to Tarron, you may be sure, to see this demonstration of affection between man and horse; to hear the low, smothered voice of Ingram speaking to the black monster, and to see the ears of the stallion pricked forward.

He waited to see this; then he slipped away through the night, went past the house, and stood for a moment at the side of the gray stallion, watching the light pouring through the door of the old shack and spilling down the hillside.

In that moment, Tarron came marvelously close to giving up the work which was before him. The sounds of singing from the house and the cheerful knowledge that there was good bread and better wine in the place had nearly unnerved him and made him sharply and miserably aware of his own hunger and his own misery.

However, there is a force of habit which makes even hard things easier. We are carried along by instinct, as it were, in the course which has been first begun. And when Tarron turned Jimmy's head, he pointed it, almost against his will, toward the mouth of the pass of Santa Maria.

However, the good gray had not taken a dozen steps, trotting down the valley, before Tarron's heart grew more resolute. He was ready to stick to his purpose now, and to stick to it with all his might.

So, in an astonishingly short time, he came again within the danger zone at the mouth of the pass.

Dawn was beginning to break at last over that night which had seen him pass through so much; and now, looking up the face of the rock, he watched the water bounding down with a rushing and roaring. It was no great body of water, but the distance and the sheerness of the fall made the noise like that of a plunging torrent.

He hardly dared to pause, because if he had waited his resolution might have slipped from him. He gave Jimmy a farewell hug, and then advanced to his work. He pushed through the scattering vines which masked the bottom of the rock. And within these, he found the precipice beginning. However, it was really not a precipice at all. Though the general lines of the rock were, at a distance, sheer enough to daunt any heart, still, close at hand, he found that the dashing water of the fall had, by centuries of patient labor, broken a way through the solid rock upon either hand, so that the foot and the hand found an easy stairway prepared. He had climbed a hundred feet with great speed when a frantic neighing beneath him called him back toward the stallion.

Jimmy stood beneath, whinnying as though his heart would break to bring his master once more to his side. Tarron glanced anxiously up and down. He could not tell when that clarion summons would bring suspicious spies to investigate the nature of the disturbance here. There was nothing in sight, but still he was greatly worried; and he had to shout to Jimmy until the good horse became quiet once more.

Then Tarron turned to the task before him. Every instant it grew easier. The hardest portion seemed to be the first ladderlike stretch of rock. In most parts of the world, this might have been a commonly used path, but here in the West, where men lived on horseback, it was a different matter. Only where a horse could go would men travel.

He gained the top of the first ascent, and looking before

him, he saw that the dreadful pass which old Gregorio had described was, in reality, nothing more or less than a long, high, ascending plateau, which stretched away toward the west and south. And he laughed aloud in the pink of the morning light as he thought of the dreadful prophecies which the old man had made.

He tightened his belt, and as he did so, a big mountain grouse rose from a shrub. It did not fly far. The empty stomach of Tarron lent him speed and he brought the Colt from his holster with a swift gesture. As the gun exploded, the grouse tumbled from the air through which it was slanting upward, and fell heavily upon the ground.

Tarron's attention was taken from his prey for the moment, however, for now he heard a great scratching and scrambling over the stones behind him, mingled with a heavy snorting; and turning in haste and in some dread he saw the magnificent head of Jimmy rising above the edge of the rock wall!

Whinnying with joy, the fine gray bounded to him. Tarron went back and looked over the edge down the ragged, broken ascent. Looking down, it seemed surely that no horse could have managed the thing. But here was Jimmy in the flesh, more beautiful than ever, and arching his neck as though perfectly conscious that he had done a wonderful thing deserving of the highest praise.

Jimmy was turned out to graze in the patch of grass at the top of the cliff, and there, on the verge of the height, Tarron devoured the dead bird "neat." That is to say, it went down uncooked, and to the famine-sharpened maw of the young man, there had never been any meal so perfectly delicious—or so without the need of cookery.

Sleepiness and a trembling fatigue came over him the moment he had finished his meal. He found a deep dell among the rocks, and there he concealed himself among the brush, leaving Jimmy like a watchdog, free to graze, or rest. Sure that the stallion would give the alarm, Les curled himself up and slept.

What a sleep, with hard rocks for a couch!

Many a long hour later he wakened, with a ringing in his ears and a sense of pain in his stomach. It was only returning hunger which tormented him. His body had absorbed the last meal as the face of the desert absorbs a cupful of water.

By the time he had washed his face and hands in a runlet, he was himself again. His head was clear. The pain left his stomach. And here was the stallion, in the evening of the day—for he had slept the clock almost around—as fresh as a daisy and ready for any work he might have for him.

God bless the mustang stock in that indomitable horse!

Now that Tarron was rested, he only wondered at one thing—that he should have felt the slightest awe of Ingram on the preceding night. But he attributed that to the bewildering effect of weariness and hunger. Therefore, he dismissed the qualm which had bothered him, and vowed that the next opportunity that offered would find him flying at Ingram's throat. There was no slightest doubt in him as to the result of such a battle.

Tarron had been well blooded by this time, and he was as keen as a hunting knife for the work which lay ahead. If there were danger, he would welcome it as another might welcome a banquet.

But now for Santa Maria! Now for the house of Senor Langhorne. And once in it, let God be his guide and plant his feet in the right steps!

You will wonder how such a profane young man could come to call Divinity to his aid. But so many strange things had happened to Tarron during the brief period since he had left the house of his father, that it was forced upon him and he felt, in spite of himself—that he had been selected for some great accomplishment.

Perhaps that consciousness of the ever-working hand of destiny is a great advantage, for it urges a man forward with calm nerves and no strength is wasted upon vague forebodings. Danger is accepted as it presents itself, and as a thing which must and will be conquered. Such was the state of the mind of Tarron, and no more ideal state could have been found.

He mounted the gray, and continued his journey in the most leisurely fashion, for he was not at all anxious to get to the valley beyond before the evening of the day had well closed in. As a matter of fact, it was deep in the dusk before he came to the edge of the table-land, and there he found beneath him a dangerous and shelving slide. It would be almost impossible to ascend, and perhaps fatal to descend. On the verge of it, he paused again and looked about. The lights of Santa Maria lay beneath him, gradually growing in numbers as the householders kindled their lamps. Beyond went up the dusky mountains, and on the forehead of one of those heights gleamed a triple eye of red. No stars were ever so angrily bright and threatening. No, these eyes must be made by the hand of man.

Les Tarron caught his breath with a gasp. What a half wit he had been not to have guessed at once—not to have seen that light the instant that he came into view of the inner valley.

It was the signal prearranged to summon the mountaineers to that place to search for Tarron and to guard against him. And it told him, in no uncertain words, that the men of the valley were forewarned, forearmed. His coming was expected!

Had they, perhaps, trailed up the ascent near the broader and easier pass? Les groaned with rage and despair and disappointment.

If he descended into that valley, he would be like a wingless fly, committing itself to the deeps of a great, smooth-sided bowl. He did not know the mountains and their passes which ringed the valley round about. He did not know them, and he did not know what snares were laid for him beneath. But of one thing he could be doubly sure, that the house of Senor Langhorne must be heavily guarded at this very moment. Perhaps half a hundred men were there at the disposal of the mysterious leader who had already thrown so many obstacles across the path of Tarron.

But yonder lay, in some fashion, the solution to the mystery. There was the seat of his enemies. There, also, must be the stronghold of his friends, if he could only learn their names. Yonder was the rightful possessor of the little steel box. Yonder, also, were the cunning wits and the cruel hands which would sacrifice ten thousand lives to keep the box from its rightful owner. Above all, yonder was the solution of the puzzle.

Tarron, with a thrust of his heel, sent the stallion over

the verge of the semi-precipice. Down they went caroming, like a rock cast loose from its moorings. Down they went! Behind him a small avalanche was loosed and began to crash around them, rattling volleys of stones. And then, before him, sweeping through the darkness, Tarron saw riders emerging from the trees!

Chapter XXXIV

A Beggar Afoot

THE MIND CAN go to Sirius and back again while a dog is
snapping at a fly. Tarron had time to look back to the
probable reason why this approach to the valley was
watched. Someone heard Jimmy neighing at the farther
end of the crossing. There they had found torn brush at
the bottom of the ascent, and at the top, scraped and
freshly broken rock. So they had simply sent on word to
the inner valley of Santa Maria, and the result was that
the exit was watched.

Heavily watched, too!

Tarron swung the gray to the right. Like lightning they
sprinted. And from the brush riders rose every instant
and swarmed after him. He doubled Jimmy around, for
the stallion could twist about like a dodging jack rabbit,
and back along the edge of the rock rubble at the bottom
of the long slide the gray horse flashed, running as he had
never run before. Even Tarron was amazed by his lightning
speed.

Men were not fifty yards to his right, now, and as he
rode back, he emptied two revolvers—not at them, with
aimed shots, but toward them, firing simply with a blind

haste, so that they might hear the humming of the bullets, and perhaps be turned and dazed by the whir of lead.

There was a moment's hesitancy even in that half dozen of men. As a football team stands amazed when it sees some daring opponent dash away on an unexpected flank run, so stood these men of the valley of Santa Maria.

They wavered only an instant, and then rushed in pursuit, their guns roaring. But Tarron had already been near the brush, and now he was into it. The men behind him shrieked in their madness of disappointment. They fired blindly into the woods as they galloped, and more than one in the hysteria of angry haste was knocked from his saddle by an unexpectedly low limb of a tree. Before that crowd of horsemen the gray slid through the forest like an oiled swimmer through the waves. The noise of his going was utterly drowned by the tremendous crashing behind him. Each second he was gaining yards upon the riders in his rear. If only he did not find new enemies before him!

No, in this direction the entire guard seemed to have been massed at the very point of the danger; as though they made sure that their hands would be so strong at this place of contact that they could not fail to catch and crush the fugitive.

Not fugitive, either! Rather a single wild-hearted gadfly attacking an army of tigers; flying into their den, goading them with a poisoned sting, humming its wings in their faces, scoffing at them and scorning them, and passing through their savage ranks to do some harm—some dreadful harm—against which all their powers and their trained watchfulness could not defend them and their king!

That was the feeling that came into Tarron's heart and with it, came again that thrilling suggestion of the hand of fate thrusting him forward and controlling him.

He reached the edge of a small creek. The water foamed down the center of a little gorge with banks ten feet high. Down that rocky bank went the stallion, and then whirred rapidly along, covered by this as in a sunken trench.

Les Tarron heard the noise of the pursuit break from the covert and roar into the open. Then a sudden burst of firing and the noise rolled far off to the right. They had begun to pursue some fleeting shadow in the hope that it was Tarron.

Tarron now drew up the gray and walked on with him, laughing in spite of himself, for there was not a wound of any kind upon his body except that scratch across the forehead. He had made a bandage for that hurt, and therefore he was in perfect comfort. Behind him lay utter confusion and bewilderment. Before him lay—well, what lay before him?

"They" had tried to knife him as he slept; to murder him on the way with poison. "They" had set an invincible guard in two places. Through the first he had nearly slipped, and, baffled there, he had returned again, paralyzed them with his daring as a wasp paralyzes a doomed spider, and flying into their faces he had cut through them and ridden on straight toward the heart of the town of Santa Maria.

Well, what were "they" thinking?

Were "they" now in the house of Robert Langhorne, hearing the report which some panting fellow telephoned in from the battle front—another report of failure? Did they not, then, turn their heads and stare at one another? Did they not wonder if the lonely rider might not break in upon them in spite of their strong walls and their watchful guards? Would there not be terrible though quiet misgivings among even the stoutest hearted of them? Would not the guards themselves be above all unnerved? For their fellows had watched faithfully in the distance, and Tarron had ridden through them as the prow of a ship rides through the waters.

The lights of Santa Maria were close before him when he rode Jimmy up the bank of the stream. Studying the outline of the town, he distinguished the tall front of the church at once. Behind that would be the house of Langhorne and his first goal.

In the meantime, he must secrete Jimmy, and at that thought his heart sank. Ride him into the town he hardly dared; but if he left him in some close copse near the verge of the city, there would be a great distance between the Langhorne place and Tarron's line of retreat. That was a danger which he must endure, he decided. So he set about finding a wood in which to leave the stallion. Not a furlong away, between two small houses, he saw a shadowy growth of trees and started for it. As he moved behind the first house he tripped over the shafts of a cart. He stopped to nurse his barked shins and swear silently, shaking his fist in a boyish fury at the cart. Then a new thought came to him.

He had no time to examine these inspirations in detail. He stripped off his riding boots and socks. That left him barefooted, but bare feet were a small hindrance to him, for in his home shoes had been more or less of a luxury. He took off his hip holsters and slung a Colt under each arm, where, after all, they were even more conveniently placed for a quick draw. After that, he unsaddled Jimmy, and entered the little shed at the side.

There he found a broken, tattered harness, patched with bits of rope. This he placed on the stallion, and Jimmy, with turned head, watched this proceeding with amazement and disgust. He had never borne such a weight on his back before.

After that, Tarron took the bandage from around his head and washed his wounded forehead in a pool of rain water. Next he ripped and tore at his sleeves, until they were dangling shreds that reached no lower than his elbows. His hair he rumpled and combed down with his fingers until it fell across his eyes.

Now Tarron hitched Jimmy to the cart and shook his head in concern as he saw the fine animal shudder with dread and crouch between the shafts. In the cart he placed the saddle, with the rifle in its case. Some rubbish from the shed was heaped over the saddle, and on top of all Les placed a thick layer of charcoal which he found in a corner of the little outhouse.

Thus equipped he went to Jimmy's head, took the lead rope in his hand and whispered. Jimmy started, felt the tug of the lumbering cart, and lurched ahead in terror, snorting. The cart followed, with a prodigious rumbling and squeaking of wooden axles on wooden hubs.

"Hello!" cried the voice of one within the house. "Who is that?"

"Drunken Felipe, most likely," said another, "getting home late."

Tarron, holding his breath, thanked the kind Lord who

had brought him safely past his first danger. He led Jimmy fast growing accustomed to the new work but still from time to time nosing at his master by way of assurance through a winding way among the trees and then he saw before him the first dimly lighted street of Santa Maria.

At the same moment, from the bell tower of the old church, bells began to clang and crash, not with the slow and rhythmic tolling which calls men to a Mass or funeral or wedding, but with a rapid, hurried, uneven beating, one wave of sound rushing out on the heels of the other and overtaking it and smashing against the ear in continual discord.

No call to prayer, as Tarron very well knew. No, it was a call to arms. An alarm bell, the rope tugged at by frantic hands, to send out the summons far and wide, floating above the roofs of the town, and drifting far off to the hills beyond. All would hear it, and all would answer.

There was no doubt in Tarron's mind as to the nature of that call. "They" had received the news that he had broken through their lines and was approaching the town itself, and now the danger signal was pealing. In the far distance, at either side of the valley, the triple red lights blazed forth from the foreheads of opposite hills.

The valley was roused. It was prepared to do its utmost. And even the heart of Tarron quailed in him. How can one man defy an army? But he was somewhat reassured, as he headed steadfastly down the street, leading his gray stallion.

"They" were looking for a dashing rider, on a brilliant gray horse, with a bandage about his forehead, and guns at his hip, and the hair blown behind his head by the speed of his going. What a contrast between that alert figure and this barefooted peon trudging through the dust of Santa Maria's streets, with his eyes glittering behind his tousled mass of falling hair! And as for the gray horse, how could its beauty be better disguised than by the ugly, broken, patched and rope-mended harness, while he tugged a lumbering, screeching cart behind him?

Tarron, with a steadier pulse, led Jimmy forward. But at the first turn of the street, half a dozen men swarmed out at him. Never had he seen more savage-looking fellows. And one who seemed in control stopped him with a sharp:

"Boy, did you hear the alarm bell? Where are you going?"

Chapter XXXV

Captain Courageous

As IF TO remove all doubts, at that moment the alarm
bell crashed again from the church tower and filled the air
with an uneasy dinning, and Tarron blessed the noise of
the bell, for it covered his confusion and gave his wits
time to clear a little.

When the noise had subsided, he answered, gaping:
"Senor, what can a poor boy do?"

"Take a stick or a knife," said the other, "when the bell
rings. You know that?"

"Ah, senor, how gladly would I take stick or knife, but
my father takes his rifle and goes off and leaves me to
drive the cart. I don't want to drive the cart, senor. But
what shall I do?"

"Leave it standing then, and be ready for work. The
devil is loose tonight!"

Tarron crossed himself.

"Senor, senor," said he. "I shall be beaten by my father
if I don't drive on with the cart!"

"Stuff!" said the other, while his companions grinned.
"The law is the law. No matter for your father! Where
does the cart go?"

Tarron thought swiftly. If he imagined a name, would it serve. No, this city was not so large, and a lie of that sort might bring a sharp questioning that would ruin everything.

He knew only one name in that town, and now he used it.

"For Senor Langhorne's house, senor."

There was an instant change.

"For that great house? Why didn't you say so before, young fool? Make way, there! For Senor Langhorne's house!"

And suddenly Tarron was free to go on down the street.

No, not free, for this fellow who was in charge insisted on accompanying him, and down the street they went, the pseudo-captain shouting in a great, important bellow: "Way! Way! Casa Langhorne!"

That word worked like enchantment. Even wildly galloping riders swerved respectfully to the side and sheered past the clumsy cart.

The "captain" was full of words.

"That is a good horse, my son," said he. He looked more closely. "Ha, what is such an animal doing pulling a cart!"

The heart of Tarron rapped against his teeth.

"Our good horse is sick," he declared, "and my father had to put in this poor thing."

"What? 'Poor thing?' Don't I know a horse when I see it?"

"See, senor. It is broken down in front, and notice how it hobbles!"

"Of course," said the captain, changing instantly. "I saw that at the first glance, but I wanted to learn if you knew anything about horseflesh. Well, I say it is a cruel thing to use such a beast for cart work. It should be turned loose in pasture, or put out of misery with a bullet through the head, it would make food for dogs."

"Aye, senor, and sometimes for men, too?"

The other indulged in a little laughter.

"Yes, for men, too. Well, lad, you are well out of this trouble tonight!"

"I hear," said Tarron, "that everyone is terribly excited."

205

"Tush! There—they are ringing the bell for the third time. There has never been such excitement since the rebellion—the revolution I mean to say!"

He made that addition hastily with a side glance at Tarron, but the latter pretended not to understand.

"What will be done?" asked Tarron mildly.

"Too many men! Too many men!" said the other, with a shake of the head. "These things should be left in the hands of a few brave and determined men—and God to help! God to help! I could name some of the men, some who have proved themselves!"

Thrusting out his chest he said this.

"Ah," said Tarron, "I think that my father has pointed you out. You are—let me see—"

"Juan Pilotte—he's pointed me out?"

"Yes, yes. Juan Pilotte. Senor Juan Pilotte."

"Well," said honest Juan. "A man's work will speak for itself in spite of modesty. It will talk out at the last and make itself known."

"That is true."

"If I could have a dozen men of my naming, I think that we'd handle this wild devil of a Tarron."

"Yes," said Tarron, "I should think that one such man as you would be almost enough."

"Do you think so, lad?"

"Because this Tarron—after all, he's only a man!"

"You may say that who have never stood guard against him. But I tell you, I saw him ride down the valley, crushing men like eggshells!"

"Oh, I would have liked to see that!"

"You would? You would have run home to hide your head under a blanket. I have never seen such a thing!"

"Yet he was not very big," said the son of his father.

"So you say! So you say! Well, he's not many inches over six feet in height, and he's got a horse that's about eighteen hands, at least. You may call that a small man. You may call it a small horse, too! And as for fighting, he kills men at three hundred yards with a revolver, shooting from a horse at full speed."

"Is it possible!"

"Isn't it, though? Have I eyes in my head? Can I see?"

"Of course, senor, you have judgment."

"However, bold as he is, I would face him—with a little help from man and God. Just a scant half dozen honest fellows I could name—and we'd stand to him."

"That is brave!"

"Why, a man can only die once. Only once! Better to die fighting bravely!"

"But he'll never dare to enter the town!"

"Won't he? He may be in it now!"

He shuddered violently, and cast a sharp glance over his shoulder at a tree they were passing, a tree which had an odd shape almost like a man on horseback.

"In the town now!" gasped Tarron. "And here I am in the open streets—thank God that I have you to protect me, brave Senor Pilotte!"

"Tush! Have no fear! I shall bring you right up to the door of the Casa Langhorne!"

It was the last thing that Tarron wanted, and a frown of thought came on his forehead.

"Yet," he said, "how could a man dare to come here— look!"

Down the street came rushing a little cavalry charge of half a dozen caballeros, armed to the teeth, naked rifles flashing through the dust which their horses raised.

"Let them go! Let them go!" exclaimed Pilotte. "And don't cry out suddenly again, like that. It rubs all the ends of my nerves raw!"

"Pardon me, Senor Pilotte! But that a man could dare to come into such danger!"

"He would dare anything! He dared to ride up the pass in spite of many brave men. I was there, and I had friends with me! And there were others. But fools got in our way. We could not get at him. Besides, he had magic in his horse. It went over everything, or through anything like running quicksilver! Dare to enter this town? Tush, he would dare anything! Hello! Hello! Are you going past the gate?"

They were passing a tall, wrought iron gate, flanked with powerful stone pillars. Beyond loomed a gloomy woodland.

"True! true!" said Tarron, cursing his carelessness. "But I was too interested, listening to you, senor."

"Well, turn in."

Jimmy brought the groaning cart to the gate, and there four armed men crossed the way.

"What's that?"

"Charcoal for the house."

"There was charcoal brought only yesterday."

"Well, they will burn up a load a day in that great place, I suppose. Hello, don't you know me, Olivero?"

It was Pilotte, taking charge of the whole matter.

"Juan, are you delivering charcoal? Have you gone into that business?"

"Not I. I bring this boy with his cart safely through the streets, and that is all."

"Well, nothing goes through these gates. There are orders."

"His father will beat him if he brings it back."

"Let him speak for himself."

"Alas, Senor Pilotte, if you cannot win me through, what can I do for myself?" pleaded Tarron.

"Well, that's true. You'll see that I have some authority. Listen, you—Leon!"

"I hear you."

"I know this boy. He is my nephew. I have known him all my life. And the house needs charcoal. You'll sweat for keeping him out."

"Well, let him go through. Drive on. Let me take a look at the charcoal, first."

The sharp eye of Tarron measured the distance to the trees. If the odd nature of his load were discovered as the hand of the inquisitor reached into it, he decided that he would flee for the trees and trust to God to be able to get out again, for after the alarm was given, he would never be able to enter the house. That much was sure.

However, the guard merely peered at the black heap in the cart.

"A small load," said he. "But go on. Everyone gives a short measure and a long price to Senor Langhorne. Pass on!"

So the cart passed up the driveway, and Tarron thanked his companion.

"That is nothing," said Pilotte. "A man's life is not lived in vain. We have some authority, thank God, over our fellows! Hush! What is that?"

"Where?"

"Yonder—a shadow among the trees!"

Tarron caught quickly at the fancy.

"Senor!" he whispered. "Could it be a horseman? Could Tarron have come so soon?"

Pilotte stopped with a groan of terror. Then he mastered himself.

"Go on," said he. "You will be able to see the lights of the house around the next bending. Go on! I'll return where danger may be and I shall be needed!"

And he turned and hurried down the path.

Chapter XXXVI

A Curtain Raiser

WHEN TARRON WAS left alone, he laughed until he was
weak, but then a memory of where he was and what he
had before him struck him sober. It was well enough
to have passed so many dangers almost miraculously.
And now he had entered the very grounds of the great
house. But what of the house itself? How was he to
manage that?

Well, let every bridge be crossed when it was come
to. In the meantime, he must bring his horse somewhere
close to the great house and leave the cart hidden in the
trees, as close as possible to Casa Langhorne.

As for the cart, that was a problem soon solved. In
another ten yards there was a gap among the trees and
into it Tarron drove Jimmy. Deep in the woods he un-
harnessed and unhitched the stallion, and put the saddle
on his back. Then he started straight for the house, Jimmy
following.

Tarron had not gone fifty yards before a group of
figures loomed before him, and he stopped. Jimmy, behind
him, turned to a statue of stone, and the group crossed
not a dozen yards away, but some low brush helped to
screen Tarron and his horse. Yet he could not help
worrying.

Suppose that while he was in the house the searching

patrol which was combing the woods in front of the house should come upon Jimmy—then the flight of Tarron would be cut off utterly, and he would be ruined.

Or suppose that the searching patrol found the cart and its disturbed load?

Well, let the past bury its dead, and the terrors of the future take care of themselves, one at a time!

Now, as he went ahead, the trees began to thin, and through them near rays of light commenced to break, so that Les realized he had brought the stallion as close as he dared. He did not choose a circle of trees, but in a nest of deep shrubbery he made the stallion lie down. There he was lost to view, and there he would remain like a trained dog until the voice of Tarron spoke to him again.

For a moment he remained beside the good horse, patting him and whispering in his ear. Then he slipped softly ahead, noiseless as a shadow, drifting rapidly from tree to tree and bush to bush, until he came out before the lofty face of the house of Langhorne.

There were three stories, each tall, and each faced with long windows. There was a balcony for each story and never had Tarron seen such a number of ways of entrance to a dwelling. It was a rest to his eye to examine the monster place and see in how many manners it could be attacked.

What he chose was no flank maneuver. And his reasons were excellent. Here in front of the house two great oil lamps threw a daylight blaze that revealed every detail of the surroundings, and up and down across the front of the mansion constantly paraded four men.

Four men here; therefore twice or thrice as many for the other and darker sides of the building. But it was not light that Tarron feared. It was the number and look of the guards, and above all, the way that they did their work. As for these four, they took if for granted that their numbers and the flare of the light cut off all chance of an approach to the mansion from this direction. And Tarron wanted nothing better. Danger there was, but danger had been so much his of late that this seemed nothing at all.

He saw his plan at once. Just before the main entrance and its towering portico was a circular bed of flowers, surrounded by good-sized shrubs, and the moment that the guards had passed it and marched on, arm in arm, chatting with one another gayly, Tarron slipped from his shelter and ran to this circular bed. There he crouched behind a big bush and waited until the quartet had passed him again, moving toward the farther end of the promenade. Then he was up and away like a flash and behind their backs reached the garden which fringed the foundations of the building.

After that all was easy. The crowded pillars of the portico were made to order for him. Barefooted, mighty of hand, he climbed up between two of them and gripping the edge of the cornice, swung up, and up, and drew himself onto the balcony above.

He dared not wait there long. From those windows in front of the Casa Langhorne others were watching, from time to time. But there was an open door before him, and at a stride he was through it, and crouching in a corner behind a curtain.

He had passed the barriers one by one. He was in the Casa Langhorne. It still remained to find the man he wished to confront. But that was a piece of detection which could surely be accomplished were Senor Langhorne here.

Ah, for a little more knowledge! Ah, for just five minutes of such talk as Dorn could have poured into his ears! But where should he go now, and what should he do?

He was in the second story. Most likely the master of the house was below. And he was to get there, too. This chamber in which he now crouched—as the flare of light from before the house enabled him to see—was a bedroom, beautifully furnished. And for one article Tarron gave thanks—the deep rich rug which covered the floor.

Even a heavy-footed monster could have moved over such a surface without betraying himself by a single sound. And as for Tarron, not even a whisper was roused as he crossed the room and listened at the door. There was no sound from beyond.

Little by little, he turned the well-oiled lock. He let the door move gradually open, and glancing out, he saw before him a spacious hallway—the central stairway of the mansion climbing up around the edges of a monstrous well. He saw this—and he saw two men leaning upon—no, not rifles, but sawed-off shotguns! He closed that door in great haste and fell back, biting his lip.

He had expected precautions, but these were a little more than might have been anticipated. For when he has established such advance guards as Langhorne had provided, even the most careful of men would hardly be expected to arm his very house in such a manner as this. But, as he sat in a corner of the room, resting, and rallying his thoughts, Tarron told himself fiercely that this, after all, was for the best. The most timorous of men would not have guarded himself in such a fashion. That was certain. Therefore there must be something in this house exceptionally worthy of being protected.

Tarron sighed, and set his teeth. What was the treasure? Man, woman, child? Or some priceless document?

One thing at least was determined. The hallway outside could not be used as an exit. There remained the big windows. He crossed to the farther one, which was standing open. Outside of it stretched the balcony, broken along its length by the potted shrubs at its edge, and by the rising pillars which supported the balcony of the story above.

Tarron did not hesitate long before he ventured out on it. He stepped boldly out—too boldly, alas!

For, as he passed, the door swung in a little, and the knob caught in his belt. There was a light ripping sound, and then the clang of falling metal.

He looked down, his heart stopping and saw on the floor of the balcony the little steel box, lying face up—and open! In its fall it had struck the spring which he had been unable to find, and now its secrets were exposed to him.

He did not pause to examine it, but scooping it up he sprang back, tigerlike, within the chamber, for the noise had been like a blow on a gong.

Behind the same curtain which had sheltered him before he crouched now, a Colt in his hand. Instantly there was a sound of footfalls—and voices spoke at the window which he had recently left.

"Go on in!"

"Give me the lantern. There we are!"

A bright shaft of light flashed up and down the room, and Tarron held his breath.

"Go in, I say!"

"You go first."

"You're commanding. So you've got to lead the way."

"Well, let me have a look first."

"You've had your look. You can't see behind those curtains from this distance."

"Well, I suppose I've got to."

They stepped through the window. Tarron made himself small behind the curtain; still, it seemed certain that he must make a bulge in the bottom of it.

He could see a sudden brightening of the material just before his face. A ruddy red, like blood, showed through, and he knew that they had turned the brightness of the unhooded lantern straight upon his hiding place. That moment he gave up all hopes of succeeding in his mission. But if he could shoot down these two—gain the window—slip down to the garden and from there bolt to the place where Jimmy waited for him—then God help him to the rest!

"That's something there."

"Where?"

"Behind that curtain. It moved."

"That's the wind, you fool."

"I say I see something."

"Go look, then."

"And get my head blown off, maybe?"

"Look here, you blockhead, do you really think that Tarron is in this room?"

"Why not? Didn't we hear something?"

"Well, if Tarron were here, would he sound a gong to let us know it?"

There was a moment of breathless silence.

"Anyway, I'm going to look."

Steps crossed the floor. The curtain was twitched out, and Tarron, looking up, leveled his gun into the face of a handsome young Mexican.

"You don't see a thing!" said Tarron in a whisper.

And with a shaken voice, his eyes starting from his head, the seeker called out: "There's nothing here!"

Chapter XXXVII

'Gainst Solid Steel

HE WHO STOOD at the door answered briskly: "Come away, then. I told you there'd be nothing."

The other remained staring blankly at Tarron, who shook his head.

"Face him, but don't leave!" whispered Tarron.

The handsome youth turned toward the door.

"I'm going to wait here a while," said he.

"By yourself, and be a hero, eh?" said the man at the door.

"Why not?"

"What would you do if Tarron showed up?"

"I'll handle that chance," said the young Mexican.

"You talk like a fool. Stay here if you want to! Remember what the orders were—to keep walking the rounds."

"Don't mind about me. I'll worry for myself."

There was a stifled oath, and the light flashed out. At the same time, the iron hand of Tarron fell on the shoulder of his captive. There was no escaping from that grip.

Stepping from behind the curtain, he was able to see

that the other guard had passed on. The blackness in the room was like a blanket of secrecy around them.

"Hands above your head," murmured Tarron.

He was instantly obeyed. While the victim's hands were raised at arm's length, Tarron went hastily over his body. The fellow was well enough armed. A Colt and a double-barreled pistol, short and huge of bore, rewarded the search, to say nothing of a deadly little stiletto.

"You can put your arms down," said Tarron.

"Yes, senor."

The arms obediently came down. But it was plain that the man would attempt nothing. He was trembling like a leaf.

"I'll do you no harm," said Tarron, "if you'll play square with me."

"I shall do what I can. I have no wish to die, senor!"

"You have sense. Tell me first, where can we go to talk? How can we get out from this room?"

"Through that window onto the balcony. Or through that door and into the hall."

"With guards at either place?"

"Yes, senor. There are many guards at both places."

The man had spoken the truth, as Tarron knew, and he began to feel more confident.

"What is your name?"

"I am Felipe Morales."

"Felipe Morales?"

"Yes. And your name, senor?"

"I'm Leicester Tarron."

"Oh, God receive my sinful soul!" breathed the captive, and sank limply upon his knees.

"Hush!" said Tarron, almost laughing in spite of himself when he saw what terror his name inspired. "I'll not murder you."

"No, senor. I pray God that you will not. I have an old mother, a wife, and little children! And what would one more death be to a hero like you, Senor Tarron?"

"No hero. You may be able to tell me things that will be well worth hearing."

"My very heart is open to your questioning, senor! But by what miracle did you bring yourself here?"

"By taking chances. And by taking more chances I

hope to do something before I leave the Casa Langhorne."

"I shall tell you what I know."

"Sit down here in the darkness, in this corner. So."

"Merciful God!"

"That's the muzzle of a revolver against your ribs. But I'll do you no harm with it. It's only to make sure that you keep the peace."

"I believe you! I believe you, Senor Tarron, my friend!"

"I shall ask you questions as though I knew nothing."

"Very well."

"In that way I shall know whether you are speaking the truth or not."

"I understand. But you must know, senor, that in this house of mystery there are only a few things known even to me. And yet I know more than almost all the others!"

"Good!" said Tarron, his hopes rising. "Tell me, then, why I am here?"

"That, of course, I can say. You are here to reach Antonio Lopez."

The name rang in the ears of Tarron most unexpectedly.

"Lopez? Lopez?" he thought to himself. "Why can that be? How does he enter the case?"

"And who sent me?" he added aloud.

"Andrea Alvarado, of course."

Another name! And yet both this and the other had come instantly from the lips of the prisoner.

However, it was a great step forward. God bless this man who knew so much! Andrea Alvarado, it seemed, was one of "them" who had financed and employed big Dorn and many another man to go to his death in the carrying of the steel box.

"Does Alvarado know that I am here?"

"Alas, senor, can I tell that? I know he must guess that you will have done more than all of the others. But I cannot tell you what is in the mind of Senor Alvarado, even though he is in this city!"

Again young Tarron's heart leaped.

"Where is he in this city?"

"If he is not in his house, God knows, and not I! I don't think that he would dare to leave his doors in such a time!"

"And where is his house?"

"Senor, you mock me!"

"I must test the truth that is in you, friend. Where is his house?"

"Of course. It is the low, broad white house on the western hill."

"Very good. I see that you tell the truth!"

Looking back into his mental picture of the town, Tarron could remember a tree-crowned hill to the west of Santa Maria de la Paz. And through the trees there had been touches and streaks of a white façade. There lived Alvarado, and to know that was, really, to know everything. Or so, at least, it seemed.

"I think that you are telling the truth," said Tarron. "But I must make sure."

"May the thunderbolt strike me if I leave the truth a single half inch to the side of me in what I speak."

"Why am I here instead of at the house of Alvarado?"

"Ah, senor, and what could you do there to advance the cause of Alvarado? No, we all know that the secret is to be had from the lips of old Lopez."

"And who is Lopez?"

"Well, senor, who should he be but the father of that poor, murdered Miguel?"

Murder! More and more Tarron felt that he was closing down upon the heart of the secret.

"How was Miguel murdered?" he asked.

"If I knew—well, of course I don't!"

"Tell me what you know?"

"There is very little to say. I was in the house at that time, however. I was here, and I know how Miguel had gone out into the mountains with young Carlos Alvarado. I know how he came back, too, in the night. And he and his father and Senor Langhorne went out into the little summer house in the garden. All that I know is that the shot was heard there, and young Miguel was killed by the bullet. All men know that."

"And who fired the bullet? Was it Langhorne or the father?"

"Senor Langhorne? Of course he does not have to do his killings with his own hand. And would a father murder his own son? But as for what happened, I know nothing. Only that Antonio Lopez lost his wits afterward.

And it must have been a dreadful thing that could have turned his head!"

"Do you think his wits are turned?"

"Hush, senor! I dare not say! I only know that I knew him first when his hair was black, and now it is white, and Senor Langhorne has sworn that his wits are addled. That is all that I dare to know."

"And what do you guess?"

"I guess—ah, Senor Tarron, you have guessed it also!"

"And what?"

"That he is not crazy more than you or I. And that he is kept here so that Andrea Alvarado cannot speak with him. And for what other purpose, God and the steel box knows, as the saying runs."

"The steel box?"

"Yes, senor. I have heard the saying, but what it means, I cannot tell."

"Morales, I believe that you have said nothing except what you know or think."

"May heaven strike me otherwise."

"Then tell me how I may reach Antonio Lopez."

"Alas, I knew that you would ask for that. But also I knew that I could not give the right answer. How can I tell you how to leave this room without being seen? And to be seen is to be shot at. The men are instructed to shoot first at strangers and to ask afterward."

"I understand. Tell me at least where I shall find Lopez if I can leave this room?"

"You know, of course, senor. He is always kept in that same room, where the sun can never reach him. But still his spirit is not broken after five years! And it will bend, but never break. For the old man is all steel!"

"And what room is that?"

"It is the cellar room, senor."

"Of course. How may it be known?"

"On the second floor down in the cellar, I myself have seen the door of it—all one slab of strong steel. It will turn the edge of a chisel."

"Do they trust to the strong door now?"

"Not since you have come near the city. No, no! Two men are in the room constantly, and they are changed every four hours."

"At what hours?"

"The next change is at ten, senor."

"Then lie down on the floor, my friend. And lie still. I am not going to choke you, but only to tie and gag you. Do you protest? Look! One slip of your old knife and I could put you on the floor, past all speaking!"

Chapter XXXVIII

Three on the Lookout

HE LEFT YOUNG Morales, the honest man, lying swathed in strips of velvet curtain and securely gagged. Not a finger or a toe could the fellow move.

But now that Tarron was free of hand once more, he hesitated at the window. He had, at last, enough information to act upon. He knew who was to be reached in this house. He knew where to find Alvarado, the man who had sent out the steel box. And this was a treasure of information to him. However, what was he to do with it?

First of all, he must get from the room and to the cellar. And that was a task for a giant. Tarron chose the most roundabout method. To go down or around would be tremendously dangerous, but having gone thus far up the side of the building, he trusted that he might be able to go still higher—and then to pass down over the roof, and to the rear of the Casa Langhorne.

He had to shrink back into the dark of the room the next moment, as a guard walked down the balcony. Then, crouching where the light from the strong lamps outside the house threw a reflection into the chamber, he took the steel box from his pocket and examined it.

His heart almost stopped! For within the box there was nothing except a soiled, tattered, much rubbed piece of paper; and when he unfolded it, he saw nothing upon it other than a crooked line checked with a few crosses.

He felt frantically in the pocket into which he had dropped the box after its fall. But the pocket was empty, and now Tarron guessed that the real treasure which the box had held had bounced out when it fell on the balcony and had dropped to the ground below. There, no doubt, it had been buried in the soft muck of the garden strip which ran along the wall of the house. It was lost, and lost in a place where he could never expect to search for it!

Bitter moments have come to other men, but surely there was never any more completely heartbreaking than this of Tarron's, when, come at last to the door of his quest, he found himself empty handed!

The pain of the old wound in his forehead, which he had utterly forgotten, now stabbed through his very brain; and all at once he felt sick with weariness, trembling with the weakness of hunger.

Little by little he mastered himself. And, although he might lose everything by unlucky chance, still he determined to force his way ahead. In that cellar room, closely guarded, was Antonio Lopez, by whom many mysteries might be unveiled. If he reached the place ten minutes before the hour for the change of guards; if he knocked at the steel door and demanded entrance as the new guard, stepped through with a pair of guns leveled and—

Ah, well, it was a chance more desperate than any that he had yet taken. But he was determined to push on. He was too far committed in his own mind. He could not turn back!

He slipped out of the window now, and slid like a ghost down the narrow balcony to the pillars that ran sheer up the face of the house. Once more they served him as a tree trunk serves a monkey. Bare toes and talonlike fingers gripped securely the deep flutings of the wooden columns, and Les has climbed rapidly to the top. He swung himself up over the eaves and now lay panting at full length on the gutter of the great house. Turning his head aside, he glanced down a dizzy distance to the garden beneath and the four guards who still strode confidently up and down, not knowing that the fish had passed through their net long ago!

His danger was so terrible that it cleared his mind, and the weakness and the fatigue passed from him. The first ridge of the roof arose above him, and over the tiles he crept until he had reached that vantage point. Peering over, he saw that the uppermost reach of the roof was occupied by a rectangular platform, a sort of captain's bridge, from which the eye could command the entire town and the valley beyond it.

He made for that point, and while he was lying just under the narrow balustrade that fringed the edge of it, he heard a sudden grating as of a door opened, and then a noise of steps and a burst of voices.

Flat upon the tiles went Tarron, and lay there, hardly daring to breathe. The first eye that looked over the edge of that balustrade and down upon the roof would find him! With a soft but swift movement, he drew himself up still closer and lay stretched out just under the rail, a motionless, formless shadow.

"There isn't much wind," said a voice in perfect English.

"I thought it would be blowing more, senor."

"No, it's very comfortable. Look at the lights! Our fellows are everywhere!"

"They are, senor."

"Do you think that this young devil, this will-o'-the-wisp Tarron could break through?"

"You see for yourself, senor. If he is not entirely mad—surely he will never even attempt it!"

"Aye, but we know that he did attempt it this very evening, and that he probably broke through into the village."

"What good will that do him, senor?"

"That is true. I try to imagine what good it will do him to be in the village."

"If he is in Santa Maria, then he's lying low like a rat with ferrets prowling around it."

"That's very likely. I believe that even the old man would give up hope if he were brought here."

"I think it very likely, senor, when he sees your power shown as it's shown tonight in all those lights!"

223

"Send one of your men down to the guards. Tell them that Lopez is to be brought up here at once."

"Senor!"

"Don't gape! Do as I say."

"But he has never—"

"Never had so much liberty before? It will do him good, perhaps, to see so much of the thing that he doesn't possess. Go at once."

"Senor Langhorne, I do as you say. I trust there will be no evil consequences."

There was another stir of feet, and Tarron heard someone whistling. The great Langhorne, no doubt, taking his ease on that lookout station, was enjoying all the beauty and the majesty of this valley of which he was the overlord. Such a man was like a king and nothing less.

Langhorne standing just above him—Langhorne within the stretch of his hand. Tarron held his breath in sheer amazement. But the monarch was surrounded by stanch fighting men; and one could wager that only the best of the keen warriors of the mountains would be trusted so near the person of the king.

He heard the whistling end, after a time, and then footsteps coming upstairs, and a heavy panting breath.

"Here you are, Lopez!" said Senor Langhorne cheerfully.

"I am here, senor," said the voice of an old and broken man.

Then, after a little pause, the same voice added: "There is a God over us, after all. I had forgotten the stars. Are they not the face of God, Langhorne?"

"Tush!" chuckled Langhorne. "Isn't it better to be addled than completely poetic, like this, my friend?"

"And therefore," said Lopez, continuing his own thought, "God is watching you. That's enough to make you tremble, I should think!"

"Not a bit!"

"Perhaps not. Well—why have you brought me here?"

"Guess, my friend."

"To give me a glimpse of the stars and the beautiful open night, because that will make the filthy room in the cellar more horrible to me!"

"Not filthy, Lopez!" broke in the other sharply.

"No," admitted Lopez. "Not filthy, except that the darkness is always foul. What other purpose could you have in bringing me here?"

"I'll tell you, presently. But I think that we can make this a very short interview. I am going to convince you, at last."

"You could never do that, senor."

"We'll see. Look out yonder. There are stars of heaven —and earth stars, also."

"You mean the lights—from the fires?"

"Yes. The watch fires."

"Well, there are enough of them. What are you watching against, now?"

"I'm going to tell you that. Lopez, in these years that you have been here, you know that the Alvarados have made great efforts to get at you?"

"Yes."

"And they've sent the steel box by clever messengers—"

"Yes. You've told me that to torment me."

"And I haven't waited. I've reached out and stopped them at a distance."

"You have—so you have said."

"But finally, my friend, a young man took up the work and came like lightning through every danger up to the pass. He rode into the pass, where my men were waiting for him—"

"And was shot to pieces?"

"No, wait for the end. He rode in, was stopped, got away, and galloped like a madman down the throat of the pass again. He escaped by a miracle. He left five dead men and many wounded behind him."

"God be with that young hero! Is he still alive, senor?"

"He came straight back, having failed at the pass. He crossed the mountains by a forgotten trail and dropped down into the valley. And there he was waited for by an ambuscade, but he slipped through them like a ghost and rode into the town!"

"A hero, Langhorne."

"Beyond any question. But this is the point. Now he lies somewhere in that town, surrounded by danger, hardly daring to breathe, and my men hunt for him everywhere. You understand? He has done more than all of the others. But still the best that this wild man, this brilliant fool, could do, was to place himself hopelessly within the trap. There are my men in my city. There are my outposts far away. And when he tries to get away, he will be lost. He has not eaten food for two days, I think. He is starving, weak, worn out. Soon he will be snapped up, and the last of your hopes will go with him. I've brought you here and told you the sheer truth, Lopez. Now, like a reasonable man, capitulate!"

Chapter XXXIX

Close to the Clue!

"HE HAS SMASHED through everything, and actually got into the town!"

"Yes."

"And there he is lost?"

"Ask your own reason."

"And for that reason I should surrender?"

"Well?"

There was a sudden soft cry from the old man.

"Senor Langhorne, listen to me. If I had been in that devilish prison of yours seventy years instead of seven; if I were worn out and crushed and broken and about to surrender, and if then I heard that such a hero in such a manner had come into the valley to rescue me—a man whose face I have never seen and who has never seen me —I tell you, senor, that I would then have the strength to endure for another seventy years. There are many causes in this world that are not worth a snap of the fingers. But if I am a cause worthy of such a hero, he will not die for me any more quickly than I will die for him!"

"By the Lord!" murmured Langhorne. "Too old already —too soft-witted to understand simple logic!"

"You have always scorned me," said the Mexican. "But nevertheless you have never broken me!"

"Tonight, however, I am going to convince you, my friend."

"God give you greater strength of persuasion! I stay here and enjoy the shining of the stars and the nearness of God. You cannot tempt me, senor!"

"We'll see," retorted Langhorne.

He gave orders:

"Tie the hands of this old man against the central post, there. Then go down below and wait in easy calling distance, but not closer than the first landing. I do not wish to be overheard. Do you understand?"

"Yes, senor," came the answer, and presently there was a noise of many feet retreating. The sound of a trap door shutting heavily on a cushion of air, and then Langhorne and his prisoner were alone on their platform high above the town.

No, not entirely alone, for another man lay listening. And what a man! Rather call him a tiger as he lies in the shadow, his eyes burning!

It was all miraculous and unbelievable to Tarron. He had come so far and done so much and fought always against such dreadful odds, and now, by a contrivance of kind fortune, the two men whom he wished to have in the hollow of his hand had been placed there. Old Lopez, the mysterious prisoner, was within arm's length! And with him stood this king of the valley, Langhorne, whose agents had caused so many men to die! Both in his hand! For, with his two guns and all his craft, could he not take Langhorne utterly by surprise?

Yet Tarron lay still for a while longer, anxious to hear what he could and delaying the stroke, very much as a cat plays with a mouse—tasting his power and unwilling to use it.

Moreover, when Langhorne was helpless in his hands— what next? Of what avail to have the lord of a castle in one's power, when one stood at the crest of that lord's castle with all his armed retainers between one and freedom?

But Tarron did not care to look to the future. The present, the present only, would he cling to with a grip of iron and let tomorrow take care of itself.

"You understand, Lopez," said the master, in a quiet tone of argument, "that you have made a moral issue out of a practical affair."

"The death of a man's son," replied Lopez with feeling, "is something more than a practical affair!"

"That is an attitude," said Langhorne, "that I can sympathize with, of course."

"You cannot," replied the other, "for you have no heir, and never have had one."

"Well, well!" snapped Langhorne, apparently touched in a sore spot. "There is no need to dwell on that. However, let us meet even that point in your statement. That one concerning your son. Tell me, my friend, how your dead son benefits by your present misery?"

"How would he benefit by my surrender to you?"

"How would be be harmed? That is the question."

"Because he had committed a great sin, I must do what I may to undo his sin."

"He paid his penalty. A life for a life. No code can ask for more than that!"

"It is true. No code can ask for more than that. But I can ask for more, and I shall do more than that!"

"They killed your boy with a bullet through his back while we sat in the summer house. What could be more dastardly than that?"

"I shall tell you something more dastardly. My son went with a friend to undertake a great adventure. It was young Carlos Alvarado who had worked out the problem of the lost mine and unraveled the mystery of the chart. He had spent years on the thing. Then, out of the greatness of his heart, he asked my boy to accompany him in that final search."

"I admit that, Lopez."

"He went with young Alvarado, and when they had actually discovered the mine and the enormous wealth of it, he allowed the wealth to madden him. He killed his friend and benefactor—because Alvarado had sworn to give him a third share in the profits if their search succeeded."

229

"I remember all of the details."

"I say that the murder of Alvarado by my son was far fouler than the murder of my son by the men of Alvarado. If they had killed me, also, there would still have been a debt against our name! And now you wish me to to tell you what I know, so as to place the mine in your hands. No, no! That is not my conception of justice, my friend. And I shall never do what you wish. You may be sure of that!"

"Be reasonable, Lopez."

"I am trying to be reasonable."

"Then you will see that your case is hopeless."

"I have thought so until this night, when you told me of what that young man, that young hero, has done to reach me. His name?"

"Curse him and his name! Who would think that such a story would make you credulous! Do you dream, Lopez, that any human being can break into my house and carry you away with him?"

"He does not need to carry me away. Let me see the chart, and with one word I can give him the clue to its working!"

There was an oath from Langhorne, and then the sound of his footfall, as he strode up and down.

Tarron lay breathing fast, for the veil was being quickly torn from the face of the mystery.

"After all," said Langhorne, "your son may have dreamed of what he saw in the old mine. He may have dreamed it, and even if we should find the mine there might not be much in it!"

"So you say! But in your heart you feel otherwise. You believe so thoroughly in the report that my son made that you have been haunted all these years by the wish to get at the place. You have searched every inch of the mountains, and you have not found it. And still you keep searching!"

"One day I shall have it," said the other bitterly; "in spite of you I shall have it!"

"That I doubt."

"I shall hunt until not a mouse could be hidden from me!"

Lopez laughed.

"You have a space of ten thousand square miles to hunt over," he said, "and in any part of that space the entrance to the mine may be. Are you so sure that you can find it?"

Another snarling oath from Langhorne. Then he changed his tone.

"My friend," said he, "you must not think that it has not been against my conscience to keep you confined as I have done. It has haunted me—"

"Hush," said Lopez. "Hypocrisy is the most damnable of all sins."

"Well, you will not believe me until I give you the proof. This is it! I have offered you your freedom for your information. Now I offer you more. I offer you the third share that your son was to have had in the mine."

"Blood money!"

"Man, man, are you past all reason? What blood money is there in it?"

"I tell you, Langhorne, that even if I wished to, I could not help you. I know one of the landmarks, yes, two of them, which my son pointed out and named to me, while you were closing the door of the summer house just before the shot was fired. But, for all that, I could not connect the plan, unless I saw the chart once more."

"Give me the names of those landmarks. I remember something of the shape of the chart. I remember the scale of miles by which they said that they had worked. And with that memory, I think that I could work out the solution just as your son did. I am not a fool! No, my friend, tell me those key names, and I'll do the rest if the wit of man can accomplish it!"

Silence.

"Like a fool," said Langhorne, "you are going to cling to your darkness?"

"Perhaps so. I shall not speak. I shall not take the least chance that you should profit by anything that I could tell you. The information which I could give belongs to the Alvarados. They know it. For that reason they have been making such vast efforts to reach me. And by the pleasure of God they will win in the end! The devil cannot favor you much longer."

"Then go back to your cellar and let the darkness breed

more madness in you," gasped Langhorne, choking with rage. "And yet I'll try one last argument to convince you that—"

There was sudden hoarse shouting from beneath.

"Senor! Senor Langhorne!"

Tarron took advantage of that clamor to cover the sound he made in rising to his knees along the balustrade. Opposite him stood old Lopez, but as he saw the light glitter on the barrel of the Colt in Tarron's hand the old man made not the slightest sign and the expression of his face did not alter.

"Senor Langhorne!" came the cry from beneath.

"Yes?"

"They have found in the garden the gray horse of Tarron! He is now hiding among the trees!"

Chapter XL

If Fortune Favor

SENOR ROBERT LANGHORNE, as Tarron now saw him outlined against the brilliant stars, was a tall, slender man. On either side of his cheeks was outthrust a thin pencil of shadow—the ends of his well-trained mustache. He paused for a moment as he heard this hoarse cry from beneath, and then exclaimed softly: "The devil takes care of his own. This Tarron must be the archfiend! Has he actually brought a horse into the grounds of the house?"

He called aloud: "Send every man to search the grounds. Search them inch by inch, and in the meantime, throw a cordon around the house."

"Si, senor!"

A sound of retreating footfalls.

"You see, senor," said the prisoner, "that he was able to break through your guards, after all."

"Broke through and into the trap, like a frantic rat," said the tall man calmly. "In another ten minutes I shall have him here face to face, unless they kill him when they take him. I hope not. I want to see him—hear his voice. Odd thing, Lopez, that such a boy should have been able to give me so much trouble. But he's the desperate sort. He'll die fighting, and I'll never have the pleasure of sending him down to share your cell. Better still, I'll never have the pleasure of using him for my own work."

"Could you hire him?"

"Why not?"

"After he has killed so many of your best men?"

"That is nothing. The wheels of life turn more smoothly because there have been a few sacrifices."

"But are you not afraid? Suppose that this Tarron had broken through your line and into your house?"

"Impossible! Men are marching up and down in front of Casa Langhorne and on every side of it. The devil himself could not fly into it without being seen."

The Mexican threw back his head and broke into laughter. In the meantime, a general hubbub resounded in the garden beyond the house. But the wind was rising, and the shouts and the commands came only blurred and faint to this lofty platform.

"Why do you laugh?" asked Langhorne grimly.

"To think of your confidence, senor!"

"And what of that?"

"When you may be already in the hands of your enemy?"

"You talk like a silly fool with a weakened brain. I must send you back to your damp shadows forever!"

"No," exclaimed the Mexican. "A price has been paid for my life. Did you not say that five men died yesterday? Are they not a sufficient price even for my life?"

"Your wits have gone wandering," said Langhorne.

"Prosperity has maddened you," replied Lopez. "I have seen you come into this land without a penny in your pocket. Your success has turned your brain."

"By that brain I made my fortune grow, old man."

"By your deft fingers, rather, which helped themselves to many pockets."

"Scoundrel! Insolent dog, how dare you say that?"

"Ah, Langhorne, because I closed my eyes then, it does not mean that I was quite blind. I know how you began operations with money stolen from me. Why, senor, the salted mine that you sold me in the beginning—was I such a fool as not to see through that? But you amused me. The loss did not ruin me. I waited, hoping that I might find a way to gain back what I had lost!"

"I wish," said Langhorne, "that you were twenty years younger. But I cannot fight you. I can only show you what a dog I've always felt you to be."

Stepping closer, he struck the Mexican heavily across the face with his open hand.

"Senor," said Lopez calmly, "that is the worst folly that you have ever committed—except one other."

"What was that other, Lopez?"

"To stay here alone with me—without a guard—when you knew that Tarron had already come as far as your garden!"

"Was that a folly?"

"Yes, because it placed you in his hands!"

"That is a pleasant riddle. Explain it!"

"You would never believe my words."

"Perhaps not."

"But would you believe your own eyes?"

"Ha?" cried the tall man, starting convulsively.

"Then turn around, and see for yourself!"

Langhorne whirled about, but at that moment Tarron was stepping across the balustrade, and the master of the house fairly thrust his breast against a leveled revolver.

He did not cry out. Never did man show a more wonderfully steady nerve.

"Tarron, by all the gods!" he murmured. He waited.

"There are two things that we can do," said Tarron quietly, drawing a knife with his left hand and holding it against Langhorne's breast. "We can kill this cur and take our chances of escape. Or we can make him go with us, and have the pleasure of hearing his own voice order his own men away from us. Which do you choose?"

"My son," cried the old man, his voice trembling, "God has sent you, and God will not let you shed unnecessary blood. Do not kill him."

"Listen!" said Tarron to Langhorne. "Do you hear? You who struck him! Do you hear?"

Langhorne said not a word. In the silence, Tarron stared into the keen, burning eyes of the older man, and wondered at his quiet. Devils must have been raging in his soul, yet he made not a sound.

"Put up your hands!" commanded Tarron.

Langhorne raised them slowly above his head, but when Tarron searched him, the only weapon he found on his person was a small penknife.

Tarron turned his back on his prisoner.

"Watch him!" breathed Lopez. "He will throw himself from the roof—"

"No," said Tarron. "There's still too much that he hopes to live for! He won't do that."

He undid the bonds which fastened the hands of old Lopez.

"Now," said Tarron, "we'll walk in single file. Senor Langhorne goes first. He doesn't like it a lot. He'd be glad to make a break. But he knows that I'm walking right here behind him with a gun, and my hand on the trigger. He knows that if he makes a false move, I sink a .45-caliber chunk of lead through him. And he knows that I'd almost die myself for the pleasure of polishing him off!"

He added: "Senor Lopez, you come behind me, and as we go along, keep looking back, to see that nobody swarms too close behind us!"

"I understand."

"Langhorne!"

"Yes."

"Start down through that trap door—and go carefully!"

"My boy," said Langhorne, taking a deep breath to rally himself, "this is one of the finest things that any man ever accomplished. But it won't do! You could never get through the grounds. And if you could, what would be your advantage? Who would ever do as much for you as I'd do?"

"You'd hire me?" asked Tarron.

"At a grand salary. I don't offer you a little post. A position, not a job. Ten thousand a year, say. A groom to take care of your horses—a servant to look after your wants—freedom to do as you please—a house of your own, furnished and paid for by me—ground of your own, to farm if that pleases you, or a range stocked with cattle if you prefer. And all I'd ask from you in return is allegiance to me. Now and again—once in three years, perhaps—some small thing to do for me—"

"Like a murder, say?" suggested the boy.

Langhorne was silent.

"I know you, you rat," said Tarron. "I've been on a trail that you've made hard for me."

"Ah, my son, would you have had me throw away what is most—"

"Don't talk," broke in Tarron. "Why, it makes me sort of mad to hear you. Don't talk! There's ways of playing even the hardest sort of a game. And you ain't been playing that way. You've played crooked. A finer man than you ever was I've seen lying on his face on the floor in the moonlight with his throat cut. It was your knife that did it, Langhorne!"

"What? A midnight murder? I never put my hand to such a thing."

"You lie! Because your men done it for you! And you sold 'em the sort of work that you wanted done!"

"Tarron, will you listen? The stake we played for was possible millions. What's a life or two in such a game? And they fought me as I fought them—with every weapon that they could imagine!"

"They never poisoned. They never cut throats by night. And they never hit old men in the face—old men whose hands were tied. Now get down the stairs. I've listened to you for the last time! Get down the stairs, and if one of your men comes toward you, tell him to stand away because you're busy and can't be bothered. But if you let one of 'em come too close—I'll kill you, Langhorne; and I'll do it with a lot of pleasure."

"And then die?"

"I've got through your lines before. I could get through 'em again. And how hard would your men work for you, once they knew you were lying dead? Will you tell me that?"

Something in this last speech seemed to strike a responsive note in the breast of the older man, because he suddenly winced and without a word faced around to the trapdoor.

Down the narrow descent they went, with old Lopez struggling clumsily behind them.

They reached a door at the bottom of the stairs which opened on an upper hallway. Into that same hallway

Tarron had looked earlier in the night, but now he found it empty. The guards had been stripped away and sent by the master's own orders, to search through the garden, and guard the house from the outside.

If fortune favored them, they might now pass entirely through the house without being detected!

Chapter XLI

Through the Tall Gateway

THEY ACTUALLY PASSED through the lofty chambers of Casa Langhorne without being seen or challenged by a soul, and at the rear of the house Tarron paused and considered a new idea. To leave that place on foot was a difficult task. But to gallop from the grounds on a horse would be comparatively simple.

He said to Langhorne:

"If you call through the window, senor, one of those men would bring up my horse and two others."

"He would," said Langhorne, looking askance at Tarron as he understood the meaning of the suggestion.

"Well," said Tarron. "Give the order."

"To whisk me away with the pair of you on horseback?" said Langhorne, scowling.

"And why not?"

"Am I a rank fool, young man, to give orders such as that?"

"Think it over," said Tarron, eying him grimly. "Killing you or letting you live is pretty much the same to me. There's never a job I've had in my life that I'd like half so well as to polish you off, Senor Langhorne. There's

239

poor Dorne lying in a Mexican grave yonder in the mountains. When I think of him, I want to be at you. Is that reason enough for you to do what I want—and to ask no more questions?"

Even then Langhorne needed a moment to consider. He went to the window. But what he had commanded had already been done, and while some of his men beat over every corner of the park around the Casa Langhorne, others were drawn in a compact line around the big place.

"Orvetto!" he called.

"Senor!" answered a ready voice.

"Orvetto, have Tarron's horse brought here, and two others with saddles on them, and at once."

"Instantly, senor. Tarron's horse is already close!"

In the pause, the trio within the house could hear the many voices of the searchers through the park, and now it seemed surely beyond the range of possibility to force the owner of the house from his place against his will. Yet Langhorne was black of face as he stood scowling with folded arms, his back to the wall. Plainly he foresaw that the very worst was still a possibility.

In the meantime, the horses came. There were two black beauties, one as like the other as peas from a pod; and with them Jimmy, unkempt of mane and tail, weather stained, and seeming somewhat long and low in contrast with the others. Tarron's eye lighted with sudden joy when he saw the young stallion.

"And that's the horse!" said Langhorne, taken from his musings by the sound of the hoofs outside the window. "That's the horse with which you broke into the valley. No wonder the others couldn't take him. That's a racer, my son."

"Thanks," muttered Tarron, whose hatred for the older man was growing apace during every moment he was with him. "Now tell them to leave the horses and scatter to their work. Send everyone of them about their business, searching through the woods. Order the men from around the walls."

Langhorne set his teeth and hesitated, but again necessity was plain to him, for Tarron's eye, with murder in it, never left his face.

"Leave the horses there. Now scatter through the park,

you rascals. You've let Tarron into the park. See that you get him again, or there'll be reason for some of you to remember today as long as you live. Go!"

Langhorne let his rage come into his voice, and there was an instant scampering of frightened feet in response to his order.

"That ought to do," murmured Tarron. "Can you ride now, father?" he added to old Lopez.

The latter answered with a faint smile:

"I could rise from the grave to ride any horse like one of those three. I shall be at your side, my son, if the horse I'm on can keep me there. Are you ready?"

"Ready, yes!"

"Then lead the way out, Langhorne. And still watch yourself, and remember that my gun is on you every second!"

There was no answer, but the tall man obediently stalked forth in the lead. Just outside the door he hesitated for an instant and turned his grim face from side to side while he scanned all the woods of the park near to him. But his thundering command had effectually banished his men from that vicinity and they would not soon return to beard the lion.

Langhorne took the central black, Lopez the other, and Tarron was instantly astride the gray. Down the winding drive past the house they went. They had not entered twenty yards into the park before a dozen men spilled into the way before them and shouted "Who goes!"

"You dogs!" thundered the master. "It is I! Do you know me?"

And he reached for the nearest with the quirt which he had snatched from the bow of his saddle.

"Softly, Senor Langhorne! Softly!" said old Lopez. "One more move such as that, and you invite your soul up to the center of heaven—or hell. You were almost gone, then! Senor Tarron's finger was curling on the trigger."

Langhorne turned his head and gave Tarron the most baneful look that the latter was ever likely to receive even in a long, long life which had not been without its trials and tribulations.

"That is enough," said Tarron. "I'll give you a fair

chance, Langhorne. Something better than a dog's chance. Unless I doubt you. And then I'll let my gun do my thinking!"

They passed on down the drive. Twice again they were challenged, and twice the master of the house freed them from danger. And they came to the great gates, now closed, and guarded by a score of rifles.

"Send them away, and have them open the gates before they go," commanded Tarron. "Send them into the woods to hunt."

His orders were obeyed. Langhorne vented some of his tortured feelings in an outburst of rage at the guards which made the latter fling open the great leaves of the gate in terror and then fly.

In the meantime Tarron said to Lopez: "Now, senor, tell me how Alvarado has managed to live in the same city with Langhorne all these years when the man was the enemy of the other house?"

"Ah," said Lopez. "You do not understand. Men work for Langhorne because though he is a stranger, he can pay them for what they do. But was not Alvarado one of the first Conquistadores? They follow Alvarado for love, which is stronger than money, God be praised! They would go to hell for the money of Langhorne, but still he could not bribe them to harm an Alvarado."

"But if you and I rode to the house of Alvarado?"

"We would be as safe as though an ocean lay between us and this devil."

"And if we took Langhorne there?"

"What difference would it make? Yes, I should like to see that!"

"Then we'll do it. Keep to the side as you ride through the gateway. There's too much light, here, and more people coming!"

So said Tarron, for the tramp of many horses now passed down the road, approaching the gates. No doubt these were men who had been called in by the alarm from the Casa Langhorne. Now they were passing through the gates, Tarron to the right and old Lopez to the left of Langhorne, when the black which the latter was riding suddenly reared and struck, and the horse which carried

242

Lopez reared in alarm, and sent his startled rider toppling from the saddle.

Back went Tarron like the flash of a whip and caught Lopez before the latter could fall—caught him with one hand and caught the bridle of the rearing horse with the other—and as he brought them straight again, he heard a rush of hoofs, and looked to see Langhorne darting away bent low over his saddle.

Oh, childish trick, and how well had it worked!

As Langhorne rode, Tarron heard him shouting: "Ingram! Ingram! Faster! Faster! Tarron is behind!"

Ingram! It was a name of fear to Tarron.

"Now ride, if you want to live," said Tarron to old Lopez. "Straight for the house of Alvarado, and I'll be at your heels! Straight for the house of Alvarado! Spur every foot of the way!"

The old man did not pause to apologize for the clumsiness which had let Langhorne slip through their fingers. He bent to his work like a jockey, and set his black flying through the gates.

That instant, plunging toward them up the road at the head of half a score of followers, Tarron saw big Ingram riding, with Langhorne rushing toward them, and now safe in their midst.

Langhorne safe, and Ingram coming like an angel of vengeance! Tarron himself was riding away at the heels of the old man. He could have left them far behind in no time, but his speed was by his honor limited to the speed of Lopez, and he gritted his teeth as he saw Ingram constantly gaining. This would be the shrewdest cut of fate, if Ingram rode him down at the moment of his victory!

"Faster, Senor Lopez!"

"The black can do no more! On, Tarron, and forget me! Save yourself!"

Brave old man! Even now, he was willing to give up his precious liberty and return to the prison rather than jeopardize a comrade. But Tarron had no thought of abandoning his post. He whipped about and fired—then waited to see big Ingram crash backward in the saddle.

But Ingram did not fall!

Les Tarron fired again, aiming just beneath the brim of Ingram's hat. And still the broad-shouldered monster fol-

243

lowed close. Twice had he missed, and now a cold sweat bedecked Tarron. He changed his aim, fired lower, and saw horse and rider pitch to the ground.

But only for an instant. Ingram was up again, raving: "Go on! Ride like the devil! Take him! It's Tarron himself! It's Tarron, do you hear?"

That word did not seem to spur his followers forward, however. Instead, Tarron could see them frantically drawing rein. He watched Ingram snatch one of his followers from the saddle and mount the horse in turn. But too late! Next moment Jimmy had whisked through the tall gateway of a garden, and now they could see looming before them the front of the Casa Alvarado, gleaming white among the trees.

Chapter XLII

A Dark-Eyed Maiden

WITH HIS WINCHESTER in his hand Tarron kneeled in the patio. Servants were running here and there with lanterns in their hands. Lopez was clasped in the arms of a dignified gentleman with long white hair and a white, pointed beard. Then Tarron saw the latter walk out the patio gate and meet the raging mass of riders which Ingram had led. He heard his calm, clear, unhurried words:

"Senor, you must be a stranger to Santa Maria de la Paz. Otherwise you would know that men do not ride uninvited through my gate. No, not even the men of Senor Langhorne! I see that your men understand and are willing to leave. Do I need to invite you to follow them?"

There was a frantic burst of cursing from Ingram. But his riders were melting away behind him, and presently he himself wheeled his sweating horse around and galloped off. And after that, Tarron stepped into another phase of life, so new and so strange and so sweet to him that it seemed like a taste of heaven brought down to earth. He found it hard, afterward, to remember all that was said, and all that was done. He was only clear on one point, and that was when he met Alvarado returning to the patio and said to him: "You are Senor Alvarado?"

"Yes."

"I don't know who this belongs to," said Tarron. "You —or Lopez."

The steel box was in his hand.

"You had Dorn working for you?"

"Yes."

"And you know he died for you?"

"Yes. God be kind to him—he was a brave man! If he had remained with you that night—he would still be living, Senor Tarron. But we'll talk of him another time. Now we must talk of miracles—of yourself!"

"No," said Tarron. "I don't want to talk. I want to get rid of this—before more men die!" And he gave the steel box to Alvarado.

"It is open!" cried the tall man, and added next instant: "But the chart is here! Lopez, Lopez, the chart is here!"

They could not wait to reach the inside of the house. There in the patio they pored over it eagerly by lantern light.

Lopez said excitedly: "I remember that my boy put his hand on this cross. 'That is Mount Santa Anna,' he said. 'And this is the Santa Anna trail.' Ah, fools. That we should never have looked there!"

He turned to Tarron.

"It is in our hands! Brave Tarron! God witness that you shall not suffer though you have given up the box without asking a price first! Name it now! What will you have?"

"I don't know," said Tarron slowly. "What I want most is a bath. A good hot bath, and then something to eat!"

He began now to feel himself weakening. Pains slipped through his body, and bewildering shadows flocked across his eyes. For he had had one meal in several days, and one sleep in the midst of what labors, and how long had all his nerves been drawn taut as bow-strings!

He heard, dimly, kind sympathetic laughter, and someone saying that that was a small price; and then he was suddenly in a room where house mozos were pouring steaming water into a granite basin. He lay at length in the delicious water, and the ache was passing from his

246

body, from his soul. He dressed. In place of his blood-stained, battered, tattered rags were beautiful, soft, smooth-fitting clothes, such as he had never owned and never so much as dreamed of in all his days. He donned them, wondering. When he left the room, he had about him only two familiar things—a pair of Colts, carried in little holsters beneath the arm, slung cunningly so that they did not bulk beneath his coat.

All the house seemed to be waiting for him; shining eyes were fixed upon him, and everyone was smiling.

He entered another room, where were Alvarado and Lopez, who broke off their conversation to rise and meet him. With them was a slender girl of seventeen or eighteen, with dark, serious eyes, and a smile that passed through Tarron as lightning passes through the heart of the sky.

Then they were pressing around him, taking his hand. What would he have? What could they do?

"I'm hungry," said Tarron.

Was it by magic that he found himself at a long table spread with all dainties and before him a plate flanked by a darkly shining glass of wine? In the background, many moved with smiling faces, to attend on him. And in the foreground were Lopez, Alvarado, and the slender girl. And even they were waiting upon him, offering him food.

"What is wrong?" cried Alvarado. "There is something you wish, my child, which you don't see?"

"No," said Tarron. "But it's all queer, you know. Like Christmas! Like Christmas!"

He ate while they laughed. Not mocking laughter. Nothing that he did but seemed to rejoice them. And those Christmas faces pressed closer, watching, nodding, and beaming on him like mothers watching a famished child.

"You have not touched this cold chicken! And that ham, boiled in sweet white wine! Let him have some of those sweets. Here, my son, is the pride of our kitchen—jugged hare!"

What eating! At what a table! At what a time!

Tarron stopped.

"What is wrong? Are you ill, senor?"

"What is your name, senorita?" he asked.

247

"I am Anna Maria Alvarado, senor!"

He nodded as she curtsied.

"You've got a voice like your name, and like your face, and like your hands," said Tarron. "Wonderful, I mean!"

They laughed again. Was there nothing he could say that would not make them laugh?

He could eat no more. The wine cast a comfortable warmth of happiness into his very brain.

"There's no danger?" asked Tarron sleepily.

"No, none!"

"You," he said to Anna Maria, *"you're* not afraid of anything just now?"

"No, no, Senor Tarron!"

"There's something I want to say to you. I'll try to think what it is."

People were nodding and smiling, looking at him and at the slender girl. Her face had grown wonderfully rosy. But she was smiling and nodding at him, too, and what eyes she had for darkness and brightness and kindness!

He put his head on his hand to think. Voices withdrew to a distance. He seemed to be surrounded by whispers. And then he slept.

When he wakened, he was in a great bed, and the soft warmth of clean linen sheets embraced his body. He put out his hands. His strength had come back to him, it rippled through his body like a mountain torrent. And he laughed aloud. Let Ingram face him now, if he dared!

"Senor!" exclaimed a voice from the corner of the room.

He sat up on his elbows and saw in two corners of the room two armed men, rifles across their knees.

"Hello!" cried Tarron, grinning. "What's happened? Am I a prisoner here?"

"Prisoner?" exclaimed one of them. "We are only your guards, senor. And we are ordered to obey you as though you were the patron!"

He understood. There was still much danger in Santa Maria de la Paz. Therefore the sleep of Tarron was watched by his kind host. But let danger come as it would and when it would. He had a mind for it, a taste for it. And his strength had been given back to him.

It was afternoon. He had slept more than twelve hours, and when he strode into the next room, smiling and joyous, he found them all waiting for him—Alvarado, Lopez, and Anna Maria, smiling shyly toward him before she slipped from the room. Well, if God were willing he would find the time to see more of her hereafter!

Meanwhile there were other things to think about, other things to be done. In five minutes he stood at the topmost tower window of the house and looked forth with Alvarado on the city. In the house they were free; they could not be attacked. But how would they escape to find the mine, now that they had the chart, and the key to the chart?

"We cannot go out with a cart, as you came in," said Alvarado, and smiled. "And yet now that we have you with us, I feel that this mine is already ours, and the wealth of it in our pockets. But your share? What shall we say about that before we start?"

"I'm interested in the fun of it," said Tarron seriously. "Never mind about my share."

"Shall we say a half?"

"That's too much. I want men, first. I've gone through their lines before. Have you any men who would ride with me?"

"I have men, Tarron, who think that you could go safely through hell and back. They would follow you anywhere. And if they shouted your name, I think that they *could* ride through."

"Would you trust yourself to me and ten more?"

"I would. Tonight?"

"No, today!"

"*Madre de Dios!* By daylight? However, you know best!"

So through the bright, golden sun of the afternoon a round dozen horsemen rode down the path of the garden. They were near the gate when they heard a heavy, regular, rhythmic tolling of the great bell of the church, and a moment later a panting messenger sprang to them.

"It is the end, senor!" cried the man to Alvarado. "Senor Langhorne is dead. His heart is broken, they say, with pride and rage and shame. He died in his bed, shout-

249

ing in his sleep: 'Help! They have murdered me!' Senor, let God be thanked! Our enemy is dead!"

"And his men?" asked Alvarado.

"They are scattering already as fast as they can ride. They fear you now, every one of them. Half of them are already whirled out of Santa Maria like dead leaves in a wind. The danger is over at last!"

Chapter XLIII

One Reaches the City in the Sky

Not a shot was fired, not a hostile face was seen, when Alvarado and his troopers cantered out of Santa Maria de la Paz that day, with Tarron beside the master. And the townspeople flooded out and cheered their old patron and forgot the gold with which Langhorne had bought them.

"The name?" said Alvarado to Tarron. "It was called La Paz, many generations ago. It was only a village, then, an Indian village; there was not even a church. When the church of Santa Maria was built, the name was added; and finally the last part of the name was lost, and only the first part remained. That is the secret. But Dorn and some of the others had heard the old story, and they used the forgotten name when they talked of the place to which they were taking the box. God rest them all—brave souls!"

They took to the mountain trail.

"A hundred thousand hours have been wasted in the search of these mountains," said Alvarado. "Now let us see if my boy died for nothing, or for a priceless treasure."

And as they went up the trail, following the little, dim chart to which his dead son Carlos had provided the key, Alvarado told how his son long ago had discovered this document and had gradually ferreted out its history which went back to the days of the Conquistadores. When they first came with fire and sword, the Indians had fled before them; but before they fled they had closed the entrance to a vastly rich mine—so the story went—which was the very cause that had brought the Spainards to La Paz.

The secret of the mine was never betrayed, so the legend went, to the invaders. Finally, all the Indians who knew the secret died, and a new generation came, which had only heard of the lost mine of La Paz, but knew nothing of the place where it was actually to be found. Carlos Alvarado, by years of careful study, finally deciphered the key to the little chart done on Spanish parchment, yellow with centuries, which he had found in some Indian relics. With young Miguel Lopez he had gone to the trail. Lopez had murdered his companion, and returned, stricken with remorse, to tell his father and Langhorne what he had done and beg their protection. But is was learned that Miguel had come back alone, and an old servant of the Alvarado family, going to Casa Langhorne, had overheard the confession of murder in the summer house, and fired the fatal bullet through the window.

Such was the story to which Tarron listened while they rode up the mountain trail, and as they went, he repieced the old tale and made the figures live before his eyes. In the meantime, he was giving heed to the chart, which ended abruptly between two signs—a cross and an arrow. The riders stopped at the edge of a precipitous slope.

"Along this edge, then," said Alvarado, looking anxiously up and down the barren plateau over which they had ridden.

"Down!" said Tarron without hesitation. "That arrow at the end points down, which means that at the end the trail goes down, too. We must follow in that direction."

"Lead!" said Alvarado. "I have no right to question you in such matters as these. You have but to order, and we to obey!"

Down they clambered, leaving the horses, for no horse could follow them on such a path. A hundred yards beneath the brow of the precipice, one of the Mexicans shouted suddenly, waved his arms, and then disappeared.

When they rushed to the place, they found that there was a narrow, dark opening into the middle of the mountain. Then a light gleamed, which the Mexican had struck inside. Another shout! As they crept into the place, thrusting aside the debris that blocked the entrance, Tarron saw a great depth of tunneling before him, narrow and ancient, where a man could not stand upright. They advanced farther. There was a frantic yell from the leader, and hurrying up they saw the Mexican wildly gesticulating before such a sight as never gold miner had seen, save in some world-famous bonanza. It struck across the face of the cut like a yellow blaze—like a bit of artificial gilding—a rich, rich thread of purest gold, and above it a thick ledge of the finest gold-bearing ore!

Tarron was ignorant in such matters. But he understood, as he stared at the gleaming line, why so many lives had been lost. The riches of Croesus were under their hands, waiting ready for the pick and the drill!

What Tarron did afterward would take long to tell. It was not the end of the trail for him, in many years, but the real beginning. He went back to the North to his father and mother and brother, and rode away again, leaving them wealthy for life.

He labored over books, with a stern tutor who ruled him with no gentle hand.

And Tarron married!

One would like to describe how he went in person and found Gregorio and brought him back to that valley of heart's desire and strove to make him rich and joyous; and how old Gregorio stole away in the middle of the night and went back to the home on the mountain side to wrangle and jangle again with his savage daughter.

But there is one matter which must be described.

It is said that a big and dark-faced man rode into Santa Maria on a day, and saw, as his horse drank from the watering-trough in the center of the village, a gay young caballero dash merrily past.

The flash of a gold-trimmed Mexican jacket, the glare

of crimson sash, the sheen of a silken, shining silver stallion which the stalwart youth bestrode!

"By the eternal God!" said the stranger. "Who is that?"

"That?" cried half a dozen. "Why, that is the son of Alvarado!"

"I thought Alvarado's son was dead?" said the stranger, frowning more blackly than before.

"Oh, his own son, of course. But that is Senor Tarron—the great Tarron, the fighter. He is like a son to Alvarado now. He married into the house, you see!"

The stranger remained for a moment in black thought. Then he gave a broad-faced silver peso to a youngster who stood by.

"Go to the Casa Alvarado. Tell Tarron that I want him at the crossroads, yonder, beyond Santa Maria. You understand?"

"And who shall I say sent me, senor?" asked the boy, stricken with amazement at the peremptory tone of the big man.

"Who'll you say?"

He glowered at the boy, as though bewildered that anyone should not know his name.

"Say Ingram," he said.

And the boy fled at his bidding.

Beside the crossroad, drawn carefully out of the dust where he had fallen, they found this same stranger the next day. His body had been carefully bestowed. His hands were folded across his breast. His eyes were closed, and there was a smile of peace on his lips. Between his eyes was a purple splotch, round and even.

So was he buried, and money from an unknown source paid for a marble headstone to mark his grave. No questions were asked. None were raised in that region as a rule, when a man was found with the wound in front. Moreover, who was there in the valley of Santa Maria that cared to spread stories abroad about Senor Tarron? He was almost an Alvarado. Some considered him something less than a member of that grand old family. But there were many who considered him a great deal more.

Perhaps for Ingram there was no fitter end imaginable. He had sins enough to deserve his taking-off, and yet it was almost pitiful that Tarron's should have been the hand that ended him. For it was Ingram who had called Tarron out of his sleepy youth and given him to the long trail of the lost city and all that lay there waiting for Tarron's hand.